Wendy was born in Barnsley, South Yorkshire, England. She is married and has two grown-up children. Wendy left school at the age of 15 and had a very eclectic career. She began her working career in an office and ended her working career in an office at the age of 61. She didn't start writing until she had left work and found it a very pleasant pastime.

All the best

Wendy Gill

30/05/2023

Dedicated to my friend and neighbour
Joan Cross (03/02/1953 – 07/09/2018).
Her support and encouragement helped me on the way to
having my third book published. Thank you, Joan.

Wendy Gill

JACKSON IS MISSING

AUSTIN MACAULEY PUBLISHERS™

LONDON · CAMBRIDGE · NEW YORK · SHARJAH

A CIP catalogue record for this title is available from the British Library.

ISBN 9781528916523 (Paperback)
ISBN 9781528961585 (ePub e-book)

www.austinmacauley.com

First Published (2019)
Austin Macauley Publishers Ltd
25 Canada Square
Canary Wharf
London
E14 5LQ

Many thanks to my photographer Helen Booth at Masque Photography, and to her husband, Paul Booth, who is a Fireman at Barnsley Fire Station. Thanks for being there in case of emergency, Paul.

Chapter One

Ella descended the wide curving staircase. Her feet making no sound on the carpeted stairs, pausing for just a second to wipe the palms of her hands down the front of her dark grey, high-necked woollen dress.

Making sure her hair was tightly pulled back into a bun in the nape of her neck, she turned slightly to her right, walking across the marble-floored hallway. Raising her hand, she tapped gently on the drawing room door. Ella waited for permission to enter.

This was granted by a stern "ENTER". Ella took hold of the handle and entered the room to face her employer, knowing beforehand what the outcome would be.

Ella, having been in this situation on more than one occasion was not surprised that Lady Stern, her employer, wanted to see her.

The eldest son of the house had made advances to her and having them rejected, he had run straight to Mummy and complained that '*SHE*' is the one making advances to him.

This was the third governess position Ella had been appointed to, and this was the third complaint of the same nature, all resulting in her dismissal. Seeking employment without a reference was hard enough, but every household seemed to have an eligible son who believed governesses were fair game. Miss Ella Penrod had other ideas.

Ella had soon learnt that to deny the false allegation and try to defend herself not only resulted in her getting dismissed from her position, but also in having her wage deducted as well.

This mummy was no exception. Lady Stern stood in front of the huge fireplace with a large mirror hanging above it, her hands crossed in front of her.

"Miss Ella Penrod, I am deeply disappointed in you. I am appalled by what my son tells me. I would not have expected this lewd behaviour from a woman of your breeding. I will not have you in this house a minute longer. You will pack your bags and leave, immediately. I have nothing more to say to you, go, leave my house and do not return."

Turning her back on Ella with a swish of lavender taffeta, Lady Stern placed one hand on the mantelpiece, and the other hand she held to her ample bosom, feigning a dramatic air.

Knowing argument was futile, Ella turned silently and left the room. Her carpetbag, already packed with her meagre possessions, was waiting for her on the bed.

The first thing Ella had packed was the pair of riding breeches that once belonged to her father. He had given Ella the breeches many years ago and she had worn them when they went on long horse rides together. The breeches were her most treasured possession.

Next, she had placed her hand pistol on top of the breeches and covered them with the few clothes she still possessed. The riding breeches and pistol were the only things she had left to remind her of her father. Everything else had been sold to pay off his massive debts. They reminded Ella of happier times.

The breeches had been far too big for her, of course, but she held them up by a belt and turned the top of the breeches over the belt. Ella would turn up the breeches at the bottom to get the correct length. She had thought of cutting off the bottoms, but she decided against that, she wanted to keep them as they were given to her.

Ella took up her cape and bonnet in one hand and the carpetbag in the other and descended the wide staircase for the last time.

If truth be told, Ella could not wait to leave. From the age of nineteen, after the death of her father Ella had had to work to survive. She had found this very difficult, for in the year 1813, the only respectable occupation for a young lady of her breeding, having fallen on difficult times, was to try to find a suitable family in need of a governess.

With no references, the only positions she had been able to obtain were out in the middle of nowhere. Places where a more experienced governess would not venture. Thus, she found herself on the edge of the Longcash Moors, three miles from the nearest town of Rampton.

Ella knew she had three miles to walk over the moor, but this did not deter her.

The warm summer sun felt good on Ella's face as she walked down the long drive with her head held high and her shoulders back, but with a heavy heart, not looking forward to searching for her next position.

At least she was thankful that the weather was warm and dry for if it had been raining, the trek over the moor to reach Rampton might not have been so pleasant. Having only a few shillings in her purse, Ella was pondering her next move while she made her way towards the double wrought iron gates and off the Stern property. Her footsteps unconsciously gathering speed.

On nearing the huge gates that heralded the end of her present employment, Ella was alarmed to see James Stern, standing in her path, blocking her way off the property for the last time.

He was a handsome young man of twenty, wealthy, spoilt, arrogant and selfish. His dress sense was that of a man twice his age with his long thin legs encased in fawn, tight fitting trousers, black knee-high boots with a brown leather turnover at the top and black and tan tailcoat.

As soon as Ella saw him, she knew there was trouble ahead. She continued walking and stepped to her left to pass him by, but he stepped to his right still blocking her way. So, Ella stepped to her right, and once again the young man stepped to his left, resulting in her inability to proceed through the gates and off the property.

"You think you are little Miss Goody, Goody, don't you? Well, I have got the better of you after all. Look where your snootiness has got you now. It is a long way into Rampton, especially having to carry that heavy carpetbag as well.

"If you were to give me a kiss from those pretty little lips of yours before you go, I might think about giving you your last month's wage that m y mother gave me to give to you. Well, little Miss Goody, Goody, what about it, a kiss in exchange for your wage?" James Stern asked her.

Ella's reply to that was to lift her right knee up with as much force as she could and place it in her persecutor's groin, affording her much pleasure to see the look of disbelief on his young face.

He slowly placed his hands between his legs and bent forward, then dropped down to the ground onto his knees and finally onto his side where he lay moaning in agony.

Without saying a word, Ella stepped to the side and carried on walking. Her spirits much improved but wishing she had been given the month's wage James had said he had, it would have helped significantly to ease her lack of cash.

She would not afford James Stern the pleasure of knowing how short of money she was.

Having gone no more than fifty yards, she came upon the postman on his sturdy black horse, heading for the Stern's Mansion house.

"Good morning, Miss Penrod. Are you leaving the Mansion?" the postman asked, his eyes taking in her carpetbag.

"I am afraid so Ben, another spoilt brat getting me dismissed," Ella replied. "You don't know of anybody wanting a governess by any chance, do you?"

"Not that I have heard of, but see here, I had better give you another of your letters before you go, and you had better let the sender know you will not be at this address in future. If you are sent any more letters to this address, I will not know where to forward them on to."

"What do you mean Ben, another one of my letters? This will be the first one I have had."

"That cannot be right, Miss. I have delivered two other letters here, both addressed to you. Are you saying you have not received them? This is a serious matter, Miss. I delivered the other two letters here. You should have received them by now."

He dismounted his horse and searched through his bag until he came across a white envelope addressed to Miss E. Penrod and handed it to her.

He watched her turn it over in her hands, then reading the address on the front to make sure it was for her.

"Aren't you going to open it?" the postman asked.

"I have no idea who it can be from? The postmark is Marchum, and I do not know anybody from Marchum."

She opened the letter with trembling fingers, taking out a single sheet of folded paper. Unfolding the letter, she was amazed to find a five-pound note enclosed.

Taking the large white five-pound note away from the written word, Ella read:
"Grundy, Grundy and Grundy Solicitors,
West Street, Marchum."

She looked up at Ben and told him, "It is from a solicitor."

"Dear Miss Penrod

I write for the last time requesting you to get in touch with the above solicitors.

We have important matters to discuss with you. Once again, we enclose a five-pound note for your travel expenses.

Yours faithfully

C. Grundy, Esquire."

"Would you believe it Ben? This C. Grundy, infers not only has he sent me letters before, but there had been money enclosed in them too. Here you read it." Ella passed the letter to Ben.

"I can confirm that I have delivered two other letters here which were addressed to you in the past few weeks. Are you sure you have not received them?"

"Of course, I am. I have not been given any letters since I have been working here."

"What you need to do is go back to the mansion and get the other two letters and the money. I'll bet you Lady Stern kept both letters and money from you because she doesn't want you to leave.

"Now her son has made his accusation against you, she has changed her mind. Once you are in receipt of the other two letters, I suggest you set off for Marchum to see this solicitor. If you get the other money that is rightfully yours, there should be enough money in your pocket to get you to Marchum, and some to spare," Ben advised her.

He handed the letter back to Ella and she folded it up and placed it back in the envelope.

"Yes, the letter does infer there was money enclosed in the previous letters," confirmed Ben.

"Come on, I'll give you a lift on the back of old Sally. I shall wait for you to come out to make sure you get your letters. If Lady Stern denies having had them, you can tell her there will be trouble in store for her because she is guilty of stealing from you.

"Tell her, I am waiting outside for you and if she does not return the letters and money, I will report her to the Royal Mail. I don't think you will have much trouble with her once she knows that you know she has withheld your post and stolen your money. I shall be outside ready to take you into Rampton where you can catch the mail stagecoach to Marchum."

Ella had never heard of Marchum so why someone from there should be writing letters to her and sending her money was a puzzle and she informed Ben of this.

"I had an uncle that lived in Marchum but unfortunately he died many years ago. My mother used to visit him and take me with her. We would catch the mail stagecoach in Rampton at 9 o'clock in the morning and we reached Marchum before nightfall.

"Marchum is located on the edge of the England and Scotland border just on the edge in Scotland, two miles further south and it would be in England. It is a very pleasant little town, I think you will like it.

"If we are to get you to Marchum before the stagecoach leaves, we had better get a move on."

Ella found herself sitting on the back of the old horse behind the postman with her carpetbag clutched on her lap and her other arm round Ben's waist.

There had been no sign of James Stern as they made their way back up the long drive, back towards the Stern property so Ella could face her ex-employer.

Lady Stern, of course, had denied any knowledge of any letters until Ella told her the postman was waiting outside for her and it was him that had informed her of the other letters.

After a moment's hesitation, Lady Stern crossed the room and opened her writing desk and produced the two letters, both opened.

Lady Stern searched in her purse and then thrust both letters and two five-pound notes at Ella.

Ella took the money and letters. Lady Stern did not utter another word but turned and marched out of the room leaving Ella to find her own way out of the house.

Ben asked her if she wanted him to report the theft of the letters, but she told him no, she had her letters and the money, so she wanted no more to do with Lady Stern.

She remembered little of the journey from the Sterns' mansion on the back of the postman's horse to Rampton, where she thanked Ben, bought her ticket to Marchum and boarded the stagecoach.

Ella's mind was in turmoil. The last thing she could have dreamed of this morning while she was packing her carpetbag was having fifteen extra pounds in her purse. She felt rich indeed. But confusion still reigned as she sat in the stagecoach heading even further north, for the town of Marchum.

Ella sat and watched the world go by out of the stagecoach window and wondered what was in store for her when she reached Marchum.

She now had enough money to find some cheap lodgings for a few days until she found out what the letters were all about. As far as she knew, she had no family left alive. She was an only child and so were her mother and father. There had never been any talk about any aunts or uncles except for a Lady Whiteman, who was an aunt of her father's.

Lady Whiteman had never married, and she had frightened the living day lights out of Ella when she was a child. Not that there had ever been much contact between Lady Whiteman and her father, and that lady was now deceased. As far as Ella knew, there was no other relation she could have thrown herself upon in her hour of need. The letters remained a mystery.

Chapter Two

Ella stepped down from the stagecoach in Marchum around 7 o'clock in the evening with the warm evening sun still pleasantly shining in the clear blue sky.

Taking up her carpetbag once again, she went in search of somewhere to sleep for the night.

She looked in windows as she passed, hoping to see a sign advertising a room to let. She did not see one. She could find no house offering her a bed for the night.

Ella had passed two hostelries, but she could not bring herself to enter either of them. The smell and the noise deterred her.

It had been a very long and emotional day, but her spirits were high. The mail stagecoach had stopped twice to change the horses and while this was being attended to, the passengers had been happy to partake of two very satisfying meals.

She had had no hesitation on both occasions to purchase a substantial meal. A luxury she had not anticipated when waking up that morning.

Ella was beginning to tire by this time and the carpetbag was getting heavier and heavier when she suddenly came across West Street.

Putting her carpetbag down, she took one of her letters out of her receptacle to check the address. The letter confirmed that West Street was where the solicitor's office was located.

She found herself walking along this built-up area, checking all the buildings as she went until she came to the solicitor's office. It was a detached, two-storey building and the last house on West Street. After the solicitor's building, beautiful Scottish moorland reached as far as the eye could see.

It was an impressive location and boasted two stone pillars supporting a canopy which covered a small porch that led to wooden carved double doors. The sides and front of the pillars, except for the entrance, were bricked three quarters of the way up, with the top portion housing windows to provide light inside the porch and protection from the elements.

A plaque, fixed to the side of the door read 'Grundy, Grundy and Grundy Solicitors'.

Ella guessed it must be around 8 o'clock in the evening by now. She assumed that Grundy, Grundy and Grundy Solicitors would have locked up and gone home long ago.

She stepped up onto the porch and found that in the recesses on either side of the pillars were wooden benches which were out of sight of the road.

Deciding to take a short rest before she set off once more in search of accommodation, Ella sat down in a corner and placed her carpetbag on the floor; raising her aching feet, she used it as a footstool. Then rolling up her cape she placed it on the sidewall and rested her head on it.

She closed her eyes and let the silence engulf her, intending to stay for only a little while. She was soon fast asleep.

Charles Grundy took off his glasses and rubbed his tired eyes. He placed all the paperwork on his desk in a folder and took it to the filing cabinet, and closing the drawer, he heaved a big sigh.

He had nothing to look forward to when he returned home, and he found himself staying at the office longer and longer and tonight was no exception. He looked around to make sure everything was in order before making his way out, locking the door behind him.

He turned to go onto the street and was amazed to see a young woman with her head on one side and her feet upon a carpetbag, fast asleep and seemingly without a care in the world.

Hesitating, he approached her and touched her shoulder expecting her to wake up, but nothing happened, she was still fast asleep. Taking hold of her arm, he gently shook her until she stirred, then he stepped back so he would not alarm her.

Ella struggled to open her eyes. She took a deep breath and held it for a moment before slowly coming from a deep, dreamless sleep. Her eyes grew larger as she took in a portly gentleman with tall black hat, small round glasses and tight-fitting tailcoat, exaggerating his girth.

"I beg your pardon, sir. I did not mean any harm. I sat down to rest for a while and must have fallen asleep. It has been a long day," the young woman told him.

"Well, you cannot sleep here all night. You never know who is lurking about. May I walk you back to your home?"

"Unfortunately, I have no home to go to. I was looking for lodgings but have so far been unsuccessful. I wonder, sir, do you know of anywhere I could retire for the night? Then, in the morning I can search for somewhere to stay for a few days. If so, would you be so kind as to direct me? I am a stranger here and I am afraid I am lost."

"Where do you want to go? You may have a problem at this late hour. Have you no relations here that you could go to? Marchum is a very quiet little town I am afraid. Not much goes off here so there is no call for lodging houses, we do not get many visitors," the portly gentleman told her.

"I am here to see, Grundy, Grundy and Grundy, Solicitors. I noticed their name on the plaque on the wall, so I sat down to rest for a while. I have been travelling all day. I guess I would still have been here in the morning if you had not come by." Ella gave a weary smile, but Mr Grundy did not miss the twinkle in her eye.

"Tell me, what is your name?"

"Ella Penrod, do you think you might be able to help me, sir?"

"You are Ella Penrod? Well, I must say I am most pleased to see you my dear. My name is Charles Grundy, it is I who sent you the letters. The best thing for you to do is come home with me and we will have some supper and talk."

"Come home with you sir, I could not, I do not know you. Thank you for the kind offer but I really must decline."

"There is no impropriety involved here, for even though we have not met before, I am your uncle, so there is no need for you to be miss-ish. Your circumstances leave you without much option I am afraid. You are quite safe with me you know, I am not built to be chasing young ladies 'round the bedroom, as you can well see." Mr Grundy patted his portly stomach and gave her a devilish wink.

Ella decided she liked Mr Grundy and felt that she could trust him, but she said, "My uncle sir? I did not know I had an uncle."

"I am your uncle by marriage. But come along, it has been a long day for me too. Let us go home and have something to eat and I will explain everything to you when we are sitting comfortably. There is no need for you to feel nervous. By the end of this evening, I have a feeling that you and I are going to be great friends." He held out his hand and Ella placed her hand in it and he helped her to her feet.

Mr Grundy picked up her carpetbag, held out his arm and she tucked her hand under it and they set off, back down West Street, retracing Ella's footsteps.

By now the light was beginning to fade and the evening was starting to come alive. One or two characters passed them by as they walked the length of West Street and cast an eye in Ella's direction, she was grateful for Mr Grundy's presence.

Oddly, when they turned into Haywood Street, which comprised of two long rows of terraced houses, one on either side of the road, they didn't meet a soul. Haywood Street was deserted.

Ella and Mr Grundy did not speak until they neared the end of Haywood Street, which like West Street, heralded the end of the town. "Nearly there my dear, nearly there," he told her kindly.

Mr Grundy stopped at the last house. He opened the little wooden gate that led into a small forecourt garden. He proceeded up a narrow path with a very small lawn at either side then up two shallow steps which brought them to the front door.

Mr Grundy placed Ella's carpetbag on the top step and said, "Before we go inside, let me show you the side of the house. I know it is getting dark now and you may not be able to see much but it will give you an idea of the layout of the house."

He led her back through the gate to the side of the house where there was a further wooden fence leading onto an open meadow. But it was difficult to make anything out at the far end of the meadow in the fast fading evening light.

Mr Grundy pointed his finger to an extension added onto the side of his house and Ella saw what looked very much like a barn with a thatched roof.

"That extension was your aunt Fran's workshop, but we will go into that in the morning. I am ready for my tea. The days all seem to be long and meaningless now. But it could be I am just getting old. I am certainly not getting any younger but meeting you and bringing you home today, has lifted my spirits no end.

"Come, let us put the kettle on and have a nice little chat before we go to bed. There is a spare room that you may use tonight and then we will decide what is best to be done with you in the morning. You must be tired and hungry having travelled all the way from Rampton."

"On the contrary sir, my little nap has revived me. I have not been so wide awake for a long time. But I could not possibly go to sleep until I know what all this is about. I left my last employment in Longcash Moors on the edge of Rampton this morning with only a few shillings in my purse, no job and no prospects of finding one soon.

"Now I find myself with more than ten pounds left in my purse, thanks to you, and an offer of a bed for the night and something to eat. Although I must admit sir, I indulged myself at The Leg of Mutton Inn when we stopped to change the horses, with a very fine lunch and a most-welcome hot cup of tea.

"I have not had such an amount of money in my purse for quite a few years, not since my father died leaving me with nothing. I have had to work for my living and it has been an unpleasant three years. Being able to splash out on a nice lunch was very extravagant of me but, by Jove, did I enjoy it, then I felt guilty for I indulged in not one, but two very fine meals today. It was very extravagant of me considering the size of my purse."

Mr Grundy gave a delighted chuckle and unlocked his front door, picked up Ella's carpetbag, and entered the long dark hallway with a staircase running off to the right that led to the first-floor landing.

Mr Grundy placed the carpetbag on the bottom step of the staircase, then he lit a candle that was conveniently placed on a little side table, opposite the staircase and to the left of the entrance door. The candle gave off a warm pale glow providing light along the hallway which ran the length of the house and Ella found herself in the small homely kitchen.

More candles were set alight and Mr Grundy pulled out a chair and told her to sit down. He said he would make them some supper and then they could go into the front room and have a nice cosy chat.

Having all her offers to help turned down, Ella sat at the kitchen table and looked around her.

There was a big white pot sink with a window above and wooden draining board to the side. What looked like a backdoor leading out to the rear garden, but Ella could not confirm this because she was unable to see anything of the outside for by now it was too dark.

There was a big open fireplace with a cast iron oven to the side. The floor was stone flagged and a large dresser covered one entire wall and was piled high with cups, plates, pots and pans, in fact, anything a cook would need to prepare a meal seemed to be located on the shelves.

Glancing outside, she could see nothing, but total darkness and she felt warm and safe for the first time in the past three years. Ella gave a silent thank you and resigned herself to her present situation without any feeling of guilt or prick of conscience.

"Any minute now I am going to wake up," Ella said.

"Supper is nearly ready, there is only some cold ham, bread, butter and a cup of tea I am afraid. I was not expecting visitors. Tomorrow is Saturday; therefore, I do not have to go into work. We can both have a good lie-in in the morning, then we will go shopping so I can stock up the empty larder. You can enjoy looking around the shops and buy yourself some new clothes if you wish. Money is no object. You can get whatever you like." Mr Grundy placed a steaming cup of tea in front of her.

"Help yourself to the food. You will feel much more at ease with your situation when you have eaten something. Travelling always makes me very hungry and irritable."

"I cannot possibly impose on you like this, and I certainly cannot accept money from you. I should not really be here at all. Things seem to have gone off the rails so to speak. Really Mr Grundy, I do appreciate you putting me up for the night, indeed I do not know what I would have done had you not been working late and found me.

"You should not have been so kind to me. I am afraid I have had quite a few years of people being unkind. Your kindness took me by surprise. It was so easy to allow myself to be talked into this." Ella gave a defeated sigh as she bit into the bread and butter.

"No, no, you mistake me. I will of course be funding the cost of filling up the larder; after all, it is my larder. But the money I spoke of is yours by right. Your Aunt Fran left everything to you. We will talk about that later. Tomorrow I will also show you around your Aunt Fran's extension.

"Workshop as your Aunt Fran called it, attached to the side of the house. The one I showed you when we arrived. We had the extension built for your Aunt Fran, somewhere she loved to escape to when she needed a bit of peace and quiet. She loved to look out over the meadow, down to the stream and across at the wood. She was a very wealthy woman in her own right, besides what we had jointly."

Mr Grundy paused while he ate some supper then continued, "Unfortunately we had no children. I say unfortunately, I cannot say either of us was inclined to feel broody. We were happy with each other's company. I miss her very much, very much indeed."

He paused again and taking a deep breath, he added, "When she became ill, your Aunt Fran asked me to write to you and ask you to come and meet her. She had followed your progress over the years, but she was taken from me too quickly. By the time I had written that third letter to you, it was too late, your Aunt Fran had passed away.

"After I had posted the third letter onto you, I decided that if I had not heard from you within two weeks, I would go to Longcash Moors myself to find out if you still lived at the Sterns' mansion. I must say I am extremely pleased I did not have to undertake that journey, my poor old bones do not travel well these days."

"I never received the first two letters. Lady Stern intercepted them, read them and withheld the money you had placed inside. It was only by chance that I came upon the postman as I made my way off Lady Stern's property, and he gave me the third letter.

"The postman told me about the other two letters he had delivered for me to the Stern's residence. He took me back to the house and I told Lady Stern that the postman was waiting at the door ready to act against her if she did not give me the letters she had withheld.

"Once she knew the postman was waiting for me outside, she did not deny withholding the letters. She had kept them, and reluctantly she gave them back to me. Or I should say, practically threw them at me, together with the two five-pound notes that you had so kindly enclosed in the letters. It was a very lucky encounter with the postman for if I had not bumped into him, I would never have known that they existed.

"There was not much else she could do after I had told her that you had mentioned enclosing the money in both of the other letters she had withheld. I am most grateful to you for that Mr Grundy, thank you."

"No need for thanks my dear, the money is rightfully yours."

"I am confused to say the least, sir. Are you sure you have the right person? I am not aware that I ever had an Aunt Fran, you must be mistaken."

"No, there is no mistake. You look like her you know. It could be her sitting there now. Fran followed your every move. She was going to write to you when your father died. I am so sorry, my dear, for your loss.

"Until I met Fran, I am afraid I had been a most selfish individual, she taught me to live and love like I had never known. Now my life has gone back to what it was before your aunt and I met. I was hoping against hope you and I could become friends, you have nobody, just like me, but I do not expect a young woman like you will want to be bothered with an old fool like me.

"Let us put these pots in the sink and leave them for tomorrow. I need a good night's sleep and I am sure you must be ready for your bed. It must have been a long day for you too, travelling all that way. We will talk in the morning and work everything out. All will turn out for the best. Don't worry your pretty little head over it."

Ella looked at Mr Grundy. "I feel I can trust you Mr Grundy. The moment I opened my eyes and saw your kind face smiling at me, I felt I could trust you. With all my straight-laced upbringing, sleeping in a house with a man I have only known for two hours goes against everything I have had drilled into me about protocol.

"I am throwing all that to the wind and I am going to admit to you Mr Grundy, I would be very grateful for a bed for the night. I do not want to be a burden to you. And I do not want to have something that does not belong to me. Are you quite sure sir that I am your late Fran's niece?"

"Did your father never talk to you about his younger sister, the one who ran away from home to become an actress? I believe that her father, your grandfather, disowned her and would not have her name mentioned in his house. History has a habit of repeating itself you know.

"Believe it or not, I lived in Wanebridge some twenty years ago and met Fran, sitting in a doorway crying her eyes out. She had no money, nowhere to live and was on the verge of becoming a lady of the night.

"Her aspirations of becoming an actress never came to anything, and what money she had, soon ran out. Your grandfather had refused to let her go back home, he said she had made her bed, so she must lie on it. I was quite a man about town in those days. I offered her a bed for the night, just like I have offered one to you.

"A bed for the night was all I offered your Aunt Fran. I could not leave the young woman sitting on that doorstep, anything could have happened to her. She also accepted my offer of a bed for the night and she never left.

"We fell in love and got married. I became a solicitor and we moved down here, away from gossiping tongues and we never looked back. I am sure you will enjoy rummaging through all her things in the extension, but I digress. I am afraid where Fran is concerned, I can become a bit of a bore, do forgive me.

"There was an old aunt of Fran's, and your father of course, whom Fran kept in touch with. A Lady Whiteman, she kept Fran informed of all that went on back at your old home, Foxtails Hall. Fran has followed your progress from the day you were born. She wanted you to make your own way in the world, to learn how to survive and make a future for yourself, just like she had to.

"Before Lady Whiteman died, she told Fran her housekeeper was friends with your father's housekeeper, who had a daughter, who I believe you kept in touch with. When Lady Whiteman died, your old housekeeper's daughter kept Fran up to date with your whereabouts.

"Fran said that she had grown up being given everything she wanted, in fact, she had been a spoilt young woman not satisfied with anything she had until it was taken from her. Fran found happiness and contentment by having to survive on her own and she said I had done that for her. I always said it was the other way around, I had not known happiness until we met."

"I remember Lady Whiteman. She terrified the life out of me. She died many years ago and I am ashamed to say I had not thought of her in a long time. Yes, Lady Whiteman was an aunt of my father's. I guess your Fran must have been my aunt. You have given me much to think about Mr Grundy, I wish I had met her, Aunt Fran I mean. I only ever knew my father whilst I was growing up and he brought me up like the son he never had.

"He taught me to fly a kite, to fish, to fence, to ride a horse and shoot. He took me abroad and so I have a vast amount of knowledge in all these things. My practical work in the classroom left much to be desired. I had tutor after tutor, none willing to stay and teach me schooling, they did not agree with the way my father was bringing me up.

"I guess that is one of the reasons I am not a very good governess, but the skills he taught me have been more use to me than ABC or 1-2-3. I can fight with the best of them and since trying my hand at this governess lark, those skills have come in very handy on more than one occasion.

"In fact, in all three cases where I gained employment as a governess the eldest son of the house soon found out that I was not fair game in their love interests and they all got me dismissed," Ella told him.

Mr Grundy burst out laughing at this and stood up saying, "Come now, enough for tonight. I will show you to your room. There will be time enough tomorrow to carry on this conversation."

Mr Grundy held out his hand and she placed hers in it. Standing up Ella followed the portly gentleman out of the kitchen and up the steep narrow staircase and along the landing.

Opening a door at the head of the landing, Ella walked into a bedroom and turned to say goodnight and thank you for all he had done, but he would hear none of it.

Mr Grundy held out her carpetbag and told her, "There is a bolt on your side of the door. If it makes you feel safe, it is there to be used, goodnight my dear, sweet dreams."

Ella took her carpetbag and closed the door, but she did not put the bolt across. She would give the old gentleman the benefit of the doubt, but she would take her pistol and put it under her pillow before she rested her head on it, just in case.

Chapter Three

When Ella finally opened her eyes the following morning, the sun was shining into the bedroom through a crack in the curtains. It had been a long time since she'd had the luxury of having a lie-in on a Saturday morning.

She dressed and went over to the window to draw back the curtains. To her delight, the scene that met her eyes was a joy to behold.

Her window overlooked the thatched roof of the extension which in turn bordered a large meadow that fell away and joined what looked like a river that flowed on and disappeared in the large wood that lay at the far end of the meadow.

Birds flew overhead, and she watched as a hawk chased a sparrow and was more than pleased when the little sparrow made a dive for the thatched roof and the hawk swerved and flew away. *No little sparrow for his breakfast this morning,* thought Ella.

She was about to turn away when she observed the figure of a man limping across the meadow and one arm hanging at a funny angle by his side. He too made for the extension and was lost from sight.

Hurrying out of her bedroom, Ella headed downstairs and into the kitchen where she found Mr Grundy eating a thick slice of toast with loads of butter melting on top of it.

"Just in time for some breakfast, it would seem we have both had a lie-in this morning. Did you sleep well?"

"Yes, thank you Mr Grundy, it was a wonderful sleep. I have not felt so rested for a long time."

"Good. Sit down and have something to eat, then we will go into town and do some shopping. Once we have that out of the way, we will have the rest of the day to show you around and explain things in a little more detail."

A loud banging on the front door made Ella jump out of her skin and Mr Grundy spill his tea.

"Who the devil is that trying to break down my door?" he raged as he stood up and headed for the front door.

Ella heard raised voices and two smartly dressed gentlemen came striding into the kitchen with Mr Grundy following behind.

"You have no right to come barging in here, no right at all. There is nobody here except for my niece and I, as you can see. Will you please leave my house immediately?"

"We saw him heading this way. We are going to have to search the house before we leave. He cannot have gone much further, he had a bullet in his leg and I think we winged his shoulder too. You search upstairs Bert, and I will do the same down here," the taller of the two gentlemen said to his companion.

Bert headed up the stairs and the speaker of the pair did his rounds on the ground floor with Mr Grundy following close behind him, telling him he would hear more about this and demanding to know who they were.

The speaker ignored poor Mr Grundy and they met Bert at the bottom of the stairs. Bert shook his head and the speaker turned to Mr Grundy and asked him who lives in the building at the side of the house.

"Nobody lives there. It was my wife's workshop when she was alive. Who is it you are looking for, whoever it is, he is not here."

"We will have to have a look anyway, to make sure, lead the way," the speaker stood aside and indicated the front door to Mr Grundy.

Mr Grundy did not move.

"It would be better for you and this young woman if you comply with my request," Mr Grundy was told.

The tall thin man and Mr Grundy locked eyes.

Mr Grundy relented and went over to a cupboard at the side of the sink, opened a drawer and took out a bunch of keys. Mr Grundy then walked straight passed the speaker, pushing him against the wall with his huge bulk before heading out with the tall stranger following.

Ella looked at Bert, who was still standing on the bottom step of the stairs and he indicated to her, with a nod of the head, towards the front door. She made her exit out of the front door and round the side of the house and was just in time to see Mr Grundy fumbling with the door before he managed to open it and walk in. The tall stranger followed.

So did Ella and Bert.

Mr Grundy went to stand by the window and Ella went to join him.

As she headed his way, she saw in front of a dome-topped trunk, a few drops of blood on the floor so she went and sat on the trunk, primly folding her hands on her lap at the same time hiding the drops of blood with the hem of her gown.

"We saw him heading this way, out of the wood," the speaker told them. "He cannot have gotten very far with a bullet in his leg."

"Did you see whoever this poor man is, entering my house or this workshop?" Mr Grundy demanded.

"No," was the reply.

"Then you have no right to enter either of these properties without my consent. What I want to know is, who you are? I shall write a letter of complaint to the Chief Constable."

"I should not bother if I was you, he can't do anything about it. You should be grateful to us for making sure our prey is not hiding here, he is a dangerous character. Once we have made sure he is not here, we will be on our way," the tall gentleman said.

Ella and Mr Grundy watched the two men look under the desk and behind a curtain that hid a little kitchenette. Their search proved to be fruitless and when they could find nowhere else that could possibly hide a man, they gave up the search.

"I think your prey as you call him; will be well on his way to escape by now. You have wasted too much time here looking for someone that does not exist," Mr Grundy told them.

The speaker looked at Bert. "Let's go."

Ella and Mr Grundy watched the two unwelcome guests head back across the meadow and vanish back into the wood from which they had come.

"What do you make of that?" a shocked Mr Grundy asked.

Ella stood up and moved away from the trunk. "He's in the trunk."

"Who is in the trunk?"

"The man they are looking for. That was what I had come downstairs to tell you. I drew my curtains back and saw this man come running out of the wood, limping badly and his arm hanging loose at his side. He then disappeared beneath my bedroom window. I never saw the two men though; they must have come out of the wood while I was making my way downstairs to the kitchen."

"You mean there is someone hiding here? The door was not locked when I came to unlock it. I must have forgotten to lock it the last time I was in here, so I suppose it is possible for someone to have used the workshop as a bolt hole."

Ella nodded and indicated the drops of blood on the floor.

"He's in the trunk?" whispered Mr Grundy after observing the drops of blood.

Ella nodded again. "I am only guessing. Was that blood there the last time you came in here?"

"How the devil should I know, I do not go around looking for pools of blood at the base of trunks," said a confounded Mr Grundy.

"There is only one way to find out," Ella went towards the trunk.

"You are not going to open it, are you?"

"How else will we know if he is in there or not? Anyway, we need to see if he is alright. If he is losing blood, he must be hurt. If you think he will be of danger to us, I will go and get my pistol and that should make you feel safer."

"Very well, but I will open the trunk just in case he is dangerous. There is no need for firearms, they are nasty things, you never know when they will go off and I might be at the receiving end. You leave your pistol where it is." Mr Grundy bent down and lifted the trunk lid and stepped quickly back.

Sure enough there he was, a gentleman curled up in the foetal position, head slumped forward onto his chest and his eyes closed.

"Bless my soul, nothing like this has ever happened before," Mr Grundy said staring at the motionless figure.

"We must try to get him out of there and see what we can do to help him," Ella said.

"Go next door and get Charlie, he will know what to do," Mr Grundy told her.

"Who is Charlie? Why don't you go and get Charlie? You know him, I do not."

"I am not leaving you here on your own with the man in the trunk. What if he regains consciousness? Those two thugs said he was dangerous. A fine protector I would turn out to be. Fran would never forgive me if I let anything happen to you. Charlie will know what to do. He is my friend as well as my neighbour. Go on, hurry up and bring Charlie back."

Reluctantly Ella used the doorknocker of the house next door and waited, nothing happened. She rattled the doorknocker again and waited, still nothing happened. She began to pound the knocker continuously until the door swung open, and there stood a middle-aged man, dressed in loose fitting clothes and in need of a shave and a good hairbrush.

"What's up?" he asked.

"Are you Charlie?"

"He's in the library if you want him."

"I do, I do want him, can you tell him please?"

"You will have to wait while I go and get him then," he closed the door on her and she was left standing on the doorstep, all she could do was stand and wait.

The gentleman in the library looked up from his desk and asked, "Where is the fire Jackson?"

"Stood outside on the doorstep, said she wants you."

"It's a *she* knocking my door down, is it? And she wants me, does she? What is the verdict, Jackson?"

"She is the one."

"The devil she is."

"Aye, it took a long time coming, but she is here now."

"Who is she?"

"She is your woman not mine, so you go and see her. It is you she wants not me. Do you want me to do all the work? Besides, if Blanche found out I had been talking to a woman on the doorstep she would be none too pleased."

Charlie stood up and went to the door with Jackson tagging along behind.

When Charlie opened the door, he observed a young woman in a plain grey woollen dress, her mousey brown hair tightly tied back in a bun, pacing to and fro on his top step.

The young lady stopped pacing and observed the two gentlemen watching her. "Are you, Charlie?"

"I am *A* Charlie; whether I am *THE* Charlie you are seeking is yet to be established."

"How many Charlies live here?"

"There are other Charlies residing here, by nature rather than by name," he pointedly looked at Jackson.

"I want you," Ella told him.

Charlie was dressed in white shirt, tight black trousers and highly polished top boots.

The white shirt was open at the neck and Ella had a difficult time keeping her eyes averted from the brown chest hair that was peeping out.

"I am very gratified by the thought that you want me, especially as Jackson has given his approval."

"He has given his approval for what?"

"You of course, Jackson approves of you."

"Me! He does not know me. He has never laid eyes on me before this day so how can he give his approval of me?"

"He has not met a lot of other women either, but of the ones he has met he has never given any of them his approval, so that makes you a very interesting person."

"What exactly is he giving you his approval for?"

"For us to get married, what else could it be?"

"He has given you his approval to marry me?"

"He has."

"I gather you are not married already then?"

"No."

"So basically, your name is Charlie and you have a few other Charlies residing here, you are not married, and you have to have the approval of Jackson before you can get married?"

"That is correct."

"Do you usually conduct interviews standing on your doorstep?"

Charlie glanced down at his doorstep and asked, "You have taken offence to my doorstep? Jackson, have you been neglecting your duties and not keeping my doorstep clean?"

"Why should I put myself out to clean the doorstep? The rain does a good job of washing it and the wind blows anything away that is not tied down."

"That is fair comment, don't you think?" Charlie asked her.

Ella could not contain herself any longer and she set off in a fit of laughter that she had difficulty in controlling.

When she regained control of herself, she continued, "Are you and Jackson capable of dealing with a body in a trunk?"

"A body in a trunk you say. Is it dead or alive?"

"We do not know. The good news is he was alive when he went into the trunk, for he climbed in himself, whether he has died since we do not know. There is a certain amount of blood. We are told he has been shot. I have been sent to fetch you."

"Are you married?"

"I am not."

"So basically, you are not married, you want me, and you have an alive or dead body in a trunk."

"That is correct."

"You might just be right this time Jackson, if you are, it will be the first time in your life. She sounds just the sort of girl for me. Get your bag."

"I am totally undervalued," Jackson muttered, turning to get his bag.

"You are not surprised we have a body in a trunk?" asked Ella.

"Bodies in trunks are my speciality," he smiled down at her.

When Jackson returned with his little black bag, Ella turned and headed for the workshop with the two eccentric gentlemen following her.

"Where are we going?" asked Jackson.

"We are following this delightful young woman to the ends of the earth?" replied Charlie.

"Here we go again. You might be following her to the ends of the earth, but I am damned if I am," muttered Jackson.

Ella had a thought. She wondered how many Charlies lived in the house next door. She stopped and turned, and Charlie crashed straight into her. Instinctively, he put his arms around her to steady the collision and Jackson in turn, hurrying to keep up with them, crashed into the back of Charlie.

Ella found herself clasped to Charlie's chest and her eyes were on the level with his unbuttoned shirt and for a brief second, she allowed herself a crafty glimpse before looking up into Charlie's gentle, amused blue eyes and her mind went blank.

"Jackson, get off my back," Charlie said still looking down at Ella.

"You first," he said, "You let go of the girl and I will get off your back. Until you have learnt not to take girls in your arms after only five minutes of making their acquaintance I am sticking like glue, for the girl's sake. There is no wonder you cannot keep a girl if you go mauling her as soon as you meet her. I thought you would have known better by now, given your age and lack of success with the women."

"Jackson was found on a rubbish heap and was brought to me by Fran, the lady that lived next door. She said she did not want her precious Mr Grundy, landed with someone she had found on a rubbish dump. He was in a wretched state, even worse than he is now if you can believe that. He was unconscious and when he came to, he could not remember a thing.

"I think, his being booted off planet Mars and landing on his head in that rubbish dump has made him addled. Fran should have left him there, on the rubbish heap where he belonged. I fed him once and now for the devil of me I cannot shake him off," Charlie explained.

"When I find a kennel that offers better food and accommodation than you do, I shall be off," replied Jackson.

Charlie felt Ella's body pressed close to his, shaking with laughter and he only released her when she made a move to turn away. All thoughts of what she was going to say had completely gone out of her head.

She had not had such a good time since her father died. For the past three years it had all been very hard, depressing and boring work. She could see no happy future for herself, but the last two days had turned out to be very interesting and entertaining. She even had a body in a trunk; there are not many people of her acquaintance that could boast that.

Ella was still laughing when she opened the door to Fran's workshop and found Mr Grundy sitting at the desk, his eyes glued to the trunk.

Mr Grundy stood up when the door opened, and he wobbled across to Charlie.

"Thank goodness you were in Charlie. Look at this." He pointed to the inert body in the trunk.

"What have you been up to now Clarence? I thought you didn't like firearms of any kind?" Charlie asked poor Mr Grundy after seeing the blood seeping from the bullet holes and spreading into the inert man's clothes.

"I did not do it. Two well-dressed thugs pushed their way into my house and ransacked it, said I was hiding somebody. I have never hidden anybody in my house before, never had the need. I got the shock of my life when Ella told me there was a man in the trunk and when I opened it, there he was. I could not believe it, but there he is."

Charlie and Jackson went over to the trunk and Charlie took hold of the body under the arms and Jackson took the legs. They lifted the man out of the trunk and laid him on the floor. Blood was on both Charlie's and Jackson's sleeves.

"What do you think?" Charlie asked Jackson.

"Not good, it looks like he has lost a lot of blood. It would be better if we took him to our place where I can set about getting those bullets out of him. He will need to rest once the bullets are out. We need to keep him still," Jackson said.

"We will have to use the connecting doors, we cannot risk taking him outside, you never know who is watching," Charlie said.

"Have you got the keys Clarence?"

"They are in the kitchen."

"Better go and get them," Charlie told him. Then going over to the curtain that hung behind the desk he pulled it back.

The two uninvited guests had done the same but all they saw was a very tiny sink with a single drainer.

Jackson went and stood at the side of the window and kept a lookout just in case the uninvited guests should happen to return.

Mr Grundy reappeared with a bunch of keys and handed them to Charlie who selected one of the keys and vanished from sight behind the curtain once again.

They heard his footsteps running up a staircase and then the sound of doors opening. A few seconds later they heard footsteps descending.

Charlie threw Mr Grundy the keys and took hold of the inert body under the arms while Jackson moved from his sentry duty at the window and took up the legs.

Charlie, moving backwards went first, heading for the tiny sink. After entering the little alcove, Charlie, the body and then Jackson, all vanished.

Ella not wanting to miss anything followed in their wake.

The stairway was very narrow and Charlie, halfway up dropped the unfortunate body and Jackson only just managed to stop them all from tumbling back down.

"Damn it man, if this poor sod survives this, he will deserve to live. He will have the constitution of a horse, watch what you are doing," Jackson snapped.

"If you could keep his legs off the stairs, we might have a better chance," Charlie replied.

It was dark in the stairwell; the only light came from the open doors at the top of the stairs.

Mr Grundy had closed and locked the door to the stairwell and pulled the curtain back in place and the little kitchenette was hidden from sight. Locking the workshop door, he had made his way back into his house.

He locked his front door behind him and headed upstairs to his first-floor landing. His bulk, taking exception to the unexpected exercise, left him panting and gasping for breath when he reached the top of the stairs. He went into Ella's bedroom and saw the door to the wardrobe open. The hanging clothes were pulled to one side to reveal a second open door. This gave access to the stairwell that lead down into the workshop. He waited for the foursome to appear.

34

It took longer than expected, while ascending the stairwell they had stumbled more than once but Charlie's back eventually appeared in the doorway, then the body, Jackson and finally Ella.

Ella found herself standing in the wardrobe in her bedroom. Stepping out she closed the stairwell door they had all appeared through and pulled the hanging clothes back across to hide the door. She then closed the wardrobe doors.

It was all very intriguing, and her natural curiosity had to be reined in while she watched Mr Grundy walk to the other side of her bedroom and pull the dressing table away from the wall.

Mr Grundy bent down and opened a small door just about waist high. The body was laid in front of the opening and Charlie bent down and disappeared through the hole in the wall.

Ella saw two hands extend from the other side of the bedroom wall and take hold of the seemingly lifeless body and drag it through the opening with Jackson following.

Ella looked across at Mr Grundy who went over to the hole in the wall, then he bent down and closed the door. Finally, he pushed the dressing table back into position and the connecting hole was once more hidden from sight.

"Leave them to it, Ella. You and I will go shopping. We need some food. By the time we get back they should have some news for us. Shopping will take our minds off all this and if our house is being observed, seeing us stepping out should dispel any thoughts of hidden bodies lying about in here."

"Was he alive?" she asked.

"I have no idea. I was not going to touch him, nothing I could do for him anyway. I am not a doctor."

"What shall I call you?"

"My name is Charles Grundy, but your Aunt Fran always called me Mr Grundy."

"I thought Charlie called you Clarence."

Mr Grundy looked at the young woman standing by the kitchen door and chuckled.

"That was Jackson, when he found out my name was Charles he said he was not going to call me Charles he'd had enough Charlies in his life, so he christened me Clarence. He said he did not know anybody else called Clarence and the name follows me around."

"In that case, if it is alright with you I shall carry on calling you Mr Grundy just like Aunt Fran did. I would hate to get my Charlies mixed up," and they both laughed.

"I think it would be a good idea if I go and clean all that blood up before we set off, don't you? Whilst the water is boiling, can I ask you about the stairwell in the workshop and the hole in the wall in my bedroom?"

"I insisted that we had the stairwell built so your Aunt Fran could come and go whenever she pleased and she did not have to go outside when it was dark, or the weather was bad. The stairwell has been put to good use over the years," Mr Grundy told her.

"And the connecting hole through to Charlie's house?"

"That was your Aunt Fran's idea. She thought the world of Charlie and she insisted on having the connecting wall opened and the escape hatch installed as she called it. She said he never knew when he might need it given the line of work he was in. There is a bolt on your side of the connecting door if you feel uncomfortable with it. This is the first time the bolthole has been used since it has been installed. There has never been the need for Charlie to use it thank goodness."

With a bucket of warm soapy water in one hand, a scrubbing brush and cloth in the other, Ella was about to go out of the front door when Mr Grundy stopped her.

"Better use the stairwell Ella. After all, we do not know if we are being watched, do we? The keys to the stairwell are kept in that top drawer at the side of the sink."

Ella took possession of the keys and set off to clean up the mess.

First, she cleaned the floor at the base of the trunk, then the floor where the body had been laid. She cast her eye over the rest of the floor but could see no more drops of blood, so she lifted the lid of the trunk and looked inside.

Although there was a certain amount of blood on the floor of the trunk, there was not as much as she had expected to find but, lying there, at the bottom of the trunk was a little black book.

Picking it up carefully she took the clean cloth, dipped it in the water and twisted it as hard as she could to remove most of the water, then taking the damp cloth she wiped the book cover gently to remove the blood that had just caught the corner of the black leather jacket that housed the white note pad.

She was pleased to see that none of the sheets on the note pad had been stained. Placing the book in her dress pocket she took up her scrubbing brush and set to work.

Back in the kitchen Ella said to Mr Grundy, "Look what I found at the bottom of the trunk," and she held up the little black book.

He held out his hand and she placed the book in it. Mr Grundy put the book in his pocket. "Better not mention this to anyone. I will give it to Charlie."

"Why Charlie, why should he have it?"

"Because it is an occurrence book, and he is the best one to give it to, Charlie will know what to do with it."

"What is an occurrence book?"

"It is a book that the police use to make notes in, and then they can refer to it when writing out their report."

"How do you know that?"

"I have seen Charlie doing it."

"Charlie has an occurrence book? But that would make him a policeman."

"Inspector to be precise, Charlie is an inspector of police."

"Charlie is an inspector of police? And you sent me to get him when we had a dead body in the trunk in your workshop," Ella was astounded.

"We did not know whether he was dead or not and anyway, Charlie is still the best person to deal with the situation if it turned out to be bad news. Let's go shopping and I will explain on the way."

Chapter Four

Mr Grundy started by telling Ella that after Fran and he were married, Fran had gone to work for him in his solicitor's office, Grundy, Grundy and Grundy, only there was no Grundy and Grundy, only him, Mr Grundy. Fran had told him that it sounded more business like to add the other two Grundy's on. She said it sounded more like a solicitor's office.

"Fran was very good in the office and she helped me get a lot of business that I would not normally have had if it had been left up to me.

"Fran was in the office on her own one day when a young woman came into the office saying her brother needed a solicitor urgently. So, Fran, being Fran, put on her coat and went off with the young woman in distress.

"The young woman took Fran to a derelict building and that was the first encounter we had with Jackson. The young woman's brother was lying on the floor, his head covered in blood and although he was not unconscious he was in a bad state. Fran and the young woman helped him to his feet and between them they half carried, half dragged him back to the office.

"Once he was lying on the couch, he lost consciousness. Fran went to get a bowl of water to bathe the young man's head and when she came back into the room, the young woman had gone. I returned to the office to find Fran wiping blood off a stranger's face. I sent her to fetch Charlie. It was the natural thing to do, when in trouble or in need of help, fetch Charlie."

Mr Grundy went on to tell Ella he was left alone with a strange, funny looking unconscious man bleeding all over his couch, and he was none too happy.

"I am not a brave man and we had no idea who he was or how he came by the bleeding gash on his head. He could have been a murderer for all we knew and there I was, left alone with him on my couch. It was sheer luck the bleeding man was still unconscious when Fran came back with Charlie on her heels. I was never so pleased to see anybody in my life, I can tell you.

"But as it turned out it was an encounter that led to one of the best friendships Fran and I could have had. We all became the very best of friends.

"It was two hours before the stranger finally came to, and when he did, he could not remember a thing."

Mr Grundy giggled, "Did Charlie tell you the story that he thinks Jackson, for that is who the injured man turned out to be, was kicked off planet mars and he landed on his head in a rubbish dump?"

Ella could not help laughing.

"He did, and Mr Grundy, I have not laughed so much for a long, long time. They are both so funny. I find it hard to believe that Charlie is an inspector of police."

"In that case, you will find it even harder to believe that Jackson is a doctor."

"A doctor, Jackson is a doctor? God help his patients."

"Yes, in a way, he learned his trade during the war. He is a veterinary really, he was posted abroad to look after the horses on the battlefield, but when the doctor out there was killed, Jackson took over looking after the wounded soldiers."

"So, as well as looking after the horses, Jackson looked after the wounded soldiers?" Ella asked.

"There was nobody else there who had any medical training, so it fell to Jackson to attend to the wounded.

"Jackson has a couple of medals for his bravery and services on the front line. Anyway, back to our first meeting with Jackson.

"It turned out that Jackson had been called to attend to a patient who had been stabbed but when Jackson got there, the patient was already dead. Nothing he could have done; the wound was fatal. The culprit who had stabbed the patient now had to get rid of the doctor; he did not want any witnesses.

"Jackson was knocked unconscious and taken off in a cart to be dumped in the river but, as the thugs were taking the body out of the cart, they were disturbed by the sound of voices, so the thugs just dropped him, and he landed on the grass verge alongside the riverbank. The two thugs drove off leaving Jackson for dead.

"The young woman that came to the office had been out with her beau at the time, but she should not have been. Her parents had forbidden the young woman to see her young man again, for they did not approve of him. The clandestine meeting was brought to a quick parting of the ways when the young man saw the body lying on the grass verge.

"He took off and left the young woman on her own to deal with the body. When the body moved and groaned, the young woman helped the semiconscious man into the derelict building and you know the rest.

"That is how Fran and I became involved in the matter. As you know in 1800, Glasgow was the first city in Britain to establish a police force. Police stations sprung up all over Scotland and Marchum was fortunate enough to be one of those towns.

"Charlie was an inspector of police based at Marchum and he was put in charge of the case. He solved it eventually, thieves falling out and one stabbing the other, but it took two months for Jackson to remember all the details and at the end of the two months, Charlie and Jackson were firm friends.

"Charlie had taken Jackson back to his house until he recovered his memory and Jackson has been there ever since.

"They both have an odd sense of humour, not everyone can see the funny side of it, especially the women, for some peculiar reason women seem to be offended by it," concluded Mr Grundy.

"So, it was not really her brother at all?"

"No, she had never seen him before in her life. It was just an excuse she gave to get him some help."

"Why a solicitor's office, surely a doctor would have been a better choice?"

"When Charlie eventually tracked her down, she said she thought the injured man would need a solicitor when he regained consciousness, so that is why she chose a solicitor instead of a doctor. She said she knew someone would call a doctor to attend him but not many would think of getting him a solicitor. She is a clever girl, don't you think?"

"Yes, I do. What happened to her beau, the one that ran off?"

"She refused to see him again much to her parent's relief, only things did not go quite to plan as they hoped. The young woman in question is somewhat out of the ordinary herself. For one thing she is tall, and she has protruding top, front teeth and she is not that young, in her late twenties, nearly thirty."

"Why didn't her parents approve of her beau?" Ella wanted to know.

"Her father is a very wealthy merchant and he had found out that this particular young man was out to find himself a rich wife."

"You are saying then that he was after her money?"

"I am afraid so. The young woman's parents had tried on more than one occasion to set her up with a young man whom they thought would be a suitable husband for her, but each time she has told them she will marry whom she wants and will not entertain any of the young men they chose."

"I feel sorry for the young woman if that be the case," Ella told him.

"There is no need to feel sorry for her, Ella. She has now found her true love."

"Has she, how wonderful. Who is he?"

"Charlie found out who the young woman was, and he took Jackson to meet her. Jackson wanted to thank her for helping him in his hour of need and they have been inseparable ever since.

"When Charlie found Blanche, for that is her name, he told her Jackson would like to meet her and thank her for what she did for him. Blanche agreed to meet him, but she insisted on meeting Jackson away from her home, she didn't want her parents to be involved in her latest caper.

"You have seen Jackson, you cannot say he is a strapping fellow and his appearance has much to be desired, but funnily enough they are very well suited. Blanche and Jackson have been together ever since, about eight years."

"So, Jackson does not work for Charlie?"

"No, Jackson has his own vet's practice. I do not think it does much trade. For one thing, Jackson has no premises to work from but he does a bit of work for the police, as a doctor, if they cannot get anyone else."

"Surely Jackson can't claim to be a doctor if he has not qualified as one. Isn't it illegal to be calling himself a doctor?"

"Jackson does not call himself a doctor, he calls himself a vet. Word soon got around that he had acted on the battlefield as a doctor. So, anyone in need of medical attention and they have no money to pay for it, they appeal to Jackson. He helps if he can and does not take payment for his services.

"He is kept pretty busy I can tell you, there are a lot of people out there that cannot afford to pay for a doctor. He occasionally gets paid in kind, eggs or a side of pork or the odd cabbage, that sort of thing.

"He is an extremely good person, that is why he and Charlie get on so famously. Charlie is also an extremely good person, he is someone you can trust and depend on and your Aunt Fran loved him

41

like he was her own. In fact, she not only loved Charlie, she loved Jackson and Blanche too. We are a close knit little family."

"What about you Mr Grundy? Do you love them all too?"

"I do. I do not know what I would have done without them when my Fran died. I feel very lucky to have them as my friends. That is why I said it was a very lucky meeting when Blanche brought Jackson into our lives. We have all been the very best of friends ever since."

"Do you think I could come and work for you in your office? Like Aunt Fran did. Would you permit me to do that?"

"I should be delighted to have you. My filing system could do with sorting out, I am afraid I have neglected it since your Aunt Fran passed on. The filing was one of her jobs you see."

"Then on Monday morning I shall accompany you to work and make a start on your filing system," Ella smiled at him.

Their shopping bought and stored away in the larder, Mr Grundy and Ella made their way next door. There was no sign of anyone when Mr Grundy knocked on the door; no one came to answer it.

Mr Grundy waited a few seconds and knocked again and when there was still no sign of anyone answering his knock, he opened the door and went in.

Once inside, Mr Grundy shouted, "Hello! Is anyone home?"

"Do you think we should be entering the house when no one is around?" Ella wanted to know.

"Of course, you noticed the door was unlocked. Charlie leaves it unlocked for me to come and go as I please. I do the same, it is very rare we lock our doors, only when we go to bed or if I know Charlie is not going to be in, do I lock my door. It is a very quiet little town. Not much goes off here. That is probably why I forgot to lock the workshop door and our mystery man was able to gain entry."

"You say not much goes off in your little quiet town, you could have fooled me. I have lived in some busier towns than this and I have never come across a body in a trunk before. I don't think finding a body in a trunk is a very common event, even in a busy town."

"No, I must say it has livened things up a little." Mr Grundy started to ascend the stairs with Ella following.

Once again Mr Grundy knocked on one of the bedroom doors and when he got no response he entered.

Ella found herself in a sparsely furnished room with a single bed in it. Lying upon that bed was the gentleman from the trunk. He had been cleaned up and his shoulder had a clean white bandage made into a sling holding his arm close to his body to try and stop him moving it.

If his leg had a similar bandage on, they could not tell, for he was covered with clean white bed linen. His face was nearly as white as his bandage and the sheets.

Jackson was sitting by the window reading a book.

"Hello, I'm glad you are back from your shopping. Stay with the patient whilst I go and get something to eat, will you? Charlie doesn't give a damn if I starve to death so long as he can go to his precious police station. One of these days he is going to come home, and I will not be here, then he will miss me," Jackson grumbled heading for the door.

"We didn't think anyone was in. Why didn't you answer the door to our knock?" Ella asked his back.

"I heard you come in, you were making enough noise to wake the dead. I knew you would come to check on the patient so why should I bother getting up to answer the door, and anyway, I had just reached a very interesting chapter in my book," Jackson said before he disappeared.

Ella went over to the bed and saw the gentleman's shallow breathing and said to Mr Grundy, "He is alive, for I can see his chest moving up and down."

"Jackson knows what he is doing."

"I am surprised at Charlie, leaving him with nothing to eat."

"Don't let Jackson fool you Ella, he will have told Charlie to go and see if he can find anything out about the patient. Jackson likes to complain but it is only an act."

The bedroom door opened and in walked Charlie, his face beamed at the sight of Mr Grundy and Ella.

Charlie walked over to Ella took her hand and kissed the back of it, "Ah, my fiancé."

Ella looked him in the eye, "The very same."

"Good girl," he approved, patted her hand and went over to look at the patient.

"Have you found anything out about him?" Mr Grundy asked.

"Nothing, no crime has been reported nor anybody hearing gun shots or even seeing a man walking about bleeding," Charlie told them.

"This might help." Mr Grundy took the occurrence book out of his pocket and handed it to Charlie.

Charlie looked at Mr Grundy as he took the book from his hand.

Mr Grundy said, "Ella found it at the bottom of the trunk when she went to clean up the blood in case my two unwelcome guests returned."

Charlie opened the occurrence book and looked at the front page and read: "PC 152, Melvin Keyser. Hotshell Division.

"If this book belongs to our patient, his name is Melvin Keyser, he is a policeman and he is based at Hotshell. That is about four miles away. I wonder what he was doing on our patch. I had better go back to the station and let them know. Where is boy wonder by the way?"

"Who is boy wonder?" Ella asked.

"Jackson of course," Charlie replied.

"He has gone to get something to eat," Ella told him.

"Eating me out of house and home as usual, for an old man he can certainly put it away. Look after the patient. I shall see you when I get back."

"Another policeman. I wonder what is going on. I wonder if those other two who came and searched the house are policemen too. I wonder if our patient is a good policeman or not," Ella looked at Mr Grundy.

"There are a lot of wonders there Ella."

"Well, there is a lot to think about."

"If I were a betting man, I would say the patient is the good policeman and the other two are the villains. They might have been stylishly dressed but I do not think a good policeman would push his way into somebody's house and search it like those two did. I don't think they were policemen at all."

There was a knock on the door and Ella went over and opened it to find Jackson had returned bearing a tray with a steaming bowl of soup and a glass of milk on it.

"I am going to try and get some food down him. Will you give me a hand with these pillows? I will lift him up while you pile the pillows behind him to get him into a semi-sitting position. It should stop him from choking as I feed him the soup."

Jackson placed the tray on the table near the window then went back to the bed and gently lifted the patient up and Ella piled the pillows up behind him.

Going over to the table Jackson dragged it to the side of the bed and said, "There is nothing more for you two to do here. I will be alright now. I have had something to eat and I am sure it will not be long before Charlie is back."

"He has already been back and gone again," Mr Grundy told him.

"The devil he has. What is he up to now?"

"Ella found an occurrence book in the trunk this morning, so I gave it to Charlie. He has gone back to the police station to try and find out who he is."

Jackson looked at his patient, "He is a policeman, is he? Why didn't Charlie recognise him if he is a fellow policeman? I must admit I have never seen him before and I go to the police station occasionally."

"He is from Hotshell, or at least that is what it says in the book. But we don't know that the book does belong to him. That is another thing we do not know. So, in fact, we know nothing," replied Mr Grundy.

"We will go back home now Jackson and leave you to tend to your patient. Would you and Charlie like to come around to Mr Grundy's house around 7 o'clock this evening and I will have a meal ready for us all? Mr Grundy has bought a very nice piece of beef for dinner."

"That would be marvellous Ella, but Blanche is coming here this evening," Jackson informed her.

"Then we shall expect Blanche as well. I should very much like to meet her. Mr Grundy has told me all about her, how you and she met, besides that, I would like to meet anyone that knew my Aunt Fran," Ella replied.

"7 o'clock it is then, I shall look forward to it."

Chapter Five

Ella enjoyed herself in the kitchen pottering around preparing the evening meal. She pondered as she worked on how her life had suddenly become exciting and interesting.

Mr Grundy had given her permission to do as she wished in the kitchen. He was more than happy to let go of the reins where the kitchen was concerned. Two days ago, things had certainly been very different for her.

She was going to have to see about getting somewhere of her own to live, she could not expect to stay with Mr Grundy forever but, she decided, for at least a few weeks she was going to stay where she was and enjoy herself. She decided she didn't care a fig for what would be said about her, this was the happiest she had been since her father died.

She felt at ease and that she belonged in the company she had now found herself in. There was also a mystery to solve. Things were certainly looking up.

When their guests arrived, Ella was dwarfed by Jackson's, Blanche. In fact, Jackson was dwarfed by his Blanche. Only Charlie was just inches taller than she was.

Blanche was dressed in a bright orange and tan gown, her face was framed by mousey brown curly hair that hung down passed her shoulders in two thick ringlets, tied loosely back with a bright orange ribbon.

"This is Blanche, Blanche this is Ella. We met Ella yesterday for the first time when she landed us with that body I have been telling you about. The one that is upstairs in Charlie's spare bedroom."

The two ladies shook hands, and both had a mischievous smile on their lips and Ella said, "I am Fran's niece. Mr Grundy thankfully tracked me down and gave me the opportunity to come here. I am so pleased to meet you all. Any friend of my Aunt Fran's, I hope will be a friend of mine."

"I was wondering where old Clarence had got you from. So, you are Ella, Fran's niece, are you? I should have guessed. You look a bit like her," Charlie commented.

"Please come through into the kitchen, dinner is all about ready and Mr Grundy will pour us all a drink."

During dinner Charlie told them they knew nothing at all about the mystery man at the police station. Nobody had ever heard PC Keyser's name mentioned, so he was going to ride over to Hotshell tomorrow and take the occurrence book with him. They would be able to tell him if he did indeed work for the constabulary.

Jackson looked across at his beloved Blanche and said, "Is something wrong poppet? You are very quiet tonight."

Blanche put her knife and fork down and announced, "I am pregnant."

Everything went quiet in the kitchen and they all sat looking at Blanche who kept her head bent forward and her eyes downcast.

Ella was the first to speak, "How wonderful Blanche, congratulations."

"You would not be saying that if you knew my parents. They will be furious with me," Blanche whispered.

"It has nothing to do with your parents," Jackson said. "My God Blanche, this is wonderful news, me having a baby, who would have thought that?"

"Certainly not me," said Charlie, "I would not have thought you had it in you. Congratulations to you both, this is a happy occasion indeed, let us drink to the mother and baby."

"What about the father?" Jackson asked, "Why can't we drink to me as well? After all it is my baby too."

"My apologies Jackson, let us drink to the mother, father and baby?" Charlie amended raising his glass of wine.

Jackson stood up and took Blanche's glass of wine out of her hand.

"Not for you my poppet. No more wine for you until you have had the baby. I don't suppose you have a glass of milk Blanche could have, do you Ella?"

"Milk!" exclaimed Blanche.

"Lots of calcium for the baby," Jackson told her.

"Aren't you mad with me?" she asked looking across at Jackson.

"Mad at you, why the hell should I be mad with you? It is fantastic news. We will have to get married now, whether you want to or not."

47

"Of course, I want to marry you Jackson, I adore you. But we have nowhere to live, no money and I will not go cap in hand to my parents. This is our baby and I want to bring it up as our baby. My mother will try to take over, but I shall not let her, I shall tell her she will not see her grandchild if she starts telling me what to do and how to bring the baby up. I will not have it."

"You are putting the cart before the horse Blanche. I am sure your mother will be delighted that you are having a baby. You are too harsh on her," Charlie told her.

"She will not be delighted you know, when my mother finds out I am pregnant out of wedlock, she might well turn me out of the house," Blanche replied.

"We have been idling along for far too long. Now the situation has come to a head, we are going to have to take the bull by the horns and get married and see where it takes us. Something will turn up," Jackson told her.

"Why have you not married before now?" asked Ella.

"Jackson and I are happy as we are. I will not force him into marrying me if he does not want to. My parents keep throwing eligible young men at me, but I am not interested in any of them. I know they are only after my money, or I should say my father's money.

"Jackson is the only man I have ever met that treats me like a delicate flower. I am a giant of a woman and not very elegant and my teeth should have been removed at birth, but none of that matters to my Jackson, he makes me feel small and delicate and I love him."

"Anyone that loves Jackson and is willing to take him off my hands has my support any time, day or night," Charlie said.

The tension in the room became more relaxed and the little party laughed.

Ella asked, "Have you thought of any names for the baby Blanche?"

"If it is a boy, I will tell you what it is not going to be called and that is Charles," Jackson said.

"Well don't call it Clarence either, poor little thing," Mr Grundy remarked.

"I am going to have to get my thinking cap on now and find a suitable place to set up a veterinary practice instead of relying on word of mouth and the odd job for the police," Jackson muttered.

"What about Fran's workshop? Why not set up there, it is empty now and it would be ideal for you, surely? We could build some kennels at the back and there is also the meadow next to it which belongs to me. There are no neighbours to worry about only Charlie, and he does not count," Mr Grundy told him.

"I could not afford that, but thanks for the offer Clarence. I am going to have to start small and work my way up."

"You insult me Jackson, who mentioned money? You do not have to pay me for the use of it. It is yours if you want to use it. A gift to Blanche, you and your baby, from me and Fran. Fran would have been delighted at the thought of a baby. I am sure she would be the first to insist you use the meadow and workshop to set up a surgery.

"You were there for me when I needed you when Fran died. Now, I can repay your kindness and be there for you both in your hour of need," Mr Grundy said.

"What about you Ella? I think Fran intended you to have the workshop. She always said it was to come to you when anything happened to her and Clarence of course. I do not think she intended it for Blanche and me," said Jackson.

"I think it is a wonderful idea. Aunt Fran can still have a hand in helping you both. I think she would be delighted at the thought of her friends having a baby and being able to lend them a helping hand. Aunt Fran was very fond of you both, Mr Grundy has already told me that.

"He has also told me you have all been very kind to him and helped him through his worst days after Aunt Fran died. I think it is a very nice gesture Mr Grundy, and I think Aunt Fran would be proud of you for making it. If it will help you out Jackson, I should grab the offer with both hands," Ella told them all.

"It most certainly would. I think it is the perfect solution for us, but where are we going to live? We cannot expect misery guts here to put us all up. The house is not big enough anyway, or it will not be once the baby arrives.

"We will all have to sleep on it, but I think if you are still in the same frame of mind in the morning Clarence, Blanche and I will be most grateful and take you up on the offer. In fact, if the worst came to the worst, we could always sleep in the workshop as well until my practice gets on its feet then we could find somewhere to live," Jackson told him.

Jackson looked up at Charlie, "You have gone quiet."

"I was just thinking about the baby, a real live baby. Well done Blanche. It is a wonderful thing to have happened and I cannot wait to see it. It will be a pleasure to behold, watching Jackson change the nappies. I only hope the baby has your face Blanche and not Jackson's," Charlie said.

"I bet I do a better job of changing a nappy than you ever would," Jackson countered.

"We'll see Jackson old boy, we'll see," Charlie told him.

Blanche used to this banter, looked 'round the table and a tear came to her eye.

"Thank you all for your support. I thought I was going to have to go begging to my parents. I am willing to sleep in the workshop if Mr Grundy permits and try to keep out of everybody's way."

"What on earth are you talking about Blanche? Once you and Jackson are married, you must, of course, come to live with him. There will be time enough before the baby arrives to sort something more suitable out for you, Jackson and the baby. As for keeping out of everybody's way, why would you want to do that? I thought we were all friends?" Charlie wanted to know.

"I always felt I was in the way at home, so I kept out of the way as much as I could when my parents had visitors, I think they are ashamed of me. They wanted some tiny, dainty little thing to show off in front of their snobby friends and they got me. I am a great disappointment to them," Blanche sighed.

"I think you are doing your parents an injustice Blanche. They seem to have done a good job in bringing you up, but then again, I have not met them. Is your coming to live here with us going to make you feel you are missing out on the grand lifestyle your parents provide for you?" asked Jackson.

"Why do you think I would prefer to live with them rather than come and look after you?" asked Blanche.

"I will never be able to provide for you the way your parents do. It is going to be a struggle to make ends meet but if Mr Grundy is going to let me use his workshop and use his meadow as part of the surgery, and Charlie is letting us stay with him for a few months until the baby arrives, then things might not turn out to be so bad after all.

"I will go and see the vicar tomorrow, no, we will go and see the vicar tomorrow and see if we can get a special licence and get married as soon as we can. Is that alright with you Blanche?" Jackson wanted to know.

"You ask if it is alright with me, of course it is alright with me. I do not know what to say, this has all come so unexpectedly."

Blanche looked 'round the table again and she felt as though she had finally found her place in the world, friends, a home, a husband and soon, a baby of her own to love and cherish.

"What is your first name?" Ella asked Jackson.

"Now why did you have to go and spoil such an excellent evening's entertainment by asking a thing like that?" asked Jackson.

"How is telling us your first name going to spoil the evening?"

"Why can't you just be happy to call me Jackson?"

"The vicar will want to know your first name, for the marriage licence so we are going to find out sooner or later so why not get it over with now?" Ella was not going to let it go.

"If you must know my first name is Charles."

"You are an old dog Jackson. You told me your first name was Ned," Charlie accused him.

"The world is full of Charlies, there are three of us in this room for a start," Jackson told them.

"There might be four," Blanche patted her stomach.

"I have already told you if it is a boy we are not calling him Charles," Jackson glared at Blanche.

"We will see," she smiled.

Charlie's shoulders shook with laughter and he said, "This is what I call poetic justice, all the times you have called my name and it turns out we have identical names. That baby has started to change your life already Jackson old boy, and it is not even born yet."

"Thank you for the meal Ella. It was very nice of you to put yourself out on our behalf, but I must get Blanche home. It is getting late and she needs to rest you know. Now she is having my baby, I do not want her tired out."

Jackson wiped his mouth with his napkin and stood up, going around the table he pulled Blanche's chair out for her and held out his arm for her to take.

"For heaven's sake Jackson, I am having a baby I am not an invalid. Ella, I was going to suggest I come over tomorrow and do something with your hair. Why on earth do you wear it in a bun severely tied back like that, it does not suit you."

"This is how I wore it when I was a governess. If I went around with my hair modish, I would not have lasted very long in my employment. Having said that, I did not last very long in my employment with my hair in a bun either.

"But please come around tomorrow, I will be delighted to see you, in fact why don't you make it Monday morning and then we can spend a bit of time getting to know each other. Tomorrow you are going to see the vicar with Jackson."

"Very well. I will see you early on Monday morning and when we have sorted out your hair, why don't we go shopping afterwards? I feel much better now that I have told Jackson I am having a baby. It will give me something to look forward to. Thank you for the meal it was delicious.

"Goodnight and thank you all again for your support, especially you Mr Grundy for offering Jackson the workshop. It is a wonderful opportunity for us. I never expected all this kindness when I set off to come here this evening," Blanche told them.

"Think nothing of it my dear. I am sure Fran would be over the moon to think her workshop is being put to good use and a baby running around to boot. Bless my soul it is a miracle.

"But sit back down both of you. Another solution has just popped into my head while you were all talking, that might be just the very thing." Mr Grundy motioned them both to sit back down.

Blanche and Jackson retook their seats and Mr Grundy continued.

"I have been thinking for a while, since Fran passed on, that I might retire. Hearing you two are in a situation, I have just made the decision that the time is right for me to hang up my boots.

"The building in which my office is located belongs to me, it is bigger than this place and once I have put all my files in order and put them to storage in the basement, I can convert the building back into a house."

Mr Grundy looked around the table, but no one made any comment.

"Ella seems to have settled in nicely, she already feels like one of us so instead of her looking around for a place to live I shall convert my office into a small flat for me and then Ella can have the rest of the building to herself."

Again, Mr Grundy looked 'round the table, but no one spoke.

"Jackson and Blanche can move in here once we have things sorted out. We should be able to be out of here before the baby arrives. That way Ella will have her own place and I shall have mine, but we will be living in the same house and I will not feel that I have nobody or that I am totally alone in my old age.

"Also, Ella will not be on her own, she will be under my protection. I think that would be the ideal solution for all of us, don't you?"

"Are you sure Mr Grundy? I do not want you to think you have to move out on our account," Blanche told him.

"You could use this place for the office and Blanche will be able to help you out with the paper work as well as being at home to look after the baby and if you need to, you can always build a couple of stables in the meadow at the side. What do you think of that, Jackson?"

"Things seem to be going a little too fast for me to keep up with," Ella said, "But as a plan, I cannot fault it. Well thought out Mr Grundy."

"I am speechless," said Jackson.

"Whatever it is you just said Clarence, remember it. Anything that can make Jackson speechless, will be worth a fortune," Charlie told him.

"Well, I am not speechless, and I want to say I never thought I would have such friends as the people sitting 'round this table. Mr Grundy, I am more than willing to accept your offer, it is a perfect solution to our problem. Thank you so very much," and Blanche stood up and went over and gave Mr Grundy a hug and a kiss on the cheek, much to his discomfort.

"And you shall never be alone in your old age for you have all of us," Blanche added.

"But I do not have any money to pay for all this. It is alright in theory, but one must be practical about these things. I am alright now, my living arrangements are very cheap, in fact none existent, although I do have a lot to put up with," Jackson glanced across at Charlie.

Continuing Jackson said, "But although I have most of the medical equipment I will need, there will be medicines required, bandages and to say nothing of cages if the animals need overnight stays, I just cannot do it."

"Then Charlie and I will go into business with you and help you out," Mr Grundy told him.

"The devil we will," said Charlie.

"There, that is one stumbling block before we start," said a dejected Jackson.

"You do not have to pay me any rent for the properties Jackson. If I retire, I can come and help you look after the animals. I like animals, and Charlie, although he says he won't, I know damn well he will help with the funding of the materials you need. Ella can help with the baby if she wants to, if Blanche would like that of course. There are all sorts of things we can do to help.

"Once you are on your feet, you can get your own surgery. You need not feel you will be a burden to us because you will not. You will be able to get somewhere of your own if you want to. I can only live in one house at a time so in that respect you will be helping me out. I trust you not to wreck the place."

No one spoke. All eyes turned to Charlie and he wanted to know, "Why is everyone looking at me?"

"Jackson wants to know if he has your support," Mr Grundy told him.

"Wants my support, wants my support! What the devil does he think I have been doing these past ten years?" said a furious Charlie.

"Why should I withdraw my support now, when he needs it most? It's that fall from Mars that did it, landing on his head, it has made him addled. He has never been the same since. Not that I knew him before he fell from the sky, and maybe that was a blessing.

"I will help fund anything Jackson needs but I will not go into business with him, I have enough on my plate without starting up in business. He can pay me back when his pockets are flush.

"A thought did go through my mind when Jackson mentioned getting married and Blanche is coming to live with us, I thought I might ask her to be the housekeeper. Keep it clean and have a meal ready for me when I get in from work, do my washing and things like that. I would pay her for her services until she has the baby of course, then she will have her own house to keep in order."

Ella looked at the stunned Blanche. It was Blanche's turn to be speechless and Ella started laughing.

"Poor Blanche, she has gone from thinking she was going to be snubbed because she is having a baby out of wedlock to having a husband, her own house and now a paid job. It is enough to make anyone speechless."

"Yes, and it is a damned unthoughtful thing to do now that she is having a baby. The shock of it is enough to knock anyone for six. I am going to take her home now and I am going to tell her parents that we are getting married and if they throw her out I shall bring her back here to her friends. Goodnight to you all."

Jackson stood up and taking Blanche by the hand he dragged her out of the kitchen and the assembled party in the kitchen heard the front door slam behind them.

"I think that went well, don't you?" Mr Grundy asked.

Charlie burst out laughing, "Mr Grundy you are an old devil. Yes, I think that went very well indeed. It was worth it to see

Jackson nonplussed. That is the first time I have seen that, he usually has an answer for everything. It was a pleasure to behold."

"With all this going on our man from the trunk has been forgotten. I hope he is alright," Ella said.

"You are right Ella my darling about our man from the trunk, I had better go and have a look at him, make sure he is comfortable for the night. No doubt Jackson will check him before he retires but I had better go and see him all the same. It has been a very pleasant evening Clarence, and a delicious meal Ella. I shall look forward to having many more evenings like this." Charlie took his leave of them.

Mr Grundy looked at Ella and asked, "Are you alright with the arrangements Ella? I know I took it upon myself to organise things, but I think Blanche has had a bad time of it growing up and then to find herself in this position I thought she needed some help."

"You do not have to ask my permission to do whatever you want with your property and money, Mr Grundy. I thought it was very expertly done if you must know, and I agree with you about Blanche. I think she is having difficulty in taking it all in. I know how she feels, I have only been here a couple of days myself and a lot of things have left me speechless too."

"You have only yourself to blame for that. You were the one that found the bleeding body in the trunk and from that moment on we have not had a moment's peace. It has been one thing after another. I bet you made an excellent governess, the little cherubs in your care would not have known what had hit them."

Ella could not help laughing.

"Come on, let us get these dirty dishes in the sink and I will see to them in the morning. I admit to being tired, it must be the country air." Ella told him.

"It has nothing to do with the air," Mr Grundy groaned. "But I meant what I said about us moving into my office building together. I know you said you wanted a place of your own, but would you consider sharing the house with me. I won't be much of a trouble to you. It will be nice for me to know there is someone else in the house besides myself."

"Mr Grundy, if I had to move away now, I would be devastated. I know I have only been here a couple of days, but I feel as though I have lived here all my life and as for moving into your office building with you, I would appreciate your protection and companionship. I do not want to be on my own either, and I would feel safer if I knew there was someone else in the house as well."

"Then I shall sleep well tonight, and I might even have a lie-in in the morning, get used to being retired. I am looking forward to it now I have made up my mind."

Mr Grundy stood up and took his plate to the sink then made his way to the staircase and to his bed.

Ella watched with a smile on her face, she had become very fond of the old gentleman in such a short time.

Whilst lying in her cosy single bed, Ella thought of the impropriety of it all. She was living with an elderly gentleman who had told her he was her uncle when she knew he was only her uncle by marriage.

He is no blood relation and she had not even known her Aunt Fran had existed until a few days ago. Then there was the hole in the wall giving access to a bachelor home with a very nice bachelor living in it and his little Martian friend. Ella had not felt as safe as this since she had been left to fend for herself, this was her home now and she was going to stay, come what may. She pulled the covers snuggly around her neck and went to sleep with a contented smile on her face.

Chapter Six

Blanche and Jackson were told, on entering the Moyer's residence that Mr and Mrs Moyer were in the sitting room. Without hesitation, Blanche led Jackson across the hall and into the sitting room where Blanche's mother, dressed in a pale blue blouse and royal blue full-length skirt, was sitting reading a book.

Her father was dressed in his favourite smoking jacket that had seen better days and was nodding off in his favourite black leather armchair that had also seen better days. There was a roaring fire blazing in an open fireplace and a discarded newspaper scattered on the floor.

Mrs Moyer had given up trying to get her husband to abandon both smoking jacket and old black leather chair. Although he had plenty of new smoking jackets hanging in his wardrobe and comfortable armchairs in various other rooms in the house, he always seemed to revert to his old favourites.

"Mother, we have come to tell you, Jackson and I are getting married as soon as we can. We are going to see the vicar tomorrow to arrange a special licence. You and Father will be welcome if you wish to attend the ceremony but if you do not, then it will be your loss. Jackson and I are having a baby. It is up to you whether you wish to be a part of your grandchild's life growing up, but I will not under any circumstances allow you to interfere with any decisions Jackson and I make for the wellbeing of our baby."

Mrs Moyer looked from Blanche to Jackson, "We have done our best to try to find a suitable husband for you Blanche, and you have blocked our every turn. If this man is the one you have chosen, the one you want to spend the rest of your life with, then so be it.

"Believe it or not, your father and I have only ever wanted you to be happy and if we will be welcome at your wedding, we would be delighted to attend. As for having a grandchild, it is the best gift you could possibly have given us. Your timing is a little unorthodox to say the least, it would have been better to get married first and then have your baby afterwards, but I will say no more on that subject. If you are willing to let your father and I be part of the child's upbringing, then we ask for nothing more."

"How do you intend to provide for my daughter and grandchild?" a gruff voice came from the direction of the old black leather chair.

"It may surprise you Papa, but I have friends, friends that are prepared to stand by us and support us. We are being given a roof over our heads and Jackson has been given a workshop to turn into a veterinary surgery. Jackson is a very fine vet and once he has been able to establish his business, he will be able to provide us with everything we need. Do not worry Papa, I will try my best not to come to you for assistance," his daughter told him.

"Since when have I ever kept you short of money? Money has never been the root of the disquiet that holds us apart. There was never anything your mother or I could do that pleased you, so in the end we stopped trying.

"If this Jackson is the man you want to marry, then he will be as welcome here as you are. I hope you will allow your mother and me to see our grandchild and to tell you the truth, I hope you have more than one child. Your mother and I were not blessed with more children, as well you know.

"Maybe if we'd had a brother or sister for you to play with, things might have been better between us. Let us have none of this nonsense about your mother and I not wanting to be part of your family, of course we want to be part of your life and our grandchild's life. What sort of monsters are you trying to make us out to be?" Mr Moyer said angrily.

Standing up, Mr Moyer came forward with his hand outstretch and Jackson who had been expecting to have a battle on his hands was once again left speechless.

This was a new experience for Jackson, he had been brought up in a quiet little country village by his mother and father.

There was never any money for extravagances, but he had never gone hungry. Jackson had no brothers or sisters either and once he had qualified as a vet he had joined the army.

The opulence of the house had taken Jackson by surprise too, he could only stand and shake hands with his father-in-law to be.

Mr Moyer was no taller than Jackson and he had a slim, lithe figure that belied his fifty years.

Mrs Moyer on the other hand was as tall as her daughter and her figure was prone to the fuller figure, but nonetheless, she had a very striking presence and she clasped Jackson to her ample bosom and nearly squeezed the life out of him.

"There will be a considerable dowry for Blanche of course, and I will not stand for any nonsense from you Jackson by refusing to take it. Blanche is our only child and what we possess belongs to her as well as us. This is her home and always will be." Mr Moyer looked at Jackson and waited.

When Jackson made no comment, Mr Moyer told him, "We know all about you. You don't think Sally and I are ignorant of your character, do you? I have made it my business to find out about you and I know you are a very brave man. Colonel Gregson is a friend of mine and he has told me all about you being sent to the battlefield to look after the horses and when the doctor was killed you stepped in and saved more than one life of our brave men."

Again, Mr Moyer waited for Jackson to speak. He did not.

"I also know you have been awarded two medals for your bravery. I will be proud to be able to boast that you are my son-in-law, but it has taken you eight years to come up to scratch. Lord, we thought you would never get around to proposing to our daughter.

"I had said to Sally, on more than one occasion, that I was going to have a word with you about it, but she would hear none of it. She said if we started interfering then Blanche would cry off. It has all been a lot of damn silly nonsense if you ask me.

"Now be off with you. My daughter needs her rest now that she is with child and do not forget to come and collect her in the morning to go and see that vicar or I shall be 'round with my shotgun."

Jackson walked back home in a daze. He was glad to escape the house, the turn of events that evening had taken him completely by surprise. Blanche's parents were nothing like he had expected them to be, they were both a force to be reckoned with.

While walking home, Jackson began to feel ridiculous. He had just stood there like a dummy. He had never uttered a single word the whole time he was there. Things had been taken out of his hands and he had been carried along with all this sudden change of events in his life from the moment Blanche had told them she was pregnant.

One thing Charlie had been right about, this baby of his had started to change his life already and he had only known of its existence for a few hours. What would happen to his life once the baby was born? He did not know, but one thing he was certain about, he could not wait to see it and hold it in his arms.

Charlie was still up when Jackson reached home, and he found him in the sickroom sitting in the chair near the window reading the little black occurrence book.

"Jackson, how did it go?" Charlie wanted to know.

"I have been rendered speechless twice in the last few hours Charlie. I have been threatened with a shotgun and nearly smothered in the biggest pair of breasts you have ever seen.

Charlie's eyes danced, and he made a mental note to repeat this to Ella and Clarence, knowing they would appreciate it too.

"I have been welcomed with open arms by the Moyers, and Blanche's father says there is a considerable dowry attached to Blanche and I have not got to refuse it. Refuse it, what sort of a man does he think I am? It means there will be enough money for me to get the surgery up and running and not have to rely on you and Clarence to subsidise me. That is enough about me. How is the patient doing?"

"He has not made a sound whilst I have been sitting here reading this occurrence book."

"Have you found anything out?"

"No, there is nothing in here to help me even hazard a guess as to why he was being chased across the meadow with a couple of bullets lodged in him."

"I am going to get some warm milk and try and get him to drink it before I go to bed. Will you wait here and help me lift him into a semi-sitting position before you retire?"

"Of course, then I am going to bed. I am up early in the morning. I am going into Hotshell to try and find out if he is one of their policemen."

Things went better than Blanche had expected when they went to see the vicar. She had known the vicar since she was a child and he was delighted to be having the opportunity to conduct the marriage ceremony.

The date was set for the following Friday, giving Blanche and Jackson enough time to plan for a small celebratory party afterwards. Nothing too big or expensive, just their three close friends and Blanche's parents was what they had decided upon.

Ella spent all Sunday in Aunt Fran's workshop trying to sort out her aunt's things. Most of it was to do with her collection of drawings and illustrations she had cut out of books and stuck into scrapbooks.

She was fascinated by them. Some of them were quite spectacular, especially the black and white etchings. The faces of some of the people in the illustrations were very beautiful and some were very funny. There were also etchings of faraway places, places Ella had never heard of before and she found them all enthralling.

She came across two piles of scrapbooks completely different to the illustrated ones and these too kept her captivated. These scrapbooks had black silhouettes pasted onto the white pages of the scrapbooks. All sorts of different shapes, sizes and caricatures covered the pages.

Ella stacked them all up in a corner. She was going to ask Mr Grundy if she could take them with them when they moved to West Street.

She also decided to add to her late aunt's collection and she intended to learn how to cut out the silhouettes, it would give her something to do in the long winter evenings.

Ella worked away trying to get things sorted out, so Jackson could take possession of the workshop as soon as possible.

Mr Grundy had gone to his office with the intention of doing the same, sorting some of his files out and taking them down into the basement to store. He got as far as taking some of the files out of the cabinets and placing them on the top. He had nearly completed this task when he decided he had done enough for one day.

He was about to put on his coat and go home, then he changed his mind. There were only the bottom drawers of two of the cabinets left to empty, so he decided he would finish the job. His back was aching by bending down so he took two chairs over to the cabinets, threw a cushion on the floor and knelt on it.

Mr Grundy proceeded to empty the first drawer and he placed all the files on one of the chairs. Moving his cushion across to the last drawer, he emptied it of files and as before, he placed the files on the second chair. He then slammed the drawer shut with satisfaction. Now, he could go home with a clear conscience.

He pulled himself up by the cabinet's drawer handles, groaning at the effort but he was more than pleased with his days' work. He had no qualms about leaving all the files piled up on the cabinet tops and chairs; Ella was going to help him move them all down into the basement.

No visitors came knocking on Mr Grundy's door on Sunday and they spent a pleasant evening in each other's company. Although when they retired to the front room Mr Grundy was soon nodding off in his favourite chair.

While Mr Grundy enjoyed his catnap, Ella found one of her aunt's books and was more than content to sit and read.

While they were having their evening meal, Ella mentioned the scrapbooks to Mr Grundy and asked him if she could take them all over to West Street and carry on with the collection.

Mr Grundy told Ella that her Aunt Fran spent hours in the workshop with her scrapbooks and one of the reasons they had the workshop built in the first place was to give her aunt more daylight to work by and storage space for her precious scrapbooks.

He told Ella that her aunt would have her little desk placed in front of the window, so she could look up and see the meadow when she wanted to give her eyes a rest. He had moved the desk away from the window when Fran had passed on because every time he went into the workshop he expected to see Fran sitting at the desk and it was most upsetting.

When Mr Grundy woke from his catnap, Ella suggested they should go next door to check on the patient and they found Blanche busy in the kitchen.

"You look very domesticated Blanche," Ella smiled.

"Don't I just. I am getting some practice in before Friday when I shall be living here officially until the baby arrives. Jackson asked me to make some chicken soup for us all then he can give some to the patient. I have not seen Charlie, so I do not know if he will be in for dinner, but there will be plenty of soup to go around if he does turn up."

"How is the patient?" Mr Grundy wanted to know.

"Still unconscious but Jackson thinks there is a slight improvement. He keeps feeding him with milk and giving him plenty of water. That is why he asked me if I would make a soup for dinner tonight; he said he will try and get the patient to take some of it.

"So here I am, making soup. I only hope I do not poison everyone. I am not used to cooking but, funnily enough, I have found it relaxing. Our cook at home told me what to do so at least I have her instructions to follow."

"May I go up and see the patient for myself?" asked Mr Grundy.

"Yes, of course you may, you do not have to ask my permission Mr Grundy. I am sure Charlie would have no objection."

After Mr Grundy had left Ella asked, "How are things with you and your parents?"

"Believe it or not they have been very supportive. My father thinks Jackson is the best son-in-law he could possibly have. I think it is because Jackson has a couple of medals and he can boast about it to all the fellow members at the club, but I don't care what the reason is Ella. I am so happy they have accepted him, and my mother and I seem to have become less animated with each other.

"I think she is looking forward to having a grandchild. You are coming to our wedding Ella, aren't you? I would very much like you to be my maid of honour if you would."

"I would be honoured Blanche, thank you for asking me but I have nothing to wear."

"Tomorrow is Monday, I am coming to do something with your hair then we can go into town to go shopping. I will buy you a new outfit for the wedding, as a thank you gift. It is only right that I should provide you with your gown. I will take you to meet my mother and father and I shall ask my mother if she would like to come shopping with us.

"I shall also ask my father for some money. It is something I have not done for a long time. He gives me an allowance of course, but I never ask him for anything else. I think my father would like that, if I was to ask him for some money. Then we will all go on a spending spree. I have not been on a spending spree for quite a while but now I am looking forward to it very much. Do you mind if I ask my mother to come shopping with us Ella?"

"It is very exciting just thinking about it. Of course, I don't mind you asking your mother to join us I shall look forward to meeting her. It is also such a long time since I went shopping for something for myself. I shall explain the situation to Mr Grundy and I am sure he will supply me with some money too. He tells me that I am rich and that my Aunt Fran left me all her money, so I shall ask him if it is possible for me to have some of that money and we shall all three of us go and have a good time spending in the shops. Do you think your mother will be willing to join us?"

"I do not know but I shall ask her all the same. She is glad I am getting married and she has not told Jackson he is not welcome in their house, quite the reverse. I thought they disapproved of him, but I was wrong, so I am going to hang the white flag out and see if my mother and I can become friends from now on."

"Good, I am glad to hear it. I wish I had a mother to go shopping with. You are very lucky Blanche, that your mother is still alive," Ella told her.

"I never thought about it like that, but yes, I am lucky my mother is still alive."

Mr Grundy came back into the kitchen and they said their goodnights and went back home.

Ella said to Mr Grundy over a steaming cup of hot chocolate, "Did you know Jackson and Blanche are getting married on Friday?"

"Yes, he came into the sick room to see the patient just before I came back down to join you and Blanche in the kitchen. He told me that just the five of us are going to be there. Charlie is going to be the best man and you are to be the maid of honour with me bringing up the rear. Mr and Mrs Moyer are to be present of course, I had forgotten about them. That will make seven of us. Jackson's mother and father died years ago."

"That is right. Blanche has asked me to be her maid of honour and tomorrow we are going shopping for some new clothes for the wedding. She is going to ask her mother if she would like to come with us and she is also going to ask her father for some money too.

"Blanche is going to buy me a dress for the wedding as a thank you present. I told her I would ask you if it was possible for me to have some of my Aunt Fran's money, so I can join in and then I will not feel like a loose fish. It is such a long time since I had any spare money to spend."

"Of course, I will give you some money for tomorrow Ella. Go and enjoy it, then on Tuesday we will go to the bank and get your Aunt Fran's money transferred over to you, then you will not have to ask me for money again."

"I will pay you back when we have been to the bank. Thank you, Mr Grundy."

"You will do no such thing. I said I would give you some money and that is what I meant, not lend you some money. So, do not be ungrateful Ella. Please allow me to join in your fun. I shall get more pleasure from knowing you are enjoying yourself spending it, than I would letting it just sit in the bank doing nothing.

"What is money to me now? If I did not have any, that would be a different thing altogether, I would not be able to give you any. As I stand now, I can afford to be a little generous and give you some money to be frivolous with, in fact I shall get it for you now before I forget, then you will not have to ask me again. I know how difficult it must be to have to ask someone for money.

"You go and enjoy yourself Ella. I know your Aunt Fran would want you to, she was very proud of you, of the way you survived, after your father died. I have a few things I need to sort out tomorrow, so I will be up and out very early, our paths might not cross until evening. There is no need for you to rise early you can sleep in as long as you like."

"Luxury, sheer luxury Mr Grundy, you do not know how much it means to me to be able to lie-in for as long as I like."

"And you do not know how much it means to me to have you here, my dear. I was so lonely when Fran left me."

Mr Grundy left the kitchen and came back with a bundle of paper money and handed it to Ella.

"Mr Grundy, I cannot take all this," Ella said in dismay.

He leaned forward and taking Ella's hand in his, he closed her fingers over the bundle of money and holding it tight he said, "Take the money Ella, and go and spend it. You never know what is around the corner, you may never have this opportunity again, take every opportunity that is offered to you. Now I am going to bed and if our paths do not cross in the morning, enjoy your spending trip. Goodnight my dear, sweet dreams."

"Goodnight Mr Grundy. I know I said I would come to the office with you to start on the filing tomorrow but having my hair done and going shopping has tempted me to indulge myself instead. If we are finished with our shopping early I will head for the office and make a start on the filing."

"There is no rush to see to the filing Ella, I have taken all the files out of the cabinets and piled them on top and on a couple of chairs. We can take them down to the basement as the opportunity arises. Jackson and Blanche have a few months yet before the baby is born. You have your hair done my dear, the filing can wait."

Before Mr Grundy left her, he went over to the drawer next to the sink and took out a bunch of keys, "Here, take these, they were your Aunt Fran's keys. They fit both the office and this house, so you may come and go as you please."

When Mr Grundy had gone to bed, Ella opened her hand and counted the money and found he had given her fifty pounds. A fortune indeed. Tears welled up in her eyes but only one dropped onto the kitchen table. She put the money and the keys carefully in her pocket, washed up the teacups ready for breakfast and went upstairs to bed.

Chapter Seven

Blanche went up to her parents' bedroom and knocked on the door, she was greeted by her father's voice saying, "Come in."

Both her parents were sitting up in bed reading. There was a lit double candlestick standing on a bedside cabinet at either side of their bed. They were both shocked to see their daughter walk in and sit at the bottom of their bed. She had not done this since she was a little girl of no more than ten years old.

"Mother, Ella and I are going shopping tomorrow. Would you like to join us? I am going to buy Ella a gown for the wedding. She has agreed to be my maid of honour and buying her the dress is the least I can do for her as a thank you gift. You will like Ella, Mother, she is all I am not, she is small, pretty and very clever," Blanche told her mother.

"And what makes you think I would prefer her to you? You have some funny notions in your head about your father and me, Blanche. I have only to look in the mirror and see where your height comes from. I have never had a problem with my height and neither has your father.

"We have been extremely happy over the years but the only thing we are sorry about is not giving you a brother or sister. It just did not happen, but we had you and we have never complained over anything about you.

"And I might add you are very pretty and much more intelligent than I. No doubt I shall like Ella very much if she is a friend of yours, but I love you Blanche. I would very much like to come shopping with you both tomorrow and if Ella is going to have a new outfit for the wedding, then so are we."

"In that case Father, may I have some money?" Blanche asked.

"By Jove you shall have as much money as you want and so shall your mother."

Mr Moyer threw off the bedclothes and padded across the bedroom carpet with bare feet and dressed only in his nightshirt. He went over to a portrait of his wife and pushing it to one side, he opened a safe and came back with three rolled-up wads of bank notes.

"Here is one for you," he handed one of the rolls of money to Blanche, "one for you," he handed one to his wife, "and one for my grandson. Go and spend some money." He handed the third wad of notes to Blanche.

"Thank you Father, but there is no guarantee that you will get a grandson," Blanche told him.

"Nonsense, of course it will be a grandson. Jackson is a hero, he will not be fathering a girl, I can assure you of that," her father was adamant.

Mrs Moyer saw the distress appear on her daughter's face, "Take no notice of him, dear. If it is a girl, he will spoil her rotten and so will I."

"I am going to do something with Ella's hair first thing in the morning but as soon as she is ready, we will come back here and collect you."

"I shall be ready and waiting my dear."

Monday morning Blanche left home early and went straight to Mr Grundy's where she found Ella washing up the breakfast things.

"I am glad to see you up Ella. Where is Mr Grundy?"

"He went to the office very early this morning. He said he had something to sort out. He has given me some money to spend today. He says I have to spend it all because I might never get another opportunity to have a good time in the shops, so that is what I intend to do."

"My father has done the same and my mother is looking forward to meeting you. She has also agreed to come with us. My father not only gave me a lot of money to spend on myself, but he gave my mother some, and would you believe it, he gave me another load of money to spend on his grandson."

"Oh, you are having a boy, are you?"

Blanche laughed and said, "I cannot wait to see Jackson and tell him that my father has said I am having a boy. He said because Jackson is a war hero there is no way he is going to father a girl."

"I can imagine his reply," laughed Ella.

"Right, let us see to your hair. I am going to need some lengths of cloth to turn your hair into ringlets, do you have any?"

"There are lots of old clothes belonging to my Aunt Fran. I will nip upstairs and get an old petticoat. We can tear that into strips." Ella ran upstairs.

Ella and Blanche spent a very pleasant hour washing Ella's hair and tearing up the petticoat. Then Blanche separated Ella's hair into slim lengths and twisted the lengths of rag around it. When Ella's hair was all neatly tied up in rags, they sat at the kitchen table drinking hot chocolate and waiting for Ella's hair to dry.

An hour later, the kitchen door opened and in walked Charlie. His face lit up at the sight of Ella's ragged hair.

"You may find it amusing Charlie Blurr, but we women have to go through purgatory just to impress the male species." Ella told him not in the least put out.

"On the contrary, my little Ella, remembering holding you in my arms and feeling your body shaking with laughter has made an everlasting impression on my mind, a few rags in your hair is a mere nothing," his eyes danced with devilment.

"I am sure you did not come just to try and embarrass me, because if you did, it will not work," Ella held his gaze.

"Good, because it's true, I am not trying to embarrass you, I would dearly love to repeat that experience," he informed her.

"If you are looking for Jackson he is in the extension trying to sort it out. He wants to find out the best position for work tables and things. I have never seen him so enthusiastic about anything for a long time," Blanche told him.

But Jackson saved Charlie a trip next door because the door opened and in he walked. Going straight over to the sink, Jackson began to wash his hands.

Jackson did not notice Ella sitting at the kitchen table with her hair tied up in rags. "So, you are back. Did you find anything out?" he asked looking over at his friend.

"Not much, the only thing I could find out is that a policeman by the name of Melvin Keyser has not turned up for work today. A sergeant from Hotshell is coming to see if our patient is his missing police officer. How is he doing by the way?" Charlie wanted to know.

"His colour is much improved, and the bleeding seems to have stopped but he has not come around yet. I am going to take some more of the excellent chicken broth Blanche made last night and try and get him to take some more along with some water. His lips are beginning to crack so he needs plenty of water.

"I think he will be alright, he seems to have a strong constitution, even though you did try to throw him down the stairs a couple of times, he seems no worse for wear. Are you going to come and give me a hand? The ladies are going shopping so no doubt they want to see the back of us. I say Ella; you are not going like that, are you?" He pointed to her hair.

"No, I am not. When you two have gone, Blanche is going to make me look beautiful, for our shopping trip."

"That should not be a very hard task. You look beautiful even with the rags dangling down your head," Charlie grinned.

Ella could not help laughing and her eyes danced back at Charlie.

"We will be off then," Jackson said. "Is your mother going with you?"

"She is. My father gave us both some money to go and spend so that is what we are going to do. By the way, my father seems to have a bit of hero worship going on with you. He said I was having a boy because no one with a war medal could possibly father a girl." Blanche told her shocked beau.

Ella and Blanche heard Jackson say as the two gentlemen made their way along the passage towards the front door, "I tell you this Charlie, I think I am marrying into a madhouse."

Charlie's reply was, "In that case Jackson old boy, you will fit in perfectly."

Jackson's reply was, "Yes, from one madhouse to another."

"To hear them talk you would think they are the worst of enemies instead of the best of friends." Blanche made a start on Ella's rags.

Ella, wearing one of her Aunt Fran's day dresses and her hair hanging in ringlets and looking a delight to behold, found herself, on entering the Moyer residence, crushed to Mrs Moyer's ample bosom in a warm embrace.

"My dear you do not know how pleased I am to meet you. You are the first friend my daughter has brought home since she was in pigtails and I believe you are to be her maid of honour on Friday."

"I am very pleased to meet you too Mrs Moyer. I am so looking forward to our shopping spree. It is a long time since I have had any spare money to throw away on none essentials," Ella told her.

"In that case my dear, I will get my bonnet and we shall be off." Mrs Moyer headed for the door with Blanche and Ella following close behind.

Blanche bought Ella a pale pink satin dress, cut low at the front, suggesting untold pleasures for any male lucky enough to lay eyes on her. A slightly darker pink ribbon was tied neatly under her bust.

Mrs Moyer insisted on buying Blanche her wedding dress and Blanche insisted that it must be ivory and not white. She did not think it was appropriate to wear white she told her mother.

This too had a low neckline showing the beginning of her well-developed breasts but unlike Ella's dress, that dropped straight down to the floor and boasted only little cap sleeves, Blanche's dress had a slightly fuller skirt and long closely fitting sleeves.

Mrs Moyer's outfit was a deep red taffeta dress with a tight-fitting bodice and full skirt. Blanche was pleased with all their dresses and she told them both so.

The rest of the morning was spent looking at shoes and gloves and anything else that caught their eye, and when they were all satisfied with their purchases, Blanche told them she wanted to go to a baby store and spend some more money.

She bought loads of nappies and baby clothes and a lovely little swinging cradle with bedding to go with it.

"Whilst I am rocking my baby to sleep I shall tell him or her that this little comfy cot he or she sleeps in is from his grandma and grandpa. Thank you, mamma. I have enjoyed today, it has been a very happy day and I shall always remember it."

Blanche tucked her hand through her mother's arm and added, "Let's go home now and get Fred to go and collect all our purchases, shall we?"

Mrs Moyer patted her daughter's hand. "We shall indeed my dear."

"I will go back home too Blanche if you don't mind, and get dinner ready for Mr Grundy," Ella said, and their ways parted.

Ella changed back into her old woollen dress and set about making an evening meal for when Mr Grundy arrived back home. Halfway through the meal preparation, Charlie walked in followed by Jackson.

"Clarence not back yet?" asked Jackson.

"No. I am expecting him home any minute now."

"Did you have a good day at the shops?" Charlie asked.

"We have had an excellent day, thank you. Have you both eaten?" she asked them.

"No, Jackson said he could smell something nice coming from here, so if we were to come around on the pretence of wanting to see Clarence, he thought we might get an invite to stay," Charlie informed her.

Ella cast a glance at Jackson.

"It is all true. It will save me having to do the cooking for us and anyway, your meals taste better than mine."

Ella could not help laughing, "In that case I had better do some more vegetables and we will all have to make do with a share of the meat."

Mr Grundy was delighted to see his kitchen crammed with people and the smell of a hot meal waiting for him.

"I am ready for this. My days seem to get longer and longer." Mr Grundy eased his bulk onto the only chair available to him.

Over dinner Mr Grundy asked Charlie if he had found anything out about the body from the trunk.

Charlie was pleased to be able to report that, "Sergeant Brook from Hotshell came over to Marchum this afternoon to see if our body from the trunk was his missing officer, and it turns out it is. His name is Melvin Keyser, but the sergeant has no idea why he should be running out of our wood with two bullets in him.

"According to Sergeant Brook, Melvin Keyser was not working on anything that merited being shot at. The day he appeared in our trunk was his day off work. In fact, PC Keyser was not working over the weekend and that is why he was not missed. The plot thickens," Charlie told them.

"How is the patient by the way Jackson? He is still alive I take it?" Mr Grundy asked.

"He is, and he must have come around sometime today for when last I looked in on him, he had moved his arm. The good arm was crossed over his body and resting on the sling on his bad arm. I am guessing he must have come to his senses and wondered where he was, and then passed out again. That is a good sign at least."

"That is our news out of the way. How did your shopping go?" Charlie asked Ella.

"We had a great time. I have two new dresses, two pairs of new shoes and a new coat. I have spent all the money Mr Grundy gave me and as I had such a good time doing so I have bought him a present." Ella went over to the cupboard and produced a bottle of port and handed it over to him.

"Thank you my dear, but you should have spent the money on yourself, that is why I gave it to you. We shall go into the sitting room and open this bottle and have a glass before we retire."

"Sounds good to me," said Jackson then continued, "You must have met Blanche's mother then, Ella?"

"Yes, I did, and she did the same to me as she did to you. She gave me a warm embrace and nearly smothered me in her breast," Ella laughed.

"I cannot wait to meet her," Charlie said.

"She will not smother you in her breast Charlie boy, your arse is too high up," Jackson informed him.

Ella's eyes danced as they met Charlie's, "What he meant to say is that I am taller than him, and that does not take much doing."

Mr Grundy gave an amused chuckle. "Don't let Blanche hear you talking about her mother like that or you will all be in deep water. Let's go and open this bottle, shall we?"

But before they could leave the kitchen, a knock came to the door and Blanche entered.

"I had to escape. My mother is arranging a meal for us all after the wedding, so I have left her to it. I am sorry Jackson, but I will have to let her do the organising of the meal. It is making her happy having something to do and anyway, my parents' house has more room and I know my mother will put something special on for us."

"If they are paying for it, why should I mind? I am all for that," Jackson told her.

"You are just in time, we are about to retire to the sitting room to open this bottle of port Ella bought for me today," said Mr Grundy.

"None for you though Blanche, not until you have had the baby," Jackson was adamant.

"You are becoming my mother, Jackson," complained Blanche.

"No way, I am looking out for the wellbeing of our baby; I do not want anything to happen to either of you."

"In that case, if Blanche is not allowed to participate, then neither shall I. If you men want to leave the table and go and pull the cork, Blanche and I will stay in here and I will make us a nice cup of hot chocolate. Blanche can sit and drink her chocolate while I clear this lot away. Then Blanche and I will go and have a look at the patient," Ella told them.

The two ladies could hear laughter coming from the sitting room as they made their way out of Mr Grundy's and into Charlie's house. The door was unlocked as usual and in they went and straight up the stairs to the sickroom.

They found the patient wide awake and looking bewildered at them.

"Where am I?" he asked.

"I will run next door and get the men," Ella said.

While Ella ran next door, Blanche went over to the bed and speaking softly she told the patient, "Do not worry, you are amongst friends. You have had two bullets taken out of you and you have been very poorly, but I am glad to see you are now on the way to recovery."

"How long have I been here?" he wanted to know.

"Today is Monday and you appeared in the trunk on Saturday, so I make that three days," Blanche informed him.

Ella ran down Charlie's garden path and up Mr Grundy's then, without knocking on the sitting room door she burst in.

"The trunk man is conscious," she informed them.

All three men jumped up and Charlie said, "Lead on fair maid, we follow you once more to the ends of the earth and if you feel like throwing yourself into my arms and laughing, please feel free to do so."

Ella's eyes sparkled back at him, but she made no comment, turned and headed back out with the men following her.

The trunk man found himself the subject of five pairs of eyes, he recognised none of them.

"Do you know how you came to have two bullets lodged in you?" asked Charlie.

"No, I have just opened my eyes and I do not know where I am or who I am. I tried to get out of bed, but I soon laid my head back on the pillow to say nothing of the pain in my shoulder. How did I get here and who are all of you?" PC Keyser wanted to know.

"We have found out that you are a policeman and your name is, Melvin Keyser. You were spotted by this delightful young woman," Charlie indicated Ella, "running across, Mr Grundy's meadow and it turned out you were carrying excess baggage with you in the shape of two bullets.

"You made your way into the extension at the side of Mr Grundy's house and you hid inside a trunk. The same young lady spotted blood on the floor at the base of the trunk and if it had not been for her quickness of mind and good bit of detective work, you may well still be in the trunk, where you would no doubt have bled to death."

Charlie slapped Mr Grundy on the back and continued, "The workshop where you hid belongs to this kindly gentleman, and when the same young lady who spotted you running across the meadow found your occurrence book at the bottom of the trunk, she handed it to Mr Grundy. Mr Grundy recognised it for what it was, and he handed it to me.

"Jackson," Charlie then indicated Jackson by pointing a finger at him, "took the bullets out of you and I am a fellow policeman, my name is Inspector Blurr, and I am based at Marchum police station. You belong to Hotshell Division. We knew this because of the occurrence book that Ella found.

"I went over to Hotshell and a policeman from there came to see if you are PC Keyser and he was able to confirm that you were their missing policeman. It was a very sensible thing to do, to climb into that trunk, because you had two unlikely characters hot on your heels. We have yet to discover who they were, or why they were chasing you."

"And who is the other handsome young woman?" asked PC Keyser.

"The other handsome young woman belongs to me, so you had better not have any thoughts in that direction or I shall put those bullets back where I took them from," Jackson threatened.

"Take no notice of him PC Keyser, he is having a baby and his hormones are all over the place," Charlie told him.

"Damn right I am having a baby," confirmed the indignant Jackson.

Blanche took control of the situation by saying, "Let me introduce you to us all properly, PC Keyser. This is Mr Grundy, Inspector Charlie Blurr, Charlie Jackson, Miss Ella Penrod and myself, Miss Blanche Moyer soon to be Mrs Charlie Jackson."

"I am very pleased to meet you all and you have my thanks for what you are doing for me. I wish I could remember who I am then I might be able to remember how I came to be shot."

"You have lost a lot of blood. A couple of days rest and I am sure you will start to remember how you got here. The best thing to do now is to eat and drink, drink as much as you can to get some fluid back into your body," Jackson advised.

"If he is to drink a lot, I will go and get the port," Charlie joked knowing full well that Jackson had meant water.

"You will have to excuse him PC Keyser, he is in love and his hormones are all over the place," Jackson replied.

Charlie and Ella exchanged a quick glance.

Mr Grundy said, "We will leave you to it then. I am pleased you are now on the way to recovery PC Keyser. That port has made me sleepy, my bed is calling me."

Ella said goodnight to everybody and went home with Mr Grundy.

Both went up the stairs and to their respective beds but before they parted, Mr Grundy asked Ella, "Do you mind Charlie referring to you as his fiancée?"

Ella laughed and said, "To be truthful Mr Grundy, I love being part of their little game. I have only been here four days and it already feels like I belong here, and I am part of a family again so no Mr Grundy, I do not mind Charlie calling me his fiancée.

"I am so grateful you contacted me. I can understand why my Aunt Fran came to live with you and never left. Now I have had a taste of this wonderful little family of yours, I hope I never have to leave."

Mr Grundy patted her hand and replied, "If you leave my dear, it will be of your own choosing. You too have brought light back into my life. You have even surpassed Fran's antics. She never produced a body in a trunk. Life is full of little surprises and I am glad you are part of it Ella. If you are pleased I got in contact with you, I am equally pleased you decided to come and stay.

"If you are offended by Charlie's reference to you being his fiancée, I would have told him it was in bad taste but, if you are comfortable with it, I will say no more on the subject. First thing in the morning, we will go to the bank and get your Aunt Fran's money signed over to you, and then all will be in order. Goodnight my dear."

"Before you retire Mr Grundy, how did my Aunt Fran come to have a lot of money of her own?" Ella wanted to know.

"I paid her for working for me. I preferred to have Fran working in my office when I was absent, I knew I could trust her and she was a very good office worker if I do say so myself."

"I am sure she was," Ella said.

"Believe it or not, Fran put nearly every penny I paid her for working for me into a bank account for you. But she also inherited Lady Whiteman's estate and she put all the money she got from the estate into the bank account for you as well. She said you needed it more than she did, and you also had a right to a share of it.

"This caused another angry exchange between your father and Fran. Your father said half of the estate should have gone to him. Fran explained that she was putting it all into the bank for you to inherit but still your father would not agree to you meeting her. Fran was very upset about it, so she refused to speak to him again. Your father never tried to get back in touch with Fran so that was the end of that.

"Fran would have loved to have been part of your life Ella, but she was afraid she would not have been welcome. Your father never replied to any of the letters she sent him, but she was looking out for you and I am so pleased she did. She would have been over the moon to know that the money she saved up for you has been gratefully received."

"I shall be eternally grateful to my Aunt Fran for refusing to give my father half of Lady Whiteman's money. I loved my father dearly, but he had given no thought about what was to become of me after his death. He spent all his money and more besides. I was left with nothing. But surely now my aunt has passed on, the money belongs to you?"

"We had plenty of money coming in from the business. Fran had access to it whenever she wanted anything. It was what Fran wanted to do, and now having met you I am very pleased she did.

"Because she loved, well, we both loved Charlie, Jackson and even Blanche, having met them I am sure you can understand that, we agreed that when both of us had passed away, whatever we had would be split four ways between all of you. But her money, she wanted you alone to have that. There is a will and I shall show you where to find it, so all is in order when the time comes."

"I don't know what to say, Mr Grundy. I still cannot believe all of this is happening to me, but do you know what I like best of all, being able to have a lie-in on a morning for as long as I like. That is a luxury I never thought I would have again. Not that I have ever been one for lying in bed, but just to know I can if I want to is worth a fortune," Ella admitted.

"Well my dear, you cannot have a lie-in in the morning for we are going to the bank first thing then it is off to the office for you, to start on that filing. I will join you later in the afternoon as I have some pressing business to see to before I go back to the office," Mr Grundy told her.

"That dream did not last very long then did it?" she laughed.

"There will be plenty more mornings for you to have a lie-in. When things have settled down and Blanche and Jackson are married. PC Keyser will be out of our way and we shall be able to do whatever we wish to do.

"Do you know, I think I am going to like being retired and helping Jackson out when he needs a helping hand?"

They said their goodnights and went to bed.

In a dirty rundown room in Hotshell, Bert Cole looked across at his partner in crime.

"What are we going to do now, Danny?"

"Until we find out whether the man we shot is dead or alive, we cannot do anything. We dare not go and dig up the money if he is alive, he could have informed the constabulary of what he saw. Why didn't you shoot to kill when you saw him watching us, you idiot? Look at the mess you have got us into now."

"You are as much to blame as me Danny, you fired off a round as well and you only hit him in the leg."

"It is too late now to be putting the blame on each other, the thing is done. We are going to have to think of a way of finding out what happened to him. All that jewellery and money just lying there waiting for us to spend, and we cannot touch it. What do we know about the people who live in that end house where we thought he had gone to ground?"

"The old man is a solicitor but there is nothing known about the young woman that was there with him at the time we did our search of the house. I have not been able to find anybody who knows anything about her. She is a woman of mystery.

"The old solicitor has an office in West Street. I suppose we could try there, see if they have taken him to the office just in case we go back to the house again. We don't want to be doing that Danny, going back to their house I mean, not with their next-door neighbour being Charlie Blurr.

"You have had dealings with him before. The last thing we want is to be spotted by him. He would soon put two and two together and we would be behind bars before we could turn and run."

"Charlie Blurr?" questioned Danny.

"Yes, you remember Inspector Blurr, he came to see you once when that bank in Cartermore was raided. He found your name and address in the pocket of that prostitute. She was the wife of the leader of the gang that did Cartermore bank over.

"Charlie Blurr was the policeman that put them all away, even your prostitute. He has a reputation of always getting his man does Inspector Blurr. He saw me too you know, when he came here to see if you had anything to do with that bank robbery. We do not want him on our trail, do we?

"It's a good job too, that Inspector Blurr put the prostitute's husband behind bars, when he found out you had been sleeping with his wife he threatened to do you in. Sleeping with a prostitute and paying her for it is a lot different from sleeping with one and not paying for it. You do push things to the limit sometimes, Danny." Bert looked across at Danny.

"Inspector Blurr, I remember him now. Yes, you are right. We certainly do not want him on our trail."

"I have been thinking Danny; we should not have been tempted to rob that jeweller. We have been doing alright nipping in and out of people's houses, now we are up there with the big boys, and to be honest, I do not like it very much."

"You could be right, Bert. I did not expect Inspector Blurr to be involved with this, it is not his patch, and I don't much like it either. We have shot somebody and if he dies, then we are not only thieves, but murderers.

"Tomorrow we will go to the solicitor's office and see what we can find out. We could always say we are with the police if the solicitor is there, he will never realise we are not, so why not pretend to be the police and see where it leads."

"Let's hope to God that the man we shot does not die, I only shot him because I panicked," Bert remarked.

"Too late to be sorry now Bert, much too late," Danny informed him.

Chapter Eight

After accompanying Mr Grundy to the bank, Ella made her way to see Blanche. She was going to Mr Grundy's office to make a start on the filing system, which according to Mr Grundy did not exist. He told Ella he had let it slide since Fran had died, that had been one of Fran's jobs and he had yet to fathom it out.

Ella thought Blanche might like to help her, to give her something to do to take her mind off Friday and the wedding because Blanche had told Ella she was as nervous as a kitten about it.

"Hello Ella, this is a lovely surprise," Blanche said looking up from the embroidery she was doing.

"I have come to see if you would like to come with me to Mr Grundy's office. I am going to make a start on the filing system, it would seem it has got itself into a bit of a mess since Aunt Fran died, or so Mr Grundy informs me. Really all we are going to do is store the files down in the basement. Once the files are out of the way, we can start to turn the office into a home then you and Jackson can have the house on Haywood Street."

"I would love to have come with you Ella, but my mother has made an appointment for me to see the doctor. Both my mother and father have been so good about the baby I do not want to disappoint them. I guess I will have to go and see the doctor sometime, I only wish my mother had waited until after Jackson and I are married.

"You know how frowned upon having a baby out of wedlock is. I am surprised my mother did not wait until we are married before booking the appointment and I told her so. She said whatever we discuss with the doctor should stay with the doctor, so I need not worry about it.

"A pointless remark really, people will soon be able to tell I am with child. It is something that you cannot hide, the baby will tell the world very soon it is on the way. No way to hide it and to be honest, I don't want to hide it.

"Everyone has been so good about the baby, Ella, I feel utterly guilty for putting everyone in this position, but everything seems to have fallen into place without the least effort or argument on my part. I am very lucky, don't you think?" asked Blanche.

"Five days ago, I had no family, friends or money. Not even a job or any prospects of one. Now I have an uncle, some of the nicest people imaginable that have become my friends and loads of money. I think we are both very lucky." Ella bent down and gave Blanche a hug then headed back to West Street with a spring in her step.

Taking the keys Mr Grundy had given her out of her pocket, Ella was about to insert one of them into the lock when she heard a whimper to her left.

Turning her head towards the noise Ella saw, sitting in the same place where she had sat on her arrival in Marchum, a very thin, shabbily dressed young woman with a small child upon her knee.

"Hello," Ella said.

"Hello, I want to see Mr Grundy," the young woman informed her.

"Then you had better come in and wait for him. I am expecting him back around midday. I will get your carpet bag for you." Ella told the young woman and she unlocked the door and held it open for her and the baby to go through.

After only a short hesitation, the young woman stood up, hoisting the child up to her shoulder she patted its back in a comforting way and headed for the open door.

Ella went over and picked up the young woman's carpetbag then followed her inside the office where Ella told her to sit down while she put the kettle on and they would have a nice cup of tea. Ella brought out some homemade biscuits and placed them on the table in front of the young woman and poured her a cup of tea.

The young woman put a spoonful of sugar in the cup then after stirring it well, she lifted the cup and poured some of the tea into the saucer. She took one of the biscuits and crumbled this into the saucer also, mixing it well into the tea. When the mixture was well mashed with no lumps in it, the young woman took a spoonful, then blowing on it to make sure it was not too hot, she fed the mixture to the child.

"Thank you, I hope you don't mind me doing this, but we have had nothing to eat today, this is very welcome."

Ella poured out a second cup of tea and indicated to the young woman that it was for her.

The young woman took a sip of the hot tea and nibbled at one to the biscuits whilst she continued to feed the child.

"What is your name?" Ella asked.

"My married name is Ruth Houseway, before that it was Ruth Keyser," was the reply.

"I know it is none of my business, but may I enquire why you wish to see Mr Grundy?"

"My father told me that if one day he did not return home, I was to come here to see the solicitor, Mr Grundy. My father has, what can sometimes be, a dangerous job, and he gave me a letter and told me to pass it onto Mr Grundy. To tell him that my name was Ruth Keyser. That is all I can tell you. My father has not returned home for five days now and we have run out of food and money and I do not know what to do so I came to find Mr Grundy. But when I got here, the place was closed and I did not know what else to do so I decided the best thing was to sit and wait and hope Mr Grundy would turn up."

"When you have finished feeding the baby I think it would be best if you came with me Ruth, back to our house, it is not very far. I am Mr Grundy's niece, and Mr Grundy might even be home when we get there for it is nearly lunchtime and he sometimes calls home for something to eat. I will carry your carpet bag; you have enough on with the baby."

After the baby had been fed, Ella picked up the carpetbag and Ruth followed her outside. She waited until Ella had closed and locked the door, then they set off for home.

Ella and Ruth had just turned the corner at the bottom of West Street into Haywood Street as Danny and Bert turned into the top of West Street. They missed each other by seconds.

Danny tried the door of the solicitor's office but found it locked. The porch yielded plenty of cover from the street and it did not take Bert long to apply himself to the task of lock picking, and they were in.

They searched the building from top to bottom including the basement but found no evidence of any injured man. Back in the main office Danny showed his frustration by kicking a chair that contained a pile of paper files and the files spilled onto the floor. Some of the files burst open and scattered their contents further afield. He did the same with a second chair but this one landed on its side with a crash and more files scattered across the floor.

"That was a stupid thing to do, Danny. Now they will know someone has been here. We could have been in and out without anyone being any the wiser. I thought we were supposed to be keeping a low profile."

"In that case there is no reason why they should find a bit more mess to clear up, is there?" He went to the filing cabinets, ran his hand along the top and a cascade of files went crashing onto the floor.

"What is the point of all that? We had better get out of here before we are rumbled." Bert headed for the door.

"It is a warning. They know something about the injured man, I know they do. They are hiding our witness so now they will know we are onto them and that they had better watch out." Danny followed Bert out of the building.

Later that morning, Mr Grundy stepped onto his porch in West Street to find his office door wide open. He entered his office with strong purposeful strides expecting to find Ella there but all he found was chaos.

He was taken aback and said out loud, "What the devil…!" he turned and went back out, locking the door behind him.

Ella went straight into Charlie's house with Ruth and the child following. They found Blanche busy in the kitchen preparing the evening meal, "Hello Ella, whom have you found now. Another stray?"

"This is Ruth Keyser and her baby," Ella announced.

"Is it now?" Blanche said looking at the young woman and her child with much interest.

"You certainly know how to keep the suspense flowing Ella, I will give you that. Come and sit down my dear, you look all in. I shall make us all a nice warm drink." Blanche pulled out a chair for the young woman who sat down thankfully.

"Jackson is in the workshop," Blanche looked across at Ella.

"I will go and get him."

Ella found Jackson pulling a large wooden table into the centre of the room.

He looked up as she entered, and he told her, "Charlie's not here if you are looking for him. He's off catching criminals."

"No Jackson, I came to get you. I have come across Ruth Keyser, and she has lost her father."

"The devil you have. I have never known anyone like you for finding people. Where is she?"

"She is with Blanche, who is making hot chocolate for us all."

"Chocolate eh, I could do with a cup of chocolate. This vet business is hard work."

Ella laughed, "You have not even started yet."

"It's all in the mind," Jackson said following Ella.

"If Charlie were here, I am sure he would say he didn't know you had a mind."

"More likely he would say I had left it back on Mars."

Jackson went over and kissed Blanche. Then looked at the young woman and asked, "Are you Melvin Keyser's daughter?"

"I am. Do you know my father? Do you know where he is?" the young woman asked eagerly.

"Yes, my dear, your father is here but he has been in the wars, so he has been put to bed. While Blanche is making hot chocolate for us all, we will go up and see him. He has been injured but he is going to be alright.

"He has lost a lot of blood and he cannot remember anything of his past but seeing you might help jog his memory. If you want to hand the baby over to Ella, I am sure she will keep it entertained whilst we are in the sickroom," Jackson said.

Ella was left holding a wriggling infant. She found holding such a small bundle more difficult than she had thought.

She looked at her friend and asked, "Do you want to get some practice in while I take over making the chocolate?"

Blanche held out her arms and the little boy put his arms out to her and she cuddled him close, rocking him from side to side. His head rested on her breast and she began to sing softly to the innocent little face looking up at hers. She saw his eyelids begin to droop as the gentle swaying and her soft musical voice lulled him to sleep.

The two friends exchanged glances, "You are going to be a natural."

"I hope so Ella, I really hope so. I know I am putting a brave face on but just thinking about it scares me stiff. I know nothing about bringing up a child."

"Nobody knows anything about bringing up a child when it is their first. You will have Jackson and your mother to help you. I don't think I would be much good at it either or I would offer you my help. At least you know how to hold a baby, did you see the way I was struggling with him?"

"Once the baby has arrived, I shall appreciate any help offered. We can learn together. The experience will come in handy for you when you have a baby of your own."

Charlie walked in and seeing Blanche rocking a small bundle in her arms he said, "I can't turn my back on you for two minutes before you go having the baby. That was quick work Blanche."

Blanche laughed and said, "It's not mine silly. We think it is Melvin Keyser's grandchild. His mother is with Jackson, up in the sickroom."

"Is she now? Where did they spring from?"

"Ella found them."

"Why am I not surprised? What is it with you and stray bodies?" Charlie shot out of the kitchen and up the staircase.

"Charlie, just in time, as soon as PC Keyser saw this young woman his memory came flooding back. Good news eh?"

"Good news indeed. How are you feeling?" Charlie asked the patient.

"A lot better than I was. Now I have my Ruth here I shall soon be up and about again and back at work. I can remember what happened to me now. You are Inspector Blurr, aren't you? I have a vague memory of being introduced to you."

"I am. Are you up to telling me how you came to be shot?"

"It was my day off and you have a reputation for being a good policeman, so I was making my way to see you. I needed some help well advice really, so I came to see if you could advise me on how to proceed.

"I was in the wood making my way here when I came across these two men burying something in the ground. One of them saw me and before I could say anything to them, damn me if he didn't fire a pistol at me. The first shot caught me in the shoulder, so I ran off. I heard a second shot and felt another bullet lodge in my leg.

"I came out of the wood and saw some buildings across a meadow, so I headed straight for them. I tried the first door I came to and it was unlocked, but once inside I could see nowhere to hide and by this time I was becoming faint. I saw a trunk and I thought I would just hide inside there to give myself a rest. That is the last I can remember."

"What was it they were burying?"

"I am sorry I cannot tell you that because I did not see what it was. One minute I was strolling along, minding my own business and the next, I had two bullets in me, it all happened so fast."

"Can you remember whereabouts in the wood you were when you saw them?"

"Not really, for I have never been in that wood before. I can remember passing a big overhang with a couple of trees teetering on the edge of it. I remember this because I thought how dangerous it was, a good downpour and I could imagine a landslide, taking the trees with it. Not long after that all hell broke loose."

"I know the exact spot you mean. I must go and check this out. I shall leave you in the capable hands of Jackson and your daughter. I am glad to have you back with us PC Keyser. I take exception to a fellow police officer being shot at. We will talk when I get back."

Jackson told PC Keyser's daughter, "I have been sleeping in this put-me-up bed, but you are welcome to it if you wish to stay with your father.

"I will go and get you one of the drawers from a cabinet in the workshop and we can put some blankets in the bottom and the baby can sleep in that."

"Thank you, I would appreciate that for I have nowhere else to go and have no money to find lodgings so the put-me-up will be fine for me and I would very much like to stay with my father until he is better."

"What did you say your name is?" Jackson asked.

"Ruth Houseway and my baby's name is David."

"I will go and tell Blanche you will be staying."

In the kitchen Blanche was still rocking the baby who was by this time contentedly asleep.

"I hope ours sleeps like that," Jackson said eyeing the silent infant.

"I hope so too," Blanche smiled at him.

"I have just come to tell you Ruth and baby David will be staying until her father is better and they can all go home together. Ruth is having the put-me-up and I am just on my way to get one of the big bottom drawers from one of the cabinets in the workshop to make a cot for the baby."

"Ruth is too old to be sleeping with her father Jackson, what are you thinking of. She must have your bed and you will just have to make do with the put-me-up for a few more days, until PC Keyser can go back home," Blanche told him.

"Alright, I'll sleep in the put-me-up if I must. I will go and get the drawer for the baby. It is damned uncomfortable in that put-me-up I'll have you know. I was looking forward to my own bed tonight," Jackson grumbled as he went out.

Mr Grundy and Jackson crossed in the hallway.

"You haven't got a spare bed at your house, have you?" Jackson asked him.

"I am afraid not, no," came the reply.

"Oh well, if I can't walk down the aisle on Friday, you will all know the reason why." Jackson mumbled and carried on outside.

"What has gotten into him?" Mr Grundy wanted to know.

"He was complaining about having to sleep on the put-me-up," Ella told the flustered Mr Grundy.

"Is everything alright Mr Grundy? You look a bit flushed," Blanche asked.

"I say Blanche, if you are going to breast feed the baby, you would be better off in the privacy of your own room. When did you have that? Nobody told me you have had the baby. That was a bit quick, wasn't it?" Mr Grundy asked.

"It is not mine Mr Grundy, it is yours," Blanche informed him.

"It damn well isn't though," exclaimed a shocked Mr Grundy.

"Ella found him and his mother waiting on your doorstep in West Street. She wanted to see you. What have you been up to Clarence?"

"Ella is too damn free at finding people she knows nothing about. One of these days she is going to land us all in deep trouble. I do not know where she gets it from. Her Aunt Fran was a very restful person; Ella must take after her father. Take it back to where you found it. We have enough on our hands with the trunk man." Mr Grundy looked at the sleeping infant over the top of his glasses.

"The baby turns out to be our patient's grandson Mr Grundy. I found them sitting in the exact place where you found me, in your alcove waiting to see you, so I brought her and the baby here."

"Waiting to see me. Why was she waiting to see me? It isn't my baby. If that is what she is saying, she is telling lies." Mr Grundy was still looking over his glasses at the infant.

"No Mr Grundy she is not saying it is your baby. When she told me her maiden name was Keyser, and her father had gone missing, I brought her here to see him. She said she had a letter for you and that is all I can tell you. I gave her tea and biscuits at the office, I think it was the first meal they'd had this morning."

"So, it was you in the office. You have a damn funny way of doing the filing Ella. What were you thinking of. You will never follow that sort of filing system. Each file must contain the relevant paperwork. You cannot go throwing them all up in the air and hope for the best. And while we are talking about the office you must remember to lock the door behind you when you leave."

"What on earth are you talking about? I did not get a chance to do any filing and I certainly did not throw it all up in the air."

Mr Grundy looked suspiciously at the infant and asked, "Did he do it?"

Ella could not help laughing, "The baby can't even walk yet, how could the baby do it?"

"Children tend to run amok and scatter things about or, so I have been told." He still had his eye on the child.

"How many files are on the floor?" Ella wanted to know, "I can assure you there were none when we left."

"How many files are on the floor? How the devil should I know? I did not stop to count them all. When I saw the mess, I came straight here to see what you were playing at."

"Was there a window open, could a gust of wind have done it?" Ella enquired.

"Did you open a window?" Mr Grundy asked.

"No, I was about to unlock the door when I saw Ruth and the baby. I made us a cup of tea and whilst we were drinking our tea, I found out who they were, so I brought them straight here. I can assure you there were no files on the floor when we left, and I certainly locked the door behind me because I remember putting Ruth's carpet bag down on the doorstep while I did so."

"Then there was no window open if you did not open one, that is one thing I have never done, open a window just in case I forgot to close it when I went home. Anyway, it would have had to have been a very strong gust of wind to have scattered all those files all over the floor."

Mr Grundy took his eyes off the infant and looked across at Ella. "Somebody must have been in after you left. You locked the door behind you, you say?"

"Yes, of course I did. Are you sure the door was unlocked when you arrived?"

"Not just unlocked but wide open, I thought you were inside."

"Was anything taken?"

"There is nothing there to take only my paperwork, and that is scattered all over the floor. I leave no money at the office. Who could have done it and what could they have been looking for?"

Blanche joined in, "I bet it has something to do with PC Keyser."

"What can they possible think to find there?" Mr Grundy was puzzled.

"Those two thugs might have found out that you have an office in West Street and think you might be hiding the man they are looking for there." Blanche said logically.

"You might well be right Blanche," Ella agreed, "It makes perfect sense."

"I had better tell Charlie then," Mr Grundy decided.

"He is not here, as soon as Ruth walked into the sickroom PC Keyser remembered everything, so Charlie has gone off detecting," Ella informed him.

"He has no right to be going off detecting when there are idiots going around throwing all my paperwork in the air. If he wants to do his detecting, he should look nearer home." Mr Grundy's eyes went back to the infant.

Jackson came back carrying the drawer.

"Want to come and sort this out with me, to make it into a cot for the baby?" Jackson asked Blanche.

"Lead on, White Knight for there are more dragons to slay," Blanche said dramatically.

"More dragons to slay, what the devil are you talking about? I hope you haven't been giving her port to drink, Ella?" Jackson said.

"As if I would, being aware of you objecting strongly to Blanche partaking of anything stronger then milk."

"Is it your hormones?" Jackson asked Blanche.

"No, it is Mr Grundy's wind. I will tell you all about it while we get the cot ready." Blanche started to push Jackson towards the door with one hand while holding the baby with the other.

"Clarence's wind, have you been breaking wind in the presence of the ladies Clarence? I thought you knew better than to do that," Jackson asked him.

"It is not my wind, I do not have wind," defended a shocked Mr Grundy.

"Really Clarence, everybody has wind. But you must think about where you are before you release it. In the company of the fair sex is not one of them," reprimanded Jackson.

Ella and Blanche burst out laughing at the look of disbelief on Mr Grundy's face.

"Take no notice of them Mr Grundy," Ella said wiping away her tears, "they are teasing you. While they are sorting out sleeping arrangements, shall you and I go into the sitting room and I will pour you a brandy. Then I shall go back with you to the office and see what sort of mess we have to deal with."

"I would certainly like a drink before we go but I think it would be best if we waited until Charlie gets back and accompany him. You never know, those two scoundrels might be there waiting for us next time we go. If it was the two who came to the house of course, we have no way of knowing. I did not like them before and if it is the same two that have been sneaking about in my office, I certainly do not like them now," Mr Grundy told her.

While drinking his brandy Mr Grundy said, "I have been thinking Ella, there is only another day then it is the wedding day. Do you think it would be best if Jackson and Blanche spent the first couple of weeks on their own?"

"I think it is a brilliant idea Mr Grundy but where are they going to live?"

"They can sleep at the office. There are a couple of spacious empty rooms upstairs and there is everything they will need downstairs. The kitchen is big enough and they can always come here during the day if they want to. I have only one more case to deal with then we can get everything sorted out and make it into our home like we said. But that was before the break-in. I am not so sure that it is such a good idea now."

"I don't think the break-in will put, Blanche and Jackson, off. After all those two men entered our house without your permission and we are still living here. I think Jackson is more than capable of looking after Blanche if a situation arose. Don't you?"

"Yes, I do. Heaven help them if they so much as look at Blanche."

"But where are they going to sleep?"

"I have thought about that too. Charlie, you and I will all put together and buy them a bed for a wedding present. What do you think of that?"

"I think Mr Grundy that you are a very special man, and I am very proud to be your niece. That is a wonderful idea and instead of going to the office this afternoon you and I shall go shopping for a bed. Spend some of Charlie's money for him."

Mr Grundy's face was flushed with embarrassment and pleasure, but he added, "And I my dear, am very pleased that you and I get on so well together and you have decided to stay with me. You have made an old man very happy. That filing is never going to get done at this rate."

The bed was bought and was going to be delivered before Friday evening. Mr Grundy had to pay extra to have the bed delivered but he paid up without complaint.

Ella and Mr Grundy made their way back home, happy and content in each other's company.

On arrival they found Charlie, sitting in their kitchen eating bread and cheese.

"Hello," he greeted them, "where have you two been? I went home but I could hear Jackson and Blanche upstairs in Jackson's bedroom, so I thought it was more prudent to come here. I made myself something to eat Clarence, for I was devilish hungry, I hope you don't mind."

"You are welcome to anything we have got Charlie, you know that. Ella and I have been spending your money for you." Mr Grundy explained about the bed.

"Thank God for that. To be truthful, I did not relish listening to those two on their wedding night. The walls are very thin, as you well know."

Mr Grundy laughed at this and said, "The bed is coming tomorrow but first Charlie, you have to come and have a look at my office."

"I have seen your office Clarence it is quite suitable for them to stay for a couple of weeks, if not longer."

"Charlie, I have had a break-in."

"The devil you have. When was this?"

"Sometime this morning after Ella had left the office with that young baby that Blanche has stuck to her breast."

Charlie looked across at Ella and her eyes sparkled.

"It's true Charlie. There were no files on the floor when I left with PC Keyser's daughter, but when Mr Grundy got back to the office later this morning, the door was left wide open and some files had been scattered on the floor. I know I locked the door behind me when we left.

"Somebody has gained entry between Ruth and me leaving the office and Mr Grundy arriving there. I have not seen the mess, I said I would go back with him and have a look, but Mr Grundy would have none of it, he said we should wait until you came back."

"He did the right thing. I will certainly want to have a look at what they did. Was anything stolen?"

"There is nothing to steal. I never leave any money at the office, only paperwork and all this paperwork was scattered over the floor. Not just some of the files like Ella has just stated, but all of them. Blanche thinks it is those two thugs that pushed their way into my house looking for the trunk man. Have you found anything out about them or why they were going around shooting at people and pushing their way into someone else's house?"

"I am not sure, so I don't want to be putting ideas into your heads if they turn out to be false, let's say for the sake of it, it might be the same two men still looking for PC Keyser. He saw two men burying something in the wood and they shot at him. That is about all I can tell you now. I have no need to tell you to keep it to yourselves the fewer people who know about it the better. Come on, let's go and have a look at your office."

On arrival at Mr Grundy's office Charlie walked round the room trying to see if he could find anything that might help him to identify the culprits.

"What do you think?" Mr Grundy asked.

"I think Clarence, it is a warning. They are letting you know that they have been here and what they can do if they are threatened."

"Can I start to tidy this lot up?" Ella asked.

"Yes, I suppose so, there is no damage done that I can see. What about you, Clarence, can you see anything out of the ordinary besides the scattered files?"

"No, nothing that stands out anyway."

"I do not want you here on your own Ella, so until we get this thing sorted out I want you to keep away, they may come back, and I should hate for my fiancé to be hurt."

"How long do you think that will take, and what about, Blanche and Jackson, if they are coming to live here?"

"I will tell Jackson that Blanche is not to be left here on her own. If these two men do come back, I can assure you Jackson can take care of himself. He didn't get his medals for nothing. As for how long it will take, there is no way of knowing.

"A few files scattered around on the floor will not stop Jackson and Blanche moving in on their wedding day, after all, they will be upstairs most of the time. Don't you think?"

Chapter Nine

Danny looked up as Bert walked into the room.

"What have you found out?" he wanted to know.

"There is to be a wedding, tomorrow morning at 10 o'clock. They are all going. I followed that big woman. She went to the church with an armful of flowers. When she left, I went into the church and found the vicar. I told him that I thought the flowers were nice and he told me there was going to be a wedding tomorrow morning, and the church had been privately booked.

"There was to be a maid of honour and the bride was being given away by her father and the best man was an inspector of police. I didn't even have to ask any questions, he was all puffed up about it, he could not stop talking.

"I wish all the information I try to find out about our next job was as easy as that, all I had to do was stand and listen. They are all going to be at the church tomorrow morning, including Inspector Blurr."

Danny got up from his position at the table and started to pace the room. Bert followed him with his eyes waiting for him to decide what their next move was to be.

"There has been no mention anywhere of our witness being found, dead or alive. Maybe he just curled up in a corner somewhere and popped his clogs and nobody has found him yet. There has been no activity at the jewellers either. I think Bert, what we should do is get away from here as soon as possible, I don't like it, things are too quiet by half.

"Tomorrow while they are all at the church for the wedding, especially Inspector Blurr, I think we should risk going into the wood and digging up the jewellery and money then take off, get as far away from this town as possible."

"I think that is a very good idea," agreed Bert.

"We will go early in the morning, be at the edge of the wood well before 9 o'clock and watch for the wedding guests to depart.

When we see them, all heading for the church we will nip back into the wood and dig up the goods.

"If we go early enough, it will also give us the opportunity to see if there is anyone lurking about too. Keep our eyes open for anyone hanging about in the wood. It might be a good idea if one of us were to stand well back and keep lookout, you never know who could be knocking about.

"Look what happened when we were burying the stuff, we never expected someone to come across us, did we? If one of us had been on the lookout then, we would be in a better situation than we are right now. There is plenty of hiding places in the wood; we are going to be more careful this time."

"I agree. Who is going to be the lookout?" Bert wanted to know.

"We will pull straws, the one with the shortest straw keeps lookout."

Bert went over to one of the beds and pulled out two pieces of straw from a slit in one of the mattresses and offered them to, Danny.

Danny chose a straw and Bert showed his.

Bert had lost, he was to be the lookout, "Just my luck," he mumbled.

Ella had slept the previous night at Blanche's and they were both getting a helping hand with their hair and dresses from Blanche's maid.

Mrs Moyer kept running in and out of Blanche's bedroom making sure everything was perfect for her daughter's wedding. It was not what Mrs Moyer had wanted for her daughter, but she was happy Blanche had finally decided to settle down and get married.

A baby on the way was not ideal either. There would be gossip from more than one quarter, but Mrs Moyer decided she would rather have the gossips and have her daughter back than be at loggerheads with her.

Mrs Moyer had been surprised how easy it had been for her husband to accept the situation. The only reason Mrs Moyer could think of for this unexpected turn of circumstances was because of Jackson being a war hero. She did not care what the reason was, Blanche was getting married and Blanche was happy, Mr Moyer was happy and so was she. Mrs Moyer had not seen her daughter so happy and blooming for quite a while.

Danny and Bert stood on the edge of the wood and watched the three gentlemen set off in the direction of the church.

Without a word between them they headed back into the wood and had a good look round before making for where they had hidden the stolen goods.

It was a pity that neither Bert nor Danny had the sense to glance up in the trees for they were being watched from above.

Bert walked on and Danny, retrieving the shovel from where they had hidden it when they buried the loot, proceeded to dig for his treasure.

He dug, and he dug, but he could not find the treasure. He moved to his right and he dug, and he dug, but he could not find the treasure. He moved to his left and he dug, and he dug, but he could not find the treasure.

Throwing caution to the wind he bellowed, "Bert, come here."

Bert went at a trot to find out what the panic was all about.

"What the devil are you bellowing at? You are loud enough to wake the dead."

"It has gone, the loot has gone. Have you been back and taken it without letting me know?"

"Don't be stupid, why would I do that? Are you sure it's not there? Maybe you have been digging in the wrong place."

"Well, where would you have me dig?" Danny spread his hand in the direction of the scattered holes.

Bert glanced at all the holes Danny had dug. He made no comment.

Danny said, "I don't like this Bert, I don't like it one little bit, let's get the hell out of here."

Danny threw the shovel down and turned to leave. He did not take more than two strides and he was brought to a dead halt. Six police officers were blocking their way.

Neither Danny nor Bert put up a fight. They could see it was useless. They were outnumbered and neither of them liked the look of the pistol barrels pointing in their direction.

The meal Mrs Moyer had organised for after the ceremony was being held at the Moyer's house.

They all sat around the dining table and enjoyed a fine feast when Mr Moyer said, "That vicar had a damned quiet voice I could hardly hear what he was saying, I missed your first name Jackson."

Jackson looked across at his father-in-law and he thought he had better keep on good terms with him until he got the dowry. He needed the stable block building and he was aiming to use the dowry to pay for it.

He did not relish the thought of admitting his first name was Charles but there was nothing else for it, "Charles," he mumbled.

"Charles, I knew it, I damn well knew it," exclaimed Mr Moyer. "You are in good company my boy for my first name is Charles too."

"Should have known," Jackson said.

"All the men sitting round this table are called Charles," said Blanche, "what are the odds on that? I agree with you Jackson, there are too many Charlies in this world."

"Mr Grundy's name is Clarence, surely?" asked Mr Moyer.

"Nope, it is Charlie. Jackson christened him Clarence to stop the confusion," his daughter explained.

"To stop whose confusion?" her father wanted to know. "Why are you known as Jackson and not Charlie? Why is Charlie not known as Blurr then you can be known as Charlie?"

"We let Charlie keep his name because he is the ugliest," explained Jackson.

Mr Moyer looked from Inspector Blurr to his new son-in-law and then to Mr Grundy, and he burst out laughing and they all joined in.

Mrs Moyer looked around her dining table at the odd assortment of people all enjoying themselves and she felt a cloak of contentment settle over her. It was a long time since the walls of her house had heard laughter.

"Mr Grundy has something for you and Jackson, Blanche. We hope you like it," Ella told her friend.

Mr Grundy looked over the top of his glasses at Jackson then he said to Blanche, "Charlie, Ella and I have put together and bought you a bed as a wedding present from us all. It is being installed right now, or at least it should be, in an upstairs bedroom above my office in West Street.

"Here is a key to the office. After the bed has been installed the delivery men are to drop the key I left with them through the letterbox, so you will be able to have a key each. You may use it as temporary accommodation until we all get things sorted out." Mr Grundy passed the key to Blanche.

"Charlie's house seems to be stuffed to the rafters with bodies now. It is Ella you know, she has a habit of collecting stray bodies. She did not get the habit from her Aunt Fran. She was quite the opposite, liked her own company did Fran. That is one of the reasons we had the workshop built for her," Mr Grundy explained to Mr and Mrs Moyer.

"You can go back to Haywood Street during the day if you like and sleep at West Street at night, treat it as an overflow then no one is on top of anyone else, a honeymoon retreat. Ella and I will keep away from the office for a couple of weeks then, when the honeymoon is over you can give me the keys back or you can carry on living there and Ella can come and start moving the files down into the basement. Then we can get on with turning the office into living accommodation again. I am not looking forward to carrying all those files down into the basement, I can tell you."

"Don't you worry yourself over the files Mr Grundy; I will help Ella carry the files down into the basement while Jackson is getting everything ready in his surgery. It will give me something to do," Blanche told him.

"It is the best wedding present you could have given us Clarence. You should see what they are making me sleep on now, a put-me-up. It is not doing my poor old back any good."

"Mrs Moyer, that was a very enjoyable meal, but if you don't have any objections, I must get back to work." Charlie looked over at his hostess.

"Of course, you must go if you have to. Thank you for helping to make this a pleasant occasion. Now you know where we live, you all have an open invitation to call anytime you are passing," Mrs Moyer told him.

"Yes, nice to have met you Charlie. I have heard a lot about you. How is that grandmother of yours keeping these days?" Mr Moyer stood up and shook hands with him.

"Not as sprightly as she was I'm afraid, in body that is, her tongue could do with a rest though, and she tends to bend my ear every time I see her. Are you two ready to go back yet?" Charlie looked at Ella and Mr Grundy.

"Yes, it has been a very pleasant day, but we will leave you now. Enjoy your honeymoon and we will see you when you surface again Jackson old boy. Let us see how the back is then," Mr Grundy tittered.

Jackson had the grace to blush and found it hard to avoid the gaze of his father-in-law.

Walking back home Charlie said to them, "Mr Moyer mentioned my grandmother back there. Did you ever meet her, Clarence?"

"No, I can't say I have, never even heard of her I don't think."

"No, I try to keep my work and my social life separate from her. The trouble is she is getting on in years now and she is hounding me to go and take over the family estate. I knew it would come to this one day and to be truthful, since I have met Ella, and Jackson and Blanche have tied the knot and there is a baby on the horizon, it has been on my mind more and more.

"You know, having a wife and family of my own has never been an issue with me. I have never found anyone that I wanted to share the rest of my life with until Ella came into my life. I know it is early days yet Ella, we have only known each other a week but I am thinking about leaving the police force and settling down.

"Do you think you might be able to look at me in a more personal way, once you have got to know me better of course?"

"I have not been offended at being called your fiancé, in fact, I rather like it. In the past three years I have met a few men who thought they could take advantage of me, but they soon found out differently. Since meeting you I have not felt any of the repulsion that I felt towards them.

"In fact, Charlie, I must admit, the first time I saw you, your shirt was unbuttoned, and I had difficulty in keeping my eyes off your hairy chest, which surprised me, because that sort of thing had never been further from my mind." Ella confessed, and they carried on walking in silence.

Mr Grundy was the first to speak, "Well, that seems to settle that then."

"No not quite, there is still the question of you Clarence. We have been friends for far too long to allow you to be on your own again. Would you be willing to come and live on the estate with us? There are plenty of spare rooms and I am sure you would get on famously with my grandmother, give her something to take her mind off me. What do you say to that Clarence, fancy a taste of life in the country?" Charlie asked him.

"Never lived in the country before and I certainly have never been a chaperone to an old lady to keep her occupied from nagging someone else."

"Then it is about time you did. I will leave you now, but I shall come and see you both tonight," Charlie took hold of Ella's hand and brought it to his lips.

Back in Charlie's house Ella and Mr Grundy went straight to the sickroom and found father, daughter and baby. The baby was contentedly fast asleep in his drawer.

"Hello. How did the wedding go?" PC Keyser asked.

"Everything went swimmingly, Blanche is now Mrs Charles Jackson and they are to honeymoon over in West Street so Ruth can sleep in comfort in Jackson's bed until you return home, without her feeling guilty about it," Mr Grundy explained.

"This is very good of you all," PC Keyser said. "I believe you are the young woman that saved me from being caught by my pursuers. What made you take my side? Normally when someone is injured they are usually the culprit, you had no way of knowing I was a policeman."

"There were two of them and I thought the odds were unfair, besides which they pushed their way into Mr Grundy's house and were very rude to the both of us. I did not like them," Ella told him.

"It was a good job that you didn't like them. I thank you for what you did for me. It was very kind of you. I do not know what my little Ruth would have done if I had died. We all thank you, including little David over there."

"Why did you seek me out?" Mr Grundy wanted to know looking at Ruth.

"My father gave me a letter to deliver to you if anything happened to him, so when he did not return after a few days, I headed for here," was the reply.

Mr Grundy looked at PC Keyser and waited for an explanation.

PC Keyser tried to sit up and Ruth ran over to him and pumped up the pillows behind him.

"Inspector Blurr, Jackson and yourself, have a reputation for being very fair and understanding. Ruth's husband had an accident with a plough and was unfortunately killed. He never saw his baby son, and Ruth and the baby came to live with me. My wife, Ruth's mother, died some years ago. Things have not been too bad for us, Ruth kept house for me and I was pleased to have her and the baby's company.

"Then, Chief Inspector Freeman took over our division at the police station and he had a son, also a policeman, who took a shine to Ruth and the baby. They wanted to get married but, Chief Inspector Freeman would hear nothing of it." PC Keyser put his head back on the pillow.

"Chief Inspector Freeman said Ruth was not good enough for his son and he would not allow his son to marry someone who had a baby by someone else. Chief Inspector Freeman has been trying his best to get me removed from the police force hoping to make Ruth go away at the same time.

"Our Inspector over at Hotshell is under Chief Inspector Freeman's thumb and I cannot get any support from him, so on Saturday, which was my day off, I decided to come and see

Inspector Blurr. Ask his advice on how I should proceed, and you know the rest from there. In fact, you will be more in the know than I am as to what is happening right now."

Melvin Keyser looked enquiringly first at Mr Grundy then at Ella but neither spoke, so he continued.

"I have not seen Inspector Blurr for a couple of days and Jackson will tell me nothing. I gave Ruth a letter, my will really, to bring to you Mr Grundy in case anything happened to me. I do not trust the solicitors in Hotshell that is why I instructed Ruth to come and see you, just to be on the safe side."

"Well, we cannot tell you anything either, PC Keyser. Charlie has gone off doing his detecting and he said he would be back for tea, maybe we will find out more then. In the meantime, is there anything I can do to make you more comfortable?" Mr Grundy wanted to know.

"I wouldn't mind sitting in a chair for a while. I am sick of lying here, I need to get up, try to walk, get a bit of exercise. I am not used to lying in bed all day; my body is beginning to ache."

"I can bring a chair up for you to sit on but, until Jackson has seen you I think it would be better not to do any walking on that leg, after all you did catch a bullet in it." Mr Grundy went to fetch a chair.

"You look very pretty my dear in that lovely pink dress. I shall buy Ruth a dress like that one of these days," PC Keyser smiled across at his daughter.

No smile reached his daughter's eyes when they exchanged glances. Nor did a smile appear on her lips.

"Ruth is not very happy I am afraid. She thinks she is not going to see her beau anymore. Chief Inspector Freeman is making things very difficult for his son to sneak away and see her. It looks like their relationship is doomed."

"I am very sorry Ruth. I hope things work out for you and your boyfriend. If he really loves you, he will find a way." Ella went over to the young girl and put her arm round her shoulder.

"You have all been so very kind to us, I should be feeling very grateful, but I cannot think about anything else but Lester. He will be wondering where I am, he will think I have gone off and left him without as much as a word. I was not expecting to be away this length of time." Ruth started to cry, and Ella gave her a handkerchief.

"I am sure everything will turn out for the best, you just stay here and keep your father company until he can return to work," Ella encouraged.

"Here we are." Mr Grundy came puffing into the room bearing a wooden armless chair.

"Let me put a couple of pillows on the seat that will help make it more comfortable for you to sit on."

Ella jumped up and taking a couple of the spare pillows from the ottoman under the window, she laid them across the seat.

Mr Grundy and Ella helped PC Keyser swing his legs over the side of the bed and supported him when he tried to stand up. He leaned heavily on Mr Grundy but managed to take a couple of limping steps and sit down on the cushioned chair.

"I am going to get changed out of my lovely dress and get something ready to eat for when Charlie gets back home. We had a very nice meal at Mr and Mrs Moyers' after the wedding so I am just going to do some bread, butter and cold meats for tea.

"I don't think Jackson and Blanche will be coming so I will bring the meal up here and keep you both company. When Charlie gets back you might find something out to your advantage," Ella told them.

While Ella set about in the kitchen, Mr Grundy and Ruth dismantled a table that was in Aunt Fran's workshop and reassembled it up in the sickroom. Five places were set, and more chairs brought up and the only thing missing was Charlie.

Thirty minutes before Charlie arrived home, Jackson and Blanche made an unexpected appearance.

"Blanche, Jackson, I was not expecting you tonight. Will you be stopping for something to eat? I have only done some bread and butter and cold meats, but you are more than welcome to stay."

"If it is not inconvenient Ella, we would love to stay and have a bite with you, it will round our day off nicely. Really, we have come to see if Charlie has heard anything about the two intruders, as well as begging a free meal of course," Blanche grinned at Ella, "it is our wedding day after all."

"I was just about to take the food next door. It would not take long to cut some more bread and there is plenty of cake and biscuits to finish with. You know you are most welcome anytime, both of you. If you want to go next door and see the patient, please feel free to pop along and take some of this food with you while you are going up. Charlie is not here yet, but we are expecting him anytime."

"I will stay and help you," Blanche said.

"You will do no such thing. It is your wedding day, go and relax and put your feet up, play with the baby to get some practice in. I will join you when Charlie arrives." Ella pushed them both out of the kitchen.

Ella had just finished cutting some more bread when Charlie walked in. He looked around the kitchen and enquired, "Are you on your own?"

"Yes, I am. Blanche and Jackson turned up, so I have sent them next door. I was just cutting some more bread. Jackson took the meat plate with them and Blanche a plate full of cakes. I am pleased you are back you can help carry two more chairs next door then we can all sit and listen to what you have found out while we munch away."

Charlie made no comment but went around the table, took Ella in his arms and kissed her.

"I have been longing to do that since the first time I took you in my arms, you made a lasting impression on me, Ella Penrod, and it is just as nice to hold you in my arms now, as it was then. I look forward to repeating this action many more times, if you have no objections that is," he looked down at her flushed face.

"I shall look forward to it too, but now I think the patient and his daughter will be ready for something to eat. As it is Blanche and Jackson's wedding day, let's not keep them waiting. Grab the chairs would you, Charlie? I will bring the bread and some more cups. I don't think you will have enough to go around."

"I might do as you ask, for a price?"

"And what is that?"

"This!" and he kissed her soundly one more time.

Charlie went out and into his own home carrying two chairs, one placed upside down on top of the other and he headed upstairs. Knocking on the bedroom door with his booted foot, Jackson was the one who opened it and let them both in.

"Thank you, Jackson. Not too much of a strain on your back is it, opening the door? I don't want Blanche having to look after an invalid on her wedding night." Charlie grinned.

Jackson chose to ignore the remark and after Ella had entered the room, he slammed the door shut behind them.

During the cold meal, Charlie told them how he had put a couple of policemen to watch both his house and Clarence's house in case the two intruders should return.

"The policemen had seen Blanche call at Clarence's yesterday, her arms full of flowers but she got no answer to her knock. She had turned and headed for the church.

"My men saw a man matching the description Clarence had given us of one of the men who had pushed his way into his house, come out of a doorway and start to follow Blanche. One of my men stayed where he was observing the houses and the other followed Blanche and her pursuer.

"After Blanche came out of the church, my man watched her pursuer wait until Blanche was out of sight, then he too, went into the church. Again, my man waited outside and when he saw the man that had followed Blanche come out of the church and walk away, he entered the church and went to find the vicar.

"My man asked the vicar what the gentleman who had just left had wanted and he was told he was just admiring the flowers, but he also found out that the vicar had told him about the wedding and who was going to attend. Unfortunately, the vicar had told him everything. I say unfortunately, that is the wrong word because as it turned out it was most fortunate for us as we were able to apprehend the two culprits.

"I sent some men into the wood and told them where to dig to try and find out what the two men had been burying. They came across some stolen jewellery and cash. My men filled in the holes they had dug and covered them over with dry twigs and dead leaves and left the area as they found it. The evidence was brought back to the station.

"This morning half a dozen of my men were sent out very early to take up position in the wood around the spot where the jewellery had been hidden. I advised them to try and find a tree to climb up, keep out of sight and to wait and arrest anyone that came to retrieve the goods.

"Whilst we were in church, the two robbers did indeed go to try and dig up their loot and were promptly arrested. It turns out they were responsible for a spate of house thefts in Hotshell, and they had also broken into a jeweller's and stolen quite a lot of jewellery and cash.

"Apparently, they share a single room in Hotshell and there was nowhere to hide their haul, so they buried it in the wood. The intention was to go back for it when the police had given up trying to find out who was responsible for the crime.

"Fortunately for us, unfortunately for them, our PC Keyser just happened to be innocently passing the exact spot where they were burying the stolen goods. The culprits are being charged with attempted murder as well as theft for they did try to kill PC Keyser, and I will not have anyone on the force being shot at," Charlie told them.

"So, your reputation will be further enhanced by this poor man being shot at. You will be telling us next you have been promoted again." Jackson looked across the table at Charlie.

"That is where you are wrong Jackson old man. I am leaving the force. Another four weeks and I will be plain Charlie Blurr."

"Don't believe it," Jackson said.

"It is true. You know how my grandmother is forever telling me it is time I settled down and took over the running of the estate from her; well, I have decided to do just that. I am going to get married and settle down and have a family just like you and Blanche. I am not having you telling me you are a better man than me Jackson. I am going to get married and have some children of my own. If I don't I will never hear the end of it."

"Who will marry you?" Jackson wanted to know.

"My fiancée of course," Charlie replied.

Jackson looked to the end of the table and asked of Ella, "Don't tell me you are silly enough to marry him?"

"I am. He has not asked me yet but when or if he does, I shall say yes," Ella smiled at Charlie sitting at the other end of the table.

"I knew it, I knew it the very first time I laid eyes on you that you were the one for him, but I tell you this Charlie, you are a damn fast worker. You have only known the woman a week and you have given up your job and are thinking about having children and settling down. Have you had a knock on the head or something?" Jackson wanted to know.

"I am not going to make Ella wait for eight years before I come up to scratch like you made poor Blanche wait," Charlie informed him.

"We did not wait eight years," Jackson said in his own defence.

"No, so it would seem. You put poor Blanche through all this rush job by putting the cart before the horse. Well, Ella and I are going to do things right. I am going to court her and woo her and then we are going to get married. She is the only woman I have ever met that has been on my mind from the first moment I saw her, and I do not mind her knowing it. PC Keyser is having trouble with his superintendent, so I have recommended that PC Keyser would be a perfect replacement for me and when he is feeling better he must go into the station and get things sorted out.

"That kills two birds with one stone. He can have this house if he wants it. The house belongs to my grandmother so he can rent it if he wishes to do so. I will move out to the estate and Ella and Clarence will follow me once we are married. You and Blanche can still move into Clarence's house once Ella and Clarence have moved temporarily into the office. In fact, thinking about it I have killed four birds with one stone, PC Keyser, you and Blanche, and Clarence, Ella and myself. What have you to say to that Jackson?"

All eyes looked across at Jackson, "You have missed out young Ruth and the baby."

There was a knock on the door, so Charlie stood up and went to answer it. He returned with a young man dressed in a smart black suit, white shirt and cravat and holding a hat in his hand.

Ruth jumped up and ran over to him throwing herself into his arms and bursting into tears on his shoulder.

Jackson looked over at Charlie and snarled, "Clever sod."

Charles beamed back at his friend, he cast an eye around his table, at the people sitting there, all was right in his world, but he could not help saying to Jackson, "You will have to learn to keep your language clean from now on Jackson, young children about you know."

Part Two

Chapter Ten

It's was now or never, Charlotte thought as she ascended the steps; her heart was beating rapidly as she took hold of the doorknocker and gave it three hard raps.

She heard footsteps getting louder as they approached the front door from the inside.

When the door opened, the face she beheld was not familiar to her, which took her by surprise.

"Would you be so kind and give my card to Lord Singleton?" Charlotte held out her card.

The butler took the card, "One moment please."

He had only been working for Lord Singleton for two weeks and the first thing that had been drilled into him was that he was on no account to admit any female, no matter what age, unless permission was granted first by his lordship.

Looking up to see his butler walking into the room, the gentleman, dressed leisurely in tight trousers, white loose-fitting shirt and bootless feet asked, "Yes, Watson, what is it?"

"A young woman at the front door asked me to hand you her card, my lord." He presented the card on a silver tray.

Lord Singleton took the proffered card and read the name printed on it.

The butler was amazed to see his lordship's colour rise. He was even more amazed when the same gentleman stormed past him. He watched with open mouth when his master marched through the hall to the front door and dragged it open.

"Charlotte!" exclaimed the shocked lord.

"Isaac," responded the young woman giving a slight curtsey.

It took a few seconds for his lordship to believe his eyes as he stood staring at the young woman in front of him.

"May I come in? We seem to be attracting attention," the young woman said.

"Damn it, Charlotte, you know very well you may come in." He stood aside for her to enter.

In his confusion he snapped at the unsuspecting butler, "What the devil do you mean by keeping, Miss Palmer, standing on the doorstep. You are a blithering idiot."

Charlotte's eyes sparkled as she took in the shocked look upon the butler's face and she felt the need to say to him, "Do not take it to heart, he always was grumpy first thing in the morning."

"Let me take your coat," Lord Singleton said.

"I do not think I will be staying that long but thank you Isaac. No doubt you will be wishing me gone to the devil in ten minutes."

"Take off your damn coat, Charlotte."

Charlotte locked eyes with the gentleman, and the butler held his breath.

Smiling sweetly up at his lordship, Charlotte slowly and deliberately took off her gloves and handed them to Lord Singleton. Then she started to calmly unbutton her coat which, after this process was complete, she slipped off her shoulders and passed to him.

His lordship without ceremony promptly handed the items of clothing to the butler, then he stood awkwardly, and at a loss for something else to say.

Charlotte had to confess, that she had been in the same flustered position five minutes ago, whilst she had stood upon the doorstep, waiting to be invited in.

Coming to his lordships rescue Charlotte asked, "Where is Fisher?"

"He has broken his leg and it is very inconvenient of him. Would you like to see him?"

"Yes, I would."

His lordship indicated along the hall and Charlotte walked by his side heading towards the kitchen.

On reaching the third door to the left, his lordship rapped once, then opening the door he held it open for Charlotte to pass through into the room.

A portly gentleman who was sitting in a shabby leather chair, and his right foot elevated onto a footstool, looked up from his newspaper and his wrinkled face lit up. He was genuinely pleased to see her.

"Miss Charlotte, what a wonderful surprise," and he held out both hands to her.

"I must apologise to you for not standing when you entered the room, as you can see for yourself, unfortunately I am indisposed, and I find it difficult to stand," Fisher pointed to his elevated leg.

"And it is nice to see you too, Fisher. I am sorry to see you in this predicament. Isaac informs me that it is damned inconvenient of you to break your leg."

"Is it indeed, well he has a fitter and younger man on the door, so he should have no reason to complain." Fisher looked at his lordship over the top of his glasses.

"According to Isaac, he is a blithering idiot."

"No doubt he is doing his best under difficult circumstances. I am surprised at you, my lord."

"He kept Charlotte standing on the doorstep, closed the door in her face, would you believe. I will not have it."

"He was not to know your ruling did not include, Miss Charlotte, if you did not tell him," pointed out Fisher. "Anyway, how are you keeping my dear, you do not know how good it is to see your pretty face again."

"I am keeping in better health than you Fisher. Is there anything I can do for you to make you more comfortable?"

"Bless you no, I am being well looked after," the old retainer smiled at her.

The door opened, and the huge backside of a woman dressed in grey came into the room dragging a serving trolley behind her.

"Here we are dearie, a nice bit of bacon and eggs for your breakfast."

"Hello, Martha," Charlotte said.

The cook spun round nearly knocking over the tray and for an instant she was taken aback to see his lordship standing looking at her from his position by the fireplace.

Then seeing Charlotte, her face changed into a beaming smile and she rushed over to Charlotte and clasped her to her bosom saying, "Miss Charlotte, Miss Charlotte, well bless my soul if it isn't, Miss Charlotte. My girlie, but you are a sight for old eyes. Welcome back."

Charlotte returned the embrace and said, "Thank you, Martha. It is nice to see you too. It's no good asking you if you are in good health because I can see for myself that you are."

"Someone has to keep the house running smoothly with Fisher laid up," the cook told her.

"We will leave you to have your breakfast in peace, Fisher," Lord Singleton told him.

Fisher looked purposefully over at his lordship and he looked him up and down then asked, "Do you think that is suitable attire to be entertaining your young lady in, my lord?"

Looking down at his feet Isaac, realised they were stocking clad, his hand went up to his throat and his loose-fitting shirt was open at the neck, and he had the grace to blush.

"I was not expecting visitors," he told Fisher in his defence.

"No, I don't suppose you were. If you do not want to make a cake of yourself again with Miss Charlotte, go put some clothes on," Fisher advised. "And this time take more care of her, don't go losing her again."

Charlotte's eyes sparkled at his lordship's embarrassment and he said to her, "I hope you have seen enough of Fisher now Charlotte; for I know I have, let's go."

"Aren't you two married yet?" Charlotte asked Martha ignoring his lordships last remark.

This time it was, Martha and Fisher, that were left speechless and Charlotte saw the colour rush into Martha's cheeks.

"To save Martha any more embarrassment, they were married three years ago," Isaac informed Charlotte.

Fisher's mouth dropped open in amazement, "How the devil did you know that?"

"It is my place to know, Fisher. I like to keep track on all of my staff, make sure they are fed and well looked after." Isaac let his eyes run over the laden food trolley.

Charlotte looked up at his lordship's face and he was grinning down at her.

Lord Singleton went over to the door and held it open for Charlotte to pass through, leaving his speechless butler and cook to overcome their shock.

"You enjoyed that, did you not?" she asked.

"Oh yes! It makes a change for me to get one over on Fisher, he is my biggest critic," replied Lord Singleton with a satisfied air.

"That was one of the things I always admired you for Isaac, the way you treat your servants. There are not many houses where the servants would dare to criticise their master," Charlotte told him.

"Fisher is like a father to me, he was the only stable thing in my life when I was growing up, and I loved him more than I did my father. Martha too, they were the only people that gave me any love during my childhood. The only people I could get any comfort from. My house would be a lot worse off without Fisher and Martha, I class them as part of my family, they always will be I hope. But you know all this so why I am rambling on about it, I have no idea."

"Both Fisher and Martha looked well and truly at home if you do not mind me saying so," laughed Charlotte. "He certainly will not waste away with a breakfast like that."

Lord Singleton smiled. "Yes, at least I know my servants are well fed."

An uncomfortable silence passed between them as they made their way back along the passage towards the hall.

"Whilst we are talking about Fisher, he put me in my place as usual about my dress, for which I must apologise. He was right of course; I am most unsuitably dressed to be receiving young ladies. Would you mind waiting in the drawing room while I run upstairs and get my boots on?"

"I have no objection to the way you are dressed Isaac, in fact…" Charlotte stopped herself just in time from saying she liked the way he was dressed.

"In fact, what?" he wanted to know.

"It is of little import," he was told.

"I would like to be the judge of that. You were about to say?"

"I was going to say, I like the way you are dressed, it makes you look vulnerable."

"I have always been vulnerable where you are concerned, Charlotte."

It was Charlotte's turn to blush and to change the subject she said, "You must be wondering why I am here?"

"No, I was wondering nothing of the sort. I do not care why you are here. I am just glad you have come. If I am pondering about anything at all, I am trying to think of something that will keep you here. Will you stay and have lunch with me?"

Charlotte was about to say no, she had a lot to do but the temptation was too great. Now she had seen him again, she did not want to leave, so, after a short silence her reply was, "Thank you Isaac, that would be nice."

They had reached the hall and Watson was standing to attention at the bottom of the stairs.

"Watson, I apologise for my outburst earlier on, I was out of order. Would you tell Mrs Fisher that, Miss Palmer, will be staying for lunch?"

"Mrs Fisher, my lord?" queried Watson.

"Yes, Martha," came the reply and Isaac steered Charlotte towards the withdrawing room.

"That should set the cat amongst the pigeon's," Charlotte remarked.

Isaac looked down at the impish face smiling up at him and he had the urge to take hold of her in his arms and smother that impish face with kisses.

"Oh yes, it will set the tongues wagging but it will be a seven-day wonder. That is if the rest of the servants do not know they are married already, which I very much doubt. All the servants seem to know more about what goes on in this house than I do."

"How is your grandmamma?"

"Mentally she is as sharp as ever, physically not so good. She has trouble walking these days and she does not get out much. I bought her a wheelchair and during the warm summer days Lily will take her out for walks around the garden that she loves so much. You remember Lily, grandmamma's companion, Miss Tubby?"

"Yes, I remember Miss Tubby, guards her like a dragon."

"That's the one, but I would not be without her, neither would grandmamma."

"I am sorry to hear grandmamma is not in such good health. She must find it very frustrating, being normally such an energetic lady."

"Yes, she has her bad days but mostly she does not complain."

"Do you remember Marcy Jenson?"

"Is this a trick question?"

"No, why should it be?"

"You ask if I remember the name of your best friend. How could I forget it? I remember everything about you Charlotte, which should go without saying."

"Do you remember, Marcy Jenson?" Charlotte asked again preferring to ignore his last remark.

"Yes," was the clipped reply, "I remember she had vanished under a cloud, she left Lord Mooreway standing at the altar, didn't she?"

"You see, your tone speaks volumes. You should not judge other people's actions unless you know the full story." Charlotte's tone was as clipped as his lordships'.

"To leave a man standing at the altar with everybody who had been invited to the wedding, agog with curiosity, is not the correct thing to do. If she'd had a change of heart and she did not want to marry Lord Mooreway, she should have cried off before everyone had arrived at the church. It placed Lord Mooreway in a very embarrassing position."

"You feel sorry for Lord Mooreway, do you?"

"I do. At least you had the good manners to do the right thing and put the notice in the newspaper. I was not left standing at the altar, not like poor Henry."

"You think it is poor Henry, do you?"

"Don't you? You think Marcy was in the right to leave the poor man standing at the altar. Do you know how ridiculed he must have felt?"

"No Isaac, I do not. I think he must have felt a much-relieved man."

"Relieved, how can a man who has been let down in such a way, with his guests in place in the church, feel relieved that his bride failed to appear? He must have felt an idiot. Relieved does not come into it."

"You are of that opinion Isaac, because you do not know the whole story. You can only imagine what Henry was going through because Marcy did not turn up. You are putting yourself in his place. It is how you would have felt Isaac, not how Henry must have felt."

"And you know this because you have been made aware of the full story?"

"Yes, that is correct, I know the full story."

"Very well, I am listening, and when I have heard your story, I will see if I change my opinion. But I must warn you, it had better be a good story."

"In that case, if you wish to hear the full story, I shall tell you, but you had better make yourself comfortable for it will take a while for me to explain."

"I am at my ease, please continue."

Charlotte smoothed down her skirt and began.

"On the eve of her wedding day, Marcy came to my house, she was distraught, and it took me quite a while to calm her down. In fact, I plied her full of wine before I could get anything out of her.

"Marcy shed her cape and to my amazement her gown was torn, she had one sleeve hanging off her shoulder and there was a great tear running from the other shoulder practically to her waist.

"Marcy pointed to her lip and I noticed a slight cut to her lower lip and a larger cut to her upper lip. Also, one of her eyes was beginning to swell and turn red. I had not noticed this when she first came into my house because of the distressed state she was in.

"It turned out that your poor Henry Mooreway, on the eve of their wedding day had sent Marcy an urgent letter asking her to meet him in the park, and so off Marcy went.

113

"Henry attempted to molest her. When Marcy tried to fight him off, he hit her in the face, she eventually made good her escape but not before he had left her with a few cuts and bruises and torn clothing. Marcy came to see me, she was in a state of distress and she dare not go home. She said I was the only one she could trust.

"Marcy said she was never going to marry Henry and could she stay at my house until the evidence of the attack had cleared up. Black eye, burst lips and bruises. That sort of thing. Then she was going to go to Scotland. She has an aunt who lives there. She told me she could not go on living here with the threat of meeting Henry again hanging over her." Charlotte paused and looked at Isaac.

"I have heard rumours that Henry can be violent towards women, but I always rejected them as just that, rumours. He is one of the nicest and friendliest, members of the Foxes Club you could wish to meet. I cannot imagine him hitting women," Isaac told her.

"I know Henry's mother has a vicious tongue and I can remember her saying she would break Marcy socially for what she had done to her son. Making him a laughing stock amongst all their friends.

"At the time of her saying that, I must admit I thought it was a just punishment for Marcy. In hind sight, if that is what Henry did to Marcy, then he got his just punishment and I am sorry for Marcy."

"'*If*' that is what he did, of course that is what he did. Marcy did not beat herself up and rip her own clothes. She was madly in love with Henry. Why should she make a false accusation like that? She was devastated about the whole incident.

"You are also questioning my judgement about what took place on the eve of the wedding day. I have never lied to you, Isaac. Surely you know that?"

"No, of course I know you would not lie to me about a thing like that. Maybe I worded it wrongly, I apologise. I know Marcy is your friend but why did she come to you instead of going to her uncle's?"

"I thought you would realise that Marcy could not have gone back to her uncle's. You are aware that his wife would have had no sympathy for her. You know very well she has made Marcy's life a misery for having to providing a roof over her head when she was left alone after the death of her mother.

"Her aunt treated her like an unpaid servant. She did the right thing to come to me. She is my friend and I know you would have done the same for any friend of yours that came to you in times of trouble.

"To be truthful Isaac, I was glad it happened before they were married and not afterwards. Henry must have been desperate to get out of the marriage to do what he did on the eve of their wedding day. Did he really think that Marcy would go through with the wedding when he had treated her like that?

"There is only one reasonable explanation for it and that is, he did not want to marry Marcy and he dare not refuse to do so because he was frightened of his mother.

"How did he expect to get away with it? His bride walking down the aisle with a black eye and burst lips? People would have wanted to know how she got them. At least she has been spared that humiliation, and she also had a lucky escape, because she did not get married to the brute."

"It is interesting that he has not married yet, in fact I have not heard of him being attached to anyone else. You think he did it intentionally do, so Marcy would cry off? You could be right. Having a mother like he has, he doesn't want to get married at all and end up living the rest of his life with someone like her. You must live with someone to know them, you know. Do you think all this violence towards women could be aimed at his mother?" Isaac wanted to know.

"I don't know, but Marcy is lucky to be well out of it. She did not think so at the time, but when you see her, you will be surprised to see how much she has changed."

"This sounds promising," his lordship said.

"What sounds promising?" she asked.

"You inferred I would be seeing Marcy again. That would imply I will also be seeing you."

Charlotte had the grace to blush but was saved from making any further remark by the appearance of Watson informing them that lunch was served.

During lunch Charlotte said, "Now you know the whole story, are you still of the same opinion that it is poor, Henry?"

"I must admit if this story is true, I have done Marcy, a grave injustice."

"Why do you keep saying *'If'* the story is true? I know for a fact the story is true. I am not a tittle tattler and well you know it. I would not have told you the story, if I were in the least doubt about any aspect of the turn of events that happened that evening.

"Nor would I have repeated Marcy's story to you if I thought it would go any further than these four walls, Isaac."

"My apologies again Charlotte, it is just so hard to believe."

"And yet your logic regarding why he did it is very plausible, but you still doubt it."

"No, you are right Charlotte. I grant you your story holds water."

"Thank you. But it is not my story, it is Marcy's."

"Now we have come to an agreement, can we drop the subject of Marcy and move on to something else?"

"I am afraid not, Marcy is the reason why I am here."

"This sounds ominous."

"I told you when I first arrived here my visit might not please you."

"I had hoped you had come to see me, that you had missed me as much as I have missed you."

"I thought you would have noticed I am not wearing a ring on my finger."

"I have noticed. That at least, gave me hope."

"I have come to ask a favour of you."

"The answer is, yes, whatever it is you want, the answer is, yes."

"You might regret making that offer."

"Charlotte, you know very well if it is within my power to help you I will, I love you, I always have, and I always will."

"We have been two very foolish people. I have tried my best to make myself appreciate other men, but they have never come up to your standards. It is very annoying."

The grin that crossed Isaac's face spoke volumes, "Is this a new beginning for us Charlotte?"

"More like a continuance."

"I did not mean to hurt you, I was very young, and I had a lot of females throwing themselves at me but none of it ever meant anything to me."

"Let us put all that behind us, we have wasted enough time on it already and go back to being the very best of friends."

"No Charlotte, not the very best of friends, I insist on lovers. I will settle for nothing less than lovers."

"Very well, let us go back to being lovers."

"In that case, tell me what you require of me and let us get it out of the way. Then we can concentrate on you and me, my lovely, lovely Charlotte."

"I told you it was a very long story, so I will continue where I left off. Marcy recovered of course and did what she said she would do; she went up to Scotland to live with her aunt.

116

"Marcy told her aunt what had happened to her and why she had gone to visit her. It turned out that her aunt lived in a very large six bedroomed house called, The Retreat, located in the middle of nowhere, and she took in women who had also been physically abused. There are more victims of abuse than you can ever imagine.

"Marcy asked her aunt if she could stay and help her with The Retreat, and her aunt was more than willing to accept Marcy's offer. The women that Marcy's aunt takes in are abused, either at home, or more often the case, women who work as prostitutes and have been beaten up because of the line of work they are in. They come in off the streets, have a little respite until their wounds heal and then because of their circumstances, they go back on the streets and the whole thing starts up again.

"More and more women are hearing about The Retreat and Marcy's aunt was more than pleased to accept any help she could get, and so Marcy stayed. That is where she is living now, and that is the reason you have never seen her in Bossett since she failed to turn up on her wedding day. She is living in Scotland with her aunt and she has never been happier.

"Running The Retreat of course takes a lot of money. The women who go there usually have no money of their own to pay for their stay. So, to keep The Retreat going, Marcy decided to come back here where the money is and organise a ball and invite all the rich people to the ball and ask for donations. All the money she makes will go to help with the running costs of the home.

"To give Marcy credit, it took a lot of courage to come back here to Bossett. She understands all the cream of society who have been invited to the ball know of her nonappearance at the church. But none of them know why she did it. She is also aware that, like you, everyone blames her for letting Henry down, for showing him up. All the invitations she sent out have been accepted, and Marcy says it is curiosity that has tempted them all to accept.

"Marcy is very brave, don't you think? She is prepared to weather the storm to get some money to take back to Scotland. She is fully aware that there are going to be a lot of uncomfortable questions asked of her, but Marcy thinks The Retreat is more important than some curious tattler's questions she is going to have to find an answer to.

"The ball is tonight, and she has spent her own money on providing food and drinks for all her guests and she is hoping that people will give generously, and she can recoup her own expenses and have enough to pay off most, if not all the mortgage on the house.

"Lady Mooreway being of a vicious nature, we are all aware of that, found out that Marcy was back in Bossett and is holding a ball tonight. Henry's mother has organised a ball of her own and has invited all Marcy's guests.

"The outcome of that is Marcy's guests have given backword and Marcy thinks, well she knows, for someone has told her, that all her guests are now going to Lady Mooreway's ball. Marcy is left with a lot of food nobody is going to eat and she has had to pay for the rent of the house she has hired for a couple of days. Because of Lady Mooreway's action, there is no prospect of Marcy getting her money back nor any money for The Retreat.

"This is why I have come to see you Isaac; do you think you could pull some strings at such short notice and get some of the party guests to go to Marcy's ball instead of Lady Mooreway's? If there is anyone in Bossett that could pull it off, it is you."

"I did not receive an invitation to Marcy's ball."

"No, I asked Marcy not to invite you."

"And why was that? I would have thought she was aware of my substantial fortune and if she is after money for her project, my money is as good as anyone else's."

"Yes, Marcy is aware of your fortune, but she is also my friend and I asked her not to invite you because, once I laid eyes on you again, I knew all the defence walls I had built up against you would come tumbling down. And so, they have."

Lord Singleton made no comment but looked at Charlotte with an amused eye and gentle smile on his lips.

When Charlotte dared to glance up at him his expression turned to passion and Charlotte was unable to glance away. She was held captive, and with the sound of her own heart pounding in her chest, her passion rose to match his.

"You are taking advantage of my vulnerability now, Isaac."

"No Charlotte, I am just letting you know how I feel. No need for words between us. That is the best excuse you could possibly have given me for not being invited to the ball. Because you love me, I could ask for no more. If you have had sufficient to eat let us go into the morning room where we can continue this conversation without the servants interrupting us every two minutes. You can tell me more about those walls that have tumbled down."

"We have more important things to deal with. I am very pushed for time and I should not have stayed for lunch."

"There is nothing more important than us, we have wasted enough time. Marcy shall have her ball and if not, I will pay the mortgage off for them."

"You would do that?"

"Well yes, that is unless it is a small fortune, it depends how much it is."

"She would not accept it you know, she is very independent."

"Let us go into the morning room and let me just hold you in my arms for a while, then we will carry on discussing Marcy."

Charlotte looked across the table at him, the thought of being held in his arms again was her down fall, she nodded and replied, "I would like that."

Isaac stood up and went and pulled her chair out for her and she stood up, but things did not go exactly to plan. On exiting the dining room, the front door opened and in walked three gentlemen. One Charlotte recognised, the other two, she did not.

"Hello Freddie, how nice to see you," Charlotte held out her hands and the tallest of the three gentlemen came forward and took her hands in his.

"Charlotte, well you can knock me down with a feather," he stood looking down at her with much affection.

"Now I know why Isaac did not appear for our luncheon engagement. I cannot say I blame him; you are much prettier than I am. I don't think you have met Cedric and Stanley, have you? I found them on your doorstep Isaac, something to do with a boxing match tonight," Freddie looked across at Isaac.

"No, we have not met," Charlotte held out her hand to the two gentlemen and said, "Charlotte Palmer."

Turning back to Freddie she said, "We were just about to go into the morning room. Will you join us? I have a favour to ask of you."

"This sounds intriguing," Freddie said and they all trooped into the morning room.

"Freddie, will you come to a charity ball tonight?" asked Charlotte. "Isaac is going."

"You will not get, Lord Singleton, to go to any old ball tonight. We are going to a pugilist bout," either Cedric or Stanley told her.

"I am sorry. Which one are you?"

"Cedric Tranplan, at your service." He made a slight bow in Charlotte's direction.

"Right Cedric, I challenge you to a wager. Five pounds says Lord Singleton will be going to my ball tonight and not to your boxing match." Charlotte threw out the challenge.

"Five pounds you say, I accept the bet."

"Can I have a wager too?" Stanley wanted to know.

"If you would like to take up the wager, I am not averse to taking your money off you. But I must tell you both, I would not place a wager unless I know it is a dead cert and this, is a dead cert. Lord Singleton, will be attending a ball tonight so if either of you want to back down, please feel free to do so before we shake hands on it," Charlotte warned.

Both Cedric and Stanley held out their hand to her and Charlotte shook both their hands.

Turning to Lord Singleton, she asked, "I do not have any money on me Isaac, would you be kind enough to lend me some?"

Lord Singleton went over to his desk, opened a drawer and taking out a wad of notes he threw it to Charlotte.

She caught the roll of money deftly and pulled off the paper ring holding the money together and peeled off a five-pound note. Then exaggerating the opening of her receptacle so both Cedric and Stanley could see what she was doing, she slipped the rest of the wad of notes into her receptacle and snapped it shut.

Charlotte did not miss the glance that passed between Cedric and Stanley, but neither gentleman made comment.

After taking the two five-pound notes off the two young men, Charlotte went over to Freddie and asked, "Will you hold the stakes Freddie?" and she handed the money over to him.

"You will have lost your wager this time Miss Palmer, Lord Singleton does not attend balls, he has not done so for years," Stanley told her.

"That was before I came on the scene young man. I have invited Lord Singleton to a ball tonight and he has accepted the invitation," Charlotte told them with confidence.

Cedric looked over at Lord Singleton and asked, "Well Isaac, you seem to have doubled up on your engagements for tonight, which one will you be attending, the ball or the boxing?"

"The ball," Lord Singleton told them.

"But you never go to balls," objected Stanley.

"I did not have the incentive to attend any balls that I have now," replied Isaac.

"Give Isaac his five pounds back, would you Freddie. Bring the money with you when you come to the ball tonight. Marcy will be thrilled to bits. Ten pounds, before the ball has even started. I hope this is a good sign for this evening's entertainment. I must go now, for I have a lot to do before this evening." She turned her back on Cedric and Stanley.

Whilst her back was turned to them, she opened her receptacle and took out the wad of notes as she walked across the carpet to where Isaac was perched on the edge of his desk.

Charlotte leaned in towards him and rising on her tiptoes she kissed him full on the lips. Isaac returned the kiss, but he kept his arms crossed and Charlotte slipped the wad of notes into his hand.

She slowly took her lips away from his and she was no longer on tiptoe, but she looked up at his down turned face and mouthed, "Thank you."

Turning, she went over to Freddie and kissed him on his cheek. "I shall look forward to seeing you tonight Freddie and both of you are invited as well if you wish to attend." Charlotte turned and addressed the two defeated young men.

"But I go too fast, I forget you do not know the whole story, so I shall cut it short and leave Isaac to fill in the details, for I must be on my way. I have dallied too long. Do you remember my friend Marcy, Freddie? Well she has rented a house on Dyson Street, number 141, and she is holding a ball tonight. I hope to see you all there this evening from 7 o'clock onwards." Then without a backwards glance she headed for the door.

"You have forgotten something, surely?" Stanley commented.

"I don't think so, my coat is hung in the hallway, and I will pick it up on my way out."

"What about Isaac's money?" Stanley asked.

"What about Isaac's money?" Charlotte questioned.

"You put it in your purse," she was told.

"I have given it back to him," Charlotte replied.

"You have not," he argued.

"Would you like another wager young man? Another five-pound note might get you your money back, but remember I never place a wager unless it is a dead certainty. I can prove that I did return the money to Isaac."

"I will take that wager," Stanley told her, and he took out his money again.

"And me," Cedric said also taking out his money.

"Would you give it to Freddie? He will bring it to the ball tonight and give it to Marcy. Normally I would not have taken your wagers but as you were going to place your money on a boxing match tonight, I think the money will be put to better use for Marcy's charity," Charlotte said.

"What about your five-pound note wager?"

"As I have already told you, I have given Isaac his money back. It is pointless to get the money off him again just to give it back. Don't you think?" Charlotte asked them.

"Open your receptacle and show us before you leave then and let us see for ourselves that the money is returned," Cedric challenged.

Charlotte did as she was bid and opened her purse and showed them both the inside.

Stanley and Cedric, after looking in the receptacle and observing no money, looked up at Charlotte and she looked across at Lord Singleton. Both young men's eyes followed her gaze. They were dumbfounded to see Lord Singleton open his hand and show them the wad of notes Charlotte had placed back in his hand.

"Let that be a lesson to you both, when someone tells you they do not place a wager unless it is a certainty, think twice before parting with your money or you will never be rich." She turned and walked out of the room.

After donning her coat, Charlotte was pulling on her gloves as she proceeded across the road. Halfway across she changed her mind and turned, went back across the road and instead of re-entering Lord Singleton's house, she ventured further up the road and rang the bell of the house six doors away and waited for the door to open.

On seeing Charlotte standing on the doorstep, the old retainer's face broke into a wrinkled smile and he opened the door fully and stood aside for Charlotte to enter.

"Miss Charlotte, you are a sight these old eyes never thought they'd see again, it is a most welcome sight."

"Thank you Conport, it is good to see you too. Is her ladyship in?"

"She is indeed, Miss Charlotte. Not in prime condition these days. She finds movement very taxing, and most days are spent up in her room."

"In that case Conport, I shall run upstairs and see her. There is no need for you to trouble yourself. I know the way."

"Very good Miss Charlotte, it will cheer her up no end seeing you."

Charlotte tapped on the door and was told to "Come in" by a frail trembling voice she knew so well.

An aging lady was relaxing on a chaise longue and when she saw who her visitor was, she put her hands to her mouth and Charlotte saw tears appear in the old lady's pale blue eyes.

"Hello, grandmamma." Charlotte sat beside the old lady and hugged her.

"Charlotte," was all the old lady could think of to say and she returned the embrace.

"I hope I have not shocked you too much, coming unannounced to see you?"

"You are welcome at my house anytime of the day or night without being asked and well you know it."

"I do grandmamma. I am sorry to find you indisposed."

"You do not find me indisposed my dear, just my old bones playing tricks on me, but I do not complain, they have served me well these past eighty years. Isaac?" grandmamma ventured to ask.

"Yes grandmamma, Isaac and I have patched things up."

"Oh, my dear, you do not know how happy that makes me feel. He has been tormented you know, since your breakup."

"Well that is all forgotten and forgiven but let me tell you why I went to see him and to ask for his help, and maybe you could help also. I have not much time, but I could not leave without seeing you."

After her story was told, Charlotte was standing by the window pulling on her gloves when the door burst open and Isaac came striding into the room.

"Grandmamma, you will never guess who called to see me."

"Charlotte."

"Now how the devil did you know that? You are an old witch."

Lady Singleton did not answer, she just nodded in the direction of the window and Isaac, seeing his beloved standing there, crossed the room in three long strides and Charlotte found herself in a crushing embrace and being passionately kissed.

Isaac lifted his head and still holding Charlotte crushed against his body he said, "Grandmamma, Charlotte and I are getting married, right now. I have a special licence in my pocket and we are going to see the vicar and get married. I am not letting her get away from me ever again."

"In that case, go and sign the licence. Then get on with snatching back the entire guest list from Lady Mooreway. She is a nasty, vicious woman and she deserves all that is coming to her. Go on, get on with it man. What are you waiting for?" his grandmamma asked.

"Will you come with me Charlotte, to see the vicar and get married right now?" Isaac asked his armful.

"I have a better idea, why don't you go and bring the vicar here, so we can be married with grandmamma in attendance."

"I knew I loved you for something besides your perfect body my sweet. It must be your beautiful eyes."

Charlotte smiled, and he fleetingly brushed her lips with his and then he shot out of the door.

"Quick Charlotte, go over to the wardrobe at the far end of the bedroom, in there you will see my wedding dress. It should fit you apart from the length which will be a shade too long but that will not signify, for you will not have to walk about in it. In my jewellery case on my dressing table you will find a diamond necklace which you can borrow and if you look in that bottom drawer over there, you will see some new handkerchiefs, take one of those.

"So that is something old, the wedding dress, something new, the handkerchief and something borrowed, the diamond necklace. We only want something blue now. I know, in the second drawer down you will find some ribbons, there is bound to be a blue one, bring it here."

Charlotte found the blue ribbon and passed it to Lady Singleton.

"Hurry up girl, get the dress on before Isaac comes back, we want to have everything ready for his return. I want you to look beautiful on your wedding day, not that you aren't beautiful Charlotte, because you are, but a girl's wedding day is supposed to be special and I will not allow Isaac to bully you into a shabby wedding day."

Charlotte looked at her reflection in the mirror and was more than satisfied with the young woman looking back at her.

"Thank you, grandmamma. It is a beautiful dress. Just look at me."

"Something old, something new, something borrowed and something blue. Here, this should do the trick take hold of this bible," and grandmamma passed Charlotte a bible tied up with blue ribbon.

"Perfect, just perfect," the old lady said.

Isaac marched back into the bedroom bringing with him a person whom Charlotte took to be the vicar, Conport the butler, and Miss Tubby, Lady Singleton's companion.

On seeing his bride in all her glory, he went over to her, took her hand and raised it to his lips, his eyes telling her of his approval.

"You like what you see, my lord?" Charlotte asked.

"Yes, I like what I see," he replied huskily.

The service was short and to the point. Conport poured everyone a glass of port.

On finishing her drink Charlotte said, "Thank you all of you for making this a special occasion at such short notice. Especially to grandmamma, for the loan of her beautiful wedding dress. When I set out this morning, I thought I was going to have a battle on my hands to try and persuade Isaac to help me get Marcy's guests back, and look at me now, a married woman.

"I really must get changed and be on my way. Poor Marcy will be wondering what has happened to me. It is an open invitation for tonight so if any of you would like to attend you will be most welcome. The address is 141, Dyson Street. Marcy has rented it for three days, and she travels back to Scotland tomorrow morning."

"In that case we will get back to work Miss Charlotte, and let you get changed." Conport escorted the vicar out of the room and closed the door behind them.

Before he left the room, Isaac corrected Conport by saying, "It is Lady Singleton now Conport, not Miss Charlotte."

Conport bowed in Charlotte's direction, "My apologies, Lady Singleton."

Charlotte laughed and replied, "No need to apologise Conport, it will take a lot of getting used to, for me as well as you."

When Conport and the vicar had left, Charlotte was changing back into her day dress with the help of Miss Tubby and she was conscious of her new husband's eyes on her but at last she was dressed and ready to make her exit.

Isaac told her, "You may go straight back to Dyson Street, Lady Singleton, and make ready for tonight. I was on my way to find you and ask you to marry me but decided to call in and see grandmamma first and tell her the good news. I am afraid I have taken it upon myself to send the servants out to spread the word that if anyone would like to call at Dyson Street tonight between 7 and 8 o'clock this evening, they will be able to meet the new, Lady Singleton.

"I also told the servants to tell everyone that there will be an entry charge of five shillings per person which will go to help the less fortunate. That should set things going. I think there will be more people wanting to see whom I have married than there will be attending Lady Mooreway's ball. Don't you?"

"I think the whole of Bossett will turn up. You want to thank your lucky stars that Charlotte agreed to this rush wedding or you would have looked very foolish if you had to tell everybody you had been turned down," laughed the Dowager Lady Singleton.

"Are you coming back with me?" Charlotte asked Lord Singleton.

"No, I have a few things to sort out, I will come about 6 o'clock and it will give us a bit of time to come to terms with what we have just done today. I hope you won't regret it Charlotte. I have had that special licence at the ready for the past two years, hoping I would get the chance to use it. I would have been an idiot not to take advantage of the situation." Isaac told her.

"I will never regret it. I have tried and tried to get you out of my mind and I have failed miserably. When I decided to come and ask for your help, I was determined to set my cap at you once again. I did not expect it to be so easy. No Isaac, I will never regret getting married to you.

"You are mine now for better or, for worse and I know it is going to be for the better." She walked over to him, kissed him on the lips, and then she bent down and gave grandmamma a hug before she left the room.

Dowager Lady Singleton looked at her grandson, "Happy Isaac?"

"I am quite stunned grandmamma. I have waited for this day for four years. If Charlotte cannot believe how easy the whole thing has been for her, how do you think I feel? I am on top of the world grandmamma. What about you, are you happy for me?"

"She was always the one for you. Charlotte has always been my favourite out of all the young ladies you have brought here, none have compared to our Charlotte. Here take this and give it to her as a wedding present from me.

"They look better on her young neck than they do on mine and I shall never wear them again. All my jewellery shall be hers one day anyway, what difference does it make if she gets them now, before I am dead. None what-so-ever." The dowager handed Isaac the diamond necklace Charlotte had worn for her wedding.

Isaac took the diamond necklace, kissed his grandmamma and left.

After her grandson had left the dowager said to Miss Tubby, "Lily I have decided to go to the ball. So be it if I am being pushed in a wheelchair, I am determined to go. Now, please find me out a gown and let me push the boat out one more time."

"Do you think that is wise my lady? The doctor said you have to take things easy and not overdo it." Miss Tubby looked doubtful at her mistress.

"Lily, I am turned eighty years old, if I want to go to the ball, I shall go to the ball. It is such a long time since I attended a ball and this one is so very, very special. If I do not go I shall regret it until the day I die, so find me out a gown, for I am determined to go, with or without you."

"Very well, my lady, as you wish. Do you wish me to attend the ball with you?" Miss Tubby asked.

Miss Tubby's name did not reflect her size. Although she was on the small side, she was a very thin woman with grey hair tied back in a bun in the nape of her neck.

"Of course, I want you to attend the ball with me Lily. Who else would I want to push my wheelchair? You have pushed me around for the past thirty odd years, and I do not mean only since I have been reduced to the wheelchair. Do you have anything suitable to wear?"

"No, my lady, I do not, but this is not about me is it. I shall dress you up in your finest gown and cover you in jewels. You shall be the best dressed lady there."

"No Lily, I do not want to outshine the bride, just a nice ball gown and maybe my pearls.

"But somewhere in my wardrobe you will find some old gowns of mine that I wore when I was much, much slimmer and much, much younger. You might find one that will fit you and if it needs any amending, you will have time to put the odd stitch to it and make it fit."

"Thank you, my lady, I should love that above all things. I have never had a ball gown and I have never been to a grand ball. I am so excited I can hardly wait."

"Well then," laughed the dowager, "Go heat me some water for a bath and while I am having a soak, you may raid my wardrobe to your heart's content."

Chapter Eleven

Lord Henry Mooreway was sitting opposite his mother watching her closely, his breathing shallow, he did not know what to expect. What he did know was, when it happened he would be at the receiving end of it.

Lady Mooreway was rigged out in all her finery ready to greet her guests.

Sitting in a deep cushioned armchair, her hands resting on the arm rests, her fingers drumming out a nondescript tune. She was not moving, apart from the steady up and down movement of her fingers, her eyes looked straight forward, and her face cruel, and filled with fury.

The servants were standing to attention at the rear of the room.

Through open connecting doors stood the empty ballroom with a long table at the head of the room, covered with a snow-white tablecloth which was laden with food and drink.

There was not a single guest in attendance.

"Henry, this is all your fault, you are a worthless piece of manhood, you are just like your father. He was a waste of time too. You could not manage to lead that girl Marcy down the aisle and now she has rubbed our face in it again. I will be the laughing stock of Bossett once more, and it is all because of you," Lady Mooreway spat at her son.

"Please mamma, you cannot blame this on me, it was you who decided to try and upstage Marcy not me. I was happy to let things be," Henry whined.

Lady Mooreway stood up in a rage, "You dare to defy me? I will teach you a lesson you won't forget."

Lady Mooreway turned to the servants and screamed at them all, "Get out, get out all of you, and I do not want to see any of your faces again tonight or tomorrow for that matter. If I do, it will be for the last time. Do I make myself clear?"

The head butler bowed respectfully and said, "Very clear, Lady Mooreway."

After giving Henry a pitiful glance, the butler held the door open and all the servants filed out.

Simms had been the head butler for Lady Mooreway for too many years now and he knew that Henry was about to be on the receiving end of her ladyship's displeasure. Fury was etched on her face, no good was going to come of this, and he was in no doubt about that.

Poor Henry, Simms thought as he closed the door on his employer. But he still went to hide in the kitchen with the rest of the servants and leave poor Henry to his fate.

Simms reflected whilst he made his way down to the kitchen, of the years he had been the butler for Lady Mooreway, and he wondered why he had stopped in her employment for so long. Money, he thought, she paid him good money. He would never have got the amount of money he received from Lady Mooreway if he had changed employers. The only reason Lady Mooreway paid him what she did was because she could get nobody else to work for her.

Lady Mooreway looked across at her snivelling son.

"Useless, utterly useless that is what you are," and advanced towards him.

Henry cowed down in the chair he was sitting on, he knew what was about to happen, he had seen his mother in one of her rages too many times in the past not to know what was about to befall him.

In his short lifetime, he had learnt it was best not to try to defend himself. It only made things worse.

He held his hands over his head for protection. It was the third blow that did the trick. Henry felt all the hurt and anger that had built up in his head over the passing years, spill over and flow down his right arm. He clenched his fist to stop all the anger and resentment falling out of the ends of his fingers and soiling the carpet.

His right fist shot out and upwards, catching his mother on the chin with such force he heard her neck snap. For one split second Henry saw all the hatred leave his mother's eyes, they went blank as they looked at him. Her face had lost its fury and he saw his beautiful mother's face devoid of any emotion before she fell to the floor like a stone.

Henry did not stop at that, he knelt over his mother's motionless body and pounded her face until it was unrecognisable.

After he had vented his anger on her, he stood up and looked down at what he had done.

"Mamma, mamma, get up mamma. Why are you lying down there with blood all over your face? Mamma, mamma, please get up mamma."

His mamma did not get up.

Henry stood looking down at her.

He had to get away, he knew he had to get away, far away, but first, he would put his mother to bed, make her nice and comfortable and keep her warm while he was away.

Henry did not need the help of the servants. It was his mamma and he could put her to bed without their help. He went and opened the rooms' double doors then running up the stairs he opened his mother's bedroom door, went over to the bed and pulled the sheets back. Then he turned and retraced his steps.

There were no servants anywhere to be seen, he knew that too, his mamma had sent them all way, told them not to be seen for a couple of days.

Henry knew the servants would know better than to disobey his mother. He did not blame them. She could be very cruel could his mamma but that did not stop him loving her. He had always loved her no matter what she had done to him.

Henry carried his mother up the wide staircase and into her bedroom where he placed her gently on the bed.

While he was washing the blood from her face to make her look pretty again, his anger was turned to Marcy. His mamma had wanted him to marry Marcy, but he could not, he could not take her to bed and make love to her, she was not his mamma.

If his mamma knew he had thoughts like this in his head, he would be the victim of her mirth, he would never hear the end of it but all he wanted was for his mamma to love him, to hold him and be gentle and kind to him. That is all he had ever wanted for as long as he could remember.

Now she was no longer alive, she was never going to take him in her arms and tell him she loved him. But she was never going to use her tongue and fists against him either. The strange thing was he felt no regret. In fact, quiet the reverse. He felt elated, as though a great weight had been lifted off his shoulders and immense pleasure at what he had done. A sense of freedom enveloped him.

But it was all Marcy's fault. Marcy had made him do this to his mamma and Marcy would have to pay.

He knew she was going up to Scotland in the morning, he had heard the tattlers in the club. They thought he was out of earshot, but he had heard them.

People had never forgotten his being left standing at the altar, and they never would. It would follow him for the rest of his life, but he did not care, he preferred the gossip to the thought of being married to Marcy.

The killing of his mother would also follow him for the rest of his life now. There was no escaping that, he did not need anyone to tell him, he knew. The tattlers will have their day again at his expense. No hiding place now. The tattlers had won, he had lost, but so had Marcy. He was not going to let her get away a second time.

He had to get away. He knew he had to get away. His mamma did not need him anymore.

He decided he was going to follow Marcy. Make her pay for taking his mamma away from him, making him the target of the tattler's once again. Oh yes, she was going to have to pay alright.

The last thing Henry did for his mother was pull the bed covers over her to keep her warm and safe. "Goodnight Mother, sleep tight and long. Goodbye."

Marcy's ball on the other hand went like a dream, it far exceeded all her expectations and when all the guests had left, Marcy, Charlotte, Isaac and Freddie were sitting counting the money into the early hours of the morning.

Marcy told them she would be able to pay off the mortgage and still have some money left for other things. She could not thank them all enough.

"I have been thinking Marcy," Lord Singleton said, "would you mind if Charlotte and I came up to Scotland with you in the morning, well this morning, for it is way past midnight now. We could have it as our honeymoon. I have never been to Scotland and I am told the scenery there is out of this world. What about you Freddie, do you fancy a trip to Scotland?"

"I think that would be a good idea. Marcy will be travelling with all this money and she will need protection. We will act as guards and keep her and the money safe on the journey north. That is if Marcy has no objection." Freddie looked across the table at Marcy.

"I would very much appreciate your company. I came down on the mail stagecoach, but it was very crowded and one or two of the passengers needed a good bath. It was a very long and uncomfortable journey," Marcy told them.

"Good, we will go and get a few hours' sleep and come and pick you up around 9 o'clock. If Freddie brings his coach, Marcy can travel with Freddie, for if we all were to travel in one coach, there will not be enough room for any of our luggage. Can you be at Marcy's house just before 9 o'clock, Freddie?"

"Wild horses couldn't keep me away." Charlotte noticed Freddie was looking at Marcy when he said it.

Lord Mooreway was observing Dyson Street from an alleyway at the other end of the street. He saw Freddie's coach being loaded with Marcy's boxes, and he was not best pleased.

When he had decided to follow Marcy to Scotland, he had not bargained on the presence of Isaac Singleton and Freddie Atton. He had observed Freddie pulling up outside of Marcy's and a few minutes later he saw Isaac's coach pull up behind Freddie's. Charlotte Palmer did not signify, he could easily deal with her, but he knew both gentlemen from The Foxes Club.

Henry knew both Isaac and Freddie could handle themselves perfectly well. That was a certainty; both gentlemen were much better than he was at fencing, boxing and shooting. He had come up against them both on more than one occasion at the club and he was always the loser.

Never mind, he would follow and bide his time, find out where Marcy lived in Scotland and there would come a time when he would be able to satisfy his need, his need to avenge his mamma's death. The longer he waited the more satisfaction he would get.

Henry noted that they were travelling in two separate coaches. With a bit of luck, they would get separated and he might have a better chance of revenge if the opportunity arose. On the other hand, two coaches would be easier to follow, he would be able to keep well back and not be afraid of losing them or of being seen.

Henry had decided to travel on horseback, easier to hang well back until it was time to strike, he was travelling light, just a couple of carpet bags fastened to the back of his saddle.

It was a pleasant journey north; the weather was clement and warm for the beginning of April and Freddie was pleased about that for he had decided to drive the coach himself and leave his coachman at home.

Marcy, well wrapped up sat up top with Freddie and was enjoying the feeling of wind in her hair and the pleasant company she now found herself in. During the three days they had been travelling it had been agreed that, Isaac and Charlotte, would spend one night with Marcy, then carry on and do a tour of Scotland leaving Freddie at The Retreat.

Marcy had talked Freddie into doing a few odd jobs around the place to keep him from getting bored, to say nothing of the money they would be able to save if Freddie did the odd repair for them.

Actually, Marcy had mentioned to him as they travelled north, that her aunt had said they needed to get an odd job man to do one or two repairs, and Freddie had said he would have a look at what needed doing whilst he was there. He would see if he could help.

Isaac and Charlotte would go back to The Retreat in two weeks' time and accompany Freddie on the journey back home. It was a long way to be travelling alone for in some places it was very isolated. There was always the risk of highwaymen attacking the lone traveller; it was much safer if they travelled together.

Freddie had not needed much persuasion. He was pleased Isaac and Charlotte were going off on their own for two weeks. He was more than willing to stay behind and give Marcy and her aunt a helping hand. If Freddie had to choose between being a gooseberry by tagging along with Isaac and Charlotte on their honeymoon or staying at The Retreat with Marcy, Marcy won hands down.

Only one more day of travelling and their destination would be reached. They pulled up at the last wayside inn of their journey and were welcomed by the landlord who showed them to their rooms.

"Dinner," he told them, "would be served in a private parlour at 7 o'clock."

Around 6:30pm, Isaac went to answer their bedroom door when a pounding on it roused them from a light sleep and he was amazed to see Guy, his grandmother's stable boy standing in the doorway twisting his cap nervously in his hands.

Guy looked at Lord Singleton's surprised face and words failed him.

"Guy, it must be bad news for you to be here, come in lad," Isaac held the door open for him.

"Yes, my lord, very bad news I am sorry to say, it is your grandmother sir, she's none too good," Guy told him nervously.

"None too good, what does that mean?" Isaac wanted to know.

Guy hung his head. He could not bring himself to say the words.

"Is she dead?" Isaac whispered.

Guy keeping his head bowed nodded.

"When, when did she die?"

"She passed away my lord, on the evening of the day after the ball."

"Oh, my God, she never should have taxed herself by going to the ball. I should have insisted on taking her home straightaway."

133

"Begging your pardon my lord, but I do not think you should. She was in fine spirits all the next day, we have not seen her ladyship so happy in many a long year. She just went early to bed the day after the ball and passed away quietly in her sleep, she died happy my lord, extremely happy."

"Go and see the landlord Guy. Book yourself a room here for tonight, it is too late in the day to be setting off back home. We will accompany you back first thing in the morning. I will have to go and see Freddie." Isaac looked back at Charlotte.

There were tears running down her face, Isaac knew she had a soft spot for his grandmother.

He could not find the words that would comfort her, so he went in search of his best friend.

Freddie agreed to continue with Marcy and he would stay in Scotland until Isaac and Charlotte came to accompany him back home.

Next morning found the friends going their separate ways.

Lord Mooreway had found a bed for the night in a hostelry at the opposite end of the village to where his prey was putting up for the night. He had risen early and found a hiding place from where he was observing the departure of Isaac and Charlotte, heading back the way they had come and in the opposite direction to that of Marcy and Freddie. He could feel his goal getting nearer.

Henry had a smile on his face as he watched Lord Singleton's coach heading in one direction, and Marcy and Freddie heading in the opposite direction.

There was only Freddie left to be concerned about now. But the odds were beginning to stack in his favour.

Marcy pointed out landmarks to Freddie as they neared their destination and when the daylight began to fade she pointed to a quaint little town they were approaching.

"This is Marchum. We have only a mile to go now. Marchum is the last town before The Retreat. The Retreat is a large rambling old house on two floors. It stands at the edge of a wood and it had been unoccupied for about two years when my aunt took out a mortgage on it.

"There was a lot to do to get it into a suitable state to live in. Not that any of the women who come to The Retreat care much about the condition of the house. Even in the state it was in when my aunt took it on, was a better place to stay than the homes some of the poor girls we get coming here, live in.

"My Aunt Sylvia poured money into the project when she first started out. She has a passion for what we are doing. She had a bad experience once herself which is why she never married.

"I must admit the women we take in all love her. In fact, I would go as far as to say they adore her. You will love her too when you meet her, she is addictive.

"She powers her way along and people just follow her lead. I am so pleased we are going to be able to pay the mortgage off and help keep The Retreat going. If we lost it through the lack of money, I don't think my aunt could cope with it."

"If your aunt is anything like her niece I don't think I will have a problem with liking her. Is she totally anti men?"

"No, of course she isn't. She told me that she never found anyone she could love, anyone that she could bring herself to live with for the rest of her life."

"What was the bad experience she had?"

"When she was about twelve years old, my aunt walked into her parents' bedroom without knocking and caught her mother with one of the male servants. Apparently, the male servant was standing naked by the side of the bed and he was in a very aroused state. My aunt says every time she meets a man she thinks she could become fond of, all she gets in her head is the image of the naked male servant and it puts her off.

"My aunt was in a more fortunate position than I was when her parents died for they left her well provided for. She had sufficient funds to support herself without having to go out to work or marry someone she did not love.

"Aunt Sylvia used to run a boarding house, well not a boarding house really, but she did take in lodgers. It brought her in an income and one of the lodgers she had was a pugilist. He boarded with my aunt for about five years and in that time, he taught her the art of self-defence. She can certainly look after herself and since I have been living here with her, she has taught me some of the self-defence moves too.

"Not that I have ever had to use any self-defence since I came to live here. Marchum is a very quiet little town and nothing much ever happens. But about six months ago, there was a bit of excitement when a police officer was shot twice, once in the shoulder and once in the leg.

"But I will tell you more about that another day when we find ourselves without any conversation," she told him.

"And I will be most interested to hear all about it," Freddie said. "Did the police man die?"

"No, he was lucky enough to be found by some friends of Marchum's brilliant inspector of police, Inspector Charlie Blurr."

Marcy glanced at Freddie, "Did you know about me leaving Henry Mooreway standing at the altar?"

"I did, there are not many people in Bossett that will be ignorant of the incident. You know what the tittle tattlers are like."

"The reason why I left Henry standing at the altar and the reason why I came to live with my aunt are one and the same. It was because he attacked me on the eve of our wedding day. I fought him off and all I suffered was a cut lip, bust nose, a black eye and a few bruises. I went to Charlotte's and stayed with her until my cuts and bruises had vanished, then I came up here. I could not continue living in Bossett after that."

"I should think not, how appalling. Why didn't you go to the police about it?"

"I was too ashamed. All I wanted to do was to go into hiding. Charlotte gave me that opportunity. She kept my secret and let me heal. I shall be eternally grateful for that."

"I don't know what to say."

"There is nothing to say, it is over and done with now. My aunt was full of understanding and it has been so very, very interesting working alongside of her, and she is still in the process of teaching me all she knows. That is one of the reasons Aunt Sylvia is teaching me self-defence, she says you never know when you might need to protect yourself. This is what she keeps drilling in to me. I can tell you I have been a very eager pupil."

"Your aunt sounds a formidable person."

"Well, she is not, she is adorable. Most of the money she made running her boarding house has gone now. It has all gone into The Retreat. That is why we must find different ways of keeping the funding going. If we can hold a ball each year back in Bossett and get some money together then we will be able to keep things ticking over," she chattered on.

Marcy pointing, said, "Look."

Coming into view was a stone fronted double storey house of large proportions, raised slightly above the boundary walls and surrounded by extensive lawns to all four sides.

"Impressive," Freddie had to agree.

"Welcome to The Retreat," Marcy's smile was full of pride.

The door was opened and out stepped a lady of mature years, she was wafer thin and boasted snow-white hair which curled around her once pretty face. To the back she had soft white ringlets hanging down.

"Marcy, my dear, welcome back. I have missed you terribly," the lady held out her hands to Marcy who threw her arms around the old lady and gave her a big hug.

"Aunt Sylvia, this is Freddie Atton, he has come as my bodyguard. Four of us set out but two had to return, a family problem has arisen. So poor Freddie has had to suffer my company for the last day's journey," Marcy explained.

"I am sure your company is as good as another's." She held out her hand to Freddie. "Call me Aunt Sylvia, everyone else does."

Freddie took the proffered hand and kissed the back of it.

"I have heard a lot about you, Aunt Sylvia, and I am impressed with what I have heard. My only hope is you can live up to my expectations."

Aunt Sylvia looked at the tall, handsome, young man and remarked, "If you are intending to set your cap at this young man Marcy, you have brought him to the wrong place. All the women that frequent The Retreat will eat him for dinner.

"I am afraid you will have to see to the horses yourself young man, for we do not possess a groom. You will find the stable, across the courtyard, to the right of the house and when you have put the horses to bed for the night, come into the house. I will have a nice hot meal waiting for you and Marcy can fill me in on all the gossip." Placing one hand through her niece's arm, she watched while Freddie unloaded their luggage and dropped it onto the porch.

Both Marcy and her aunt watched as Freddie disappeared around the side of the house, and then they picked up a piece of luggage each and left the rest for Freddie to take in on his return. The dynamic old lady and Marcy disappeared into the house.

Lord Mooreway, keeping well back, took in the scene outside of the impressive stone building and thought, *It would seem we have arrived at our destination,* and he let his eyes continue past the building and boundary wall into the wood beyond.

Skirting, The Retreat well away from prying eyes, Henry headed into the wood.

The light was beginning to fade now but Henry was not afraid of the dark, he was afraid of his mother.

He knew his mother was dead, for he had killed her, but he knew she would not stay dead, he knew he would never be rid of her for good.

He knew she would always be there, hiding in the back of his mind, jumping out at him at the most unexpected moment, making him do things that he knew were wrong.

But his mother insisted, and insisted, and insisted until he could stand it no more and he had to hit out, give those women a good thrashing, like his mother had given him.

It was the only way he could get some peace of mind, to hit out at those women. Once he had vented his anger on them, he found peace. That is until his mother reared her beautiful head again and there was only one way he knew of, to rid himself of her image.

He could not stop now. He knew that, he could not stop. It was never going to go away; his mother was never going to leave him alone and let him live in peace and he did not want her to. He loved his mother, he always would, and he knew that, so it was no good pretending anything else.

Whilst thinking about his mother, Henry had wandered off the well-trodden track, for his mind was still obsessed by his beautiful mother, his dead beautiful mother. When would she ever leave his mind?

When the servants found her body, he knew the constabulary would be looking for him, but they would not find him here in this wild barren terrain. Why would they? They would not know where to look for him. Nobody knew where he had gone, he had vanished, and he was glad. He liked being invisible.

Would his mother find him here? Oh yes, she knew where he was, and he was glad about that too. He wanted his mother, she could not leave him, she would not leave him, and he knew that, she was imprinted in his mind.

Quite by accident Henry came across a shack, it was well hidden in a little clearing off the beaten track.

Dismounting his horse, he tethered it to the nearest tree and walked straight into the shack. He did not care if anyone was living there, he had decided that this shack was his shack; if anyone lived there, they would have to go. He would get rid of them. He knew what to do now. He knew how to get rid of people.

It had been built just for him, out of sight, closed in by big old trees covering his shack with their solid strength. He could hide behind any one of these trees and nobody would see him, oh yes, this was his shack alright.

As it turned out the shack was empty, it had been the gamekeepers shack once upon a time when The Retreat had been occupied by the previous owners. He felt the walls of the shack surrounding him, protecting him from prying eyes.

This shack had been made for his mother and him. They would be able to live comfortably together here until the time came to move on. It would keep his mother and him safe from the outside world.

"What do you think of your new home, Mother?" Henry asked.

"Yes, I agree, it was made for us," he answered himself.

The shutters were closed, and it was very nearly pitch black inside the shack, but this did not matter to Henry. He went outside and unsaddled his horse, taking the saddle and his carpetbags inside. He deposited them onto a table that occupied the centre of the little room. Then he went back outside in search of water.

His horse needed watering, he found an upturned bucket behind the shack and set off into the wood. On further inspection it was not a very dense wood but good enough for his requirements at this moment in time.

Henry found a stream running down from a craggy hillside, where it went he did not know or care, it was sufficient for his needs.

Once Henry had made Marcy pay for making him kill his mother, he would trek further into the wild Scottish moorland, change his name and become invisible. Nobody would know him, nobody would care anyway, and nobody here in Scotland knew his mother, so why should they care if she was dead or alive.

For the moment he was satisfied, he had found his mother a new home, they could stay and rest awhile, get to know each other again, maybe, just maybe, this time she would take him in her arms and she would tell him she loved him, that he was a good boy, that he had done well, he would look forward to that, after all he had looked forward to that moment all his life.

Chapter Twelve

Lord and Lady Singleton arrived back in Bossett and went straight to the home of the late dowager to find most of the servants had found other employment and the only three servants still residing there were Conport, Miss Tubby and the housekeeper.

As soon as Miss Tubby saw Lord Singleton, the lady burst into tears and Charlotte went and put her arms around the sobbing woman.

"I am sorry my lord, I just cannot help it, every time I think of her I burst into tears."

"There is no need to apologise Miss Tubby, you have been with grandmamma for a long time, you are bound to miss her, we all will," his lordship tried to console her.

"May I have a word in private, Conport?" Isaac asked the old retainer.

"Yes, of course, my lord." Conport followed his lordship into the morning room.

"I know this is going to sound hard hearted and unfeeling Conport, but has any arrangements been made for the funeral? I believe my grandmamma died five days ago and in this weather, I think that is long enough for her to be above ground."

"The weather was a contributory factor when I took it upon myself to make the funeral arrangements my lord; the funeral can go ahead as soon as you wish. I knew you would come straight back when the news reached you, so I held it back to enable you to attend. All you have to do my lord is send word to Mr Foster and he will arrange everything for you."

"Thank you Conport, I do not think I could have done it myself. Would you go and see Mr Foster and ask him if he could arrange the funeral for first thing tomorrow morning. There is nothing I can do to alter the facts and no good will come of holding things back.

"You have been a good servant Conport, this house is going to have to be sold. Would you consider staying here and looking after it until a buyer can be found, then we will see about getting you somewhere to retire to, if that is what you want."

"I will stay here willingly my lord until I am no longer needed, then I shall go to live with my sister and her husband. We have everything arranged my lord, I am looking forward to spending the last few years of my life with my sister, we have always been very close. Miss Dobbs is still here of course, keeping the house clean and she is coming with me. We have thought about getting married, but nothing has been finalised about that yet."

"I am glad to hear it Conport. Thank you for all you have done. I will not keep you any longer. If Mr Foster cannot arrange the funeral for tomorrow, ask him to make it, as soon as possible would you?"

"I will indeed my lord. There was one other thing if you don't mind me spreading gossip, but I think you might find this interesting."

"Please continue Conport, you have my full attention."

"The night of the ball my lord, Henry Mooreway, killed his mother."

"Good God Conport, tell me more."

"Apparently not one guest turned up to her ball. This put Lady Mooreway in a rage. All the servants were terrified of her and poor Lord Henry has been a victim of her rages since he was in short trousers. I think it all started when his father left and went off with another woman. According to her servants she has taken it out on her son ever since."

"Continue, Conport, I am listening."

"All the servants were gathered in the withdrawing room waiting to attend to the guests when they arrived, but none came. Lady Mooreway went into one of her rages. She told all the servants to get out and she did not want to see any of their faces again for the next two days.

"What happened next no one knows but next morning one of the kitchen maids crept into the dining room to light the fire and found a pool of blood on the carpet. She went to inform the butler and they cleaned it up, knowing that if the stain was still there when Lady Mooreway came downstairs, her anger would flare up again.

"They have had to clean the blood from the carpet on more than one occasion in the past when Lord Mooreway had been the victim of his mother's anger and she had burst his nose, so they thought nothing of it. There was no sign of Lord Mooreway or his mother the next day.

"On the second morning after the ball, the breakfast that had been laid out had not been touched, nor had any of the food left out the previous day. The butler decided to send one of the maids up to her ladyship's bedroom, just to ask after her.

"What the maid found was Lady Mooreway laid in bed covered up with the bed linen and her face bashed in. The screams from the maid could be heard at the end of the street.

"The hunt is now on to find Lord Mooreway. The police are in no doubt that it is Lord Henry who is responsible for his mother's death then laying her out in bed and cleaning up her face.

"There have been rumours going around for a couple of years that Lord Henry had a temper to match his mother's, but as to whether there is any truth to that I do not know. He never displayed any violent tendencies towards the servants. All the servants felt sorry for him, they all knew how his mother treated him. I am sure that you are aware of how gossip spreads from one household to another, my lord. We had heard stories of abuse towards Lord Henry by his mother."

"Thank you for the information Conport. Interesting news indeed, I shall tell my wife if she comes across him to give him a wide berth."

Charlotte took Miss Tubby up to her room and asked her, "What do you intend to do now, Miss Tubby?"

"I do not know Miss Charlotte. Lady Singleton was my friend as well as my employer. I just do not know what I am going to do without her," and Miss Tubby burst into tears again.

"Come now Miss Tubby, this is not going to get us anywhere. I loved grandmamma too you know. Isaac and I are going back to Scotland straight after the funeral because we have left Freddie Atton up there, and we are to go and accompany him back to Bossett.

"My friend Marcy was the lady who held the ball that you and grandmamma went to and she runs a house for ladies that are less fortunate than we are, she runs it with her aunt. Would you like to come up to Scotland with us when we go, and stay there and help Marcy and her aunt run The Retreat? You will like Marcy's aunt; for Marcy tells me you and she are of the same age.

"I think it would be just up your street Miss Tubby. There will be lots of ladies to look after and fuss over, help them out and give them a bit of your excellent advice. If you have nothing to stay here for I am sure, Marcy and her aunt would be most grateful for your help.

"It would not pay much just board and lodgings really. There would be no wage, for all the money goes into The Retreat, but you would be amongst friends and have a home to live in. What do you say Miss Tubby, are you going to brush yourself down and head off to Scotland and a new life with new friends? Goodness knows what else may turn up for you.

"Isaac and I will stop off at The Retreat on our way up and drop you off, then we shall carry on and do a tour of Scotland just like we had planned. We will call at The Retreat on our way home to travel back with Freddie. If you have not enjoyed your stay, then you will be welcome to return to Bossett with Isaac and me."

"You make it sound so simple Miss Charlotte. Can it be so easy?"

"There is nothing to stop you doing anything you want to do now, is there?"

"Do you think her ladyship would approve of me going up to Scotland?"

"Not only do I think she would approve Miss Tubby, I think she would say, 'If you do not take this opportunity, then you are not the woman I thought you were', she would be delighted for you."

"In that case, I shall do it," Miss Tubby dried her eyes and sat up straight.

"Thank you, Miss Charlotte, I know you are Lady Singleton now, but you will always be Miss Charlotte to me, and you know my child, you made her ladyship very, very happy by marrying Isaac. She passed peacefully away in her sleep knowing that he will be well cared for, thank you for that."

Charlotte stood up and took Miss Tubby by the hand and taking her into the dowager's bedroom she said, "Right, hopefully by tomorrow afternoon we shall be on our way back to Scotland. As you will not be getting paid at The Retreat, why don't you pack as many of these clothes of grandmamma's that you want into a couple of trunks and take them with you. Except for her wedding dress, I should like to keep that myself. Anything else of hers that you want Miss Tubby, you pack. I know grandmamma would want you to have all her clothes rather than throw them away.

"They will be far too big for you, but you will have ample time to alter them to fit you, or even pass some on to any of the women at The Retreat you think might benefit from them. Get packing Miss Tubby, you had better be ready to go straight after the funeral, or we shall leave you behind, there's no time to waste."

Part Three

Chapter Thirteen

It was six months since Ella and Mr Grundy had moved into Mr Grundy's house on West Street. Jackson and Blanche had moved into Mr Grundy's end terrace house on Haywood Street and PC Keyser had moved into Charlie's old house. Ruth, PC Keyser's daughter had married her policeman and had moved back to Hotshell with him.

Before they had moved, Charlie had blocked off the bolthole he had made leading into Clarence's house. Fran had insisted on him making the bolthole in case he needed a way of escape one day. She had said that he met some very nasty characters in his line of work. Fortunately, he had never had cause to use it, but he was glad to know it had been there if ever he did.

Jackson had agreed that Charlie should brick the wall up connecting the two bedrooms up again. He told Charlie he didn't want PC Keyser creeping into his house and molesting Blanche whilst he was at work, for he had seen the way PC Keyser had looked at Blanche that first day he had laid eyes on her in the sickroom.

Jackson had made a good job of turning Fran's workshop into a veterinary surgery, and his reputation was slowly growing.

But the side stairway that connects the workshop to the house had been left in place. Jackson had no intention of blocking that off. It was handy for both he and Blanche to nip from the house to the workshop, it would be very useful when the weather turned inclement, especially in the winter months. Living in Scotland, Jackson had seen some harsh winter months.

Blanche was getting a bigger tummy every week and she would be glad when the baby finally arrived. She was finding it more and more difficult to get out of chairs but once she was standing, she was very mobile. Being pregnant had not slowed her down any.

Mrs Moyer was a regular visitor and Mr Moyer was monitoring the situation from afar.

Charlie had gone to live with his grandmother and was busy working the estate. Arrangements had been made for Charlie and Ella to be married and that was three weeks away.

Lord Mooreway woke early next morning, sleeping the sleep of the innocent, dreamless and restful and he was raring to go. He ate his last crust of bread and drank a mug of cold clean spring water.

He was sitting at the table while contemplating his next move, inviting his mother to join in and agree with him. She did not. He decided it would be best if he got his bearings, study the lay of the land. Find the best entry into this Retreat. That was his goal.

Henry had to try to find out when the best time to strike would be, in and out without anyone seeing him, no witness, that was his plan. Nobody to inform on him, he would be invisible, then the tittle tattlers would not be able to wag their tongues.

But he intended to let Marcy know who it was that had attacked her. His intention was to strike from behind, knock her to the floor then sit on her, just like he had done to his mother, then she would know who her attacker was, but she would be in no condition to tell anybody.

There would only be his mother and he that would know who had done such damage to that little face, and the thought pleased him. His mother would be proud of him.

Henry had decided he was not going to kill Marcy straight off, he was just going to take her back to his shack and teach her a lesson she wouldn't forget. He would make her pay, repeatedly. He would make her understand why he was doing it, why she had to pay.

He had thought that it might be difficult to get her back to his shack, but he did not dwell on this problem for very long. Just the thought of catching her and seeing the look on her face when she saw him, soon emptied his mind of anything else. He relished the chase and capture. He would let events take their course.

Marcy had been the cause of all his troubles. If it had not been for her, he would not have had to kill his mother, and his mother would still be alive today.

Henry was so angry with Marcy he decided once he had her tied up in his shack, he was going to go to The Retreat and smash the place up. Why should Marcy have a nice home to live in when she had made him kill his mother? Not only had he lost his mother because of her, he had also lost his home and his money. If he went to the bank, the police would arrest him, and he was not going to let that happen, he was going to do what he had to do, then he would disappear.

Henry would ask his mother to keep watch for him, let him know if anyone was about, if it was safe for him to make his move, let him know when Marcy was on her own. That would show his mother how good he was. Yes, that is what they would do. He and his mother would work together as a team from now on. His mother would be impressed by the way he worked, and she would tell him so.

Henry was hungry. He had eaten the last of the food he had brought with him, so necessity made him venture into Marchum. Showing himself in public was the last thing that Henry wanted but as luck would have it, there was a farmer's market on, and he was lost in the crowd. Spending the last of his money on provisions, he was now prepared to bide his time.

He had no money left but that did not concern Henry, he would just break into somebody's house and take what he wanted, he was now invisible.

Six days later Henry stood up and went outside and headed for the edge of the wood. It was still early, the dawn chorus was in full swing and he listened to the sweet song of the birds while he stood, leaning against one of the tall wide trees, watching The Retreat. Henry had stood and watched and waited next to the same tree every morning for the past six days.

He had seen Marcy on more than one occasion, but she had always been with somebody else. He wanted to get her on her own, he did not want any witnesses, he was going to do what he had to do, and then he was going to disappear. There would be no witnesses to what he had done, that was his intention.

His patience was rewarded at last when he saw Marcy, shopping basket in her hand, walk the length of the drive and head in the opposite direction to where he was standing.

Time to strike he decided, there was nobody around. The area was isolated but beautiful, heather was scattered all around on the rough undulating landscape.

Marcy was keeping to the barely visible footpath in the lush green grass. It was only kept trodden down by people walking into Marchum from The Retreat and back.

Henry was gaining on Marcy; his feet were moving swiftly in her direction gaining on her with every rapid stride. His footfall was silent as he moved ever closer to her across the damp grass.

Henry's heart was racing, the anticipation that was running through his body and mind made him throw all caution to the wind, he had his goal in sight, and nothing else mattered, nothing else existed in his world except Marcy and himself.

Henry had forgotten all his well thought out plans. His excitement was so great nothing else was in his head, only the chase. All he could think about was catching her and teaching her a lesson.

"Not long now Mother, not long now, Mother," he whispered to himself. His excitement growing at the thought of seeing the shock and surprise on Marcy's face at the first blow he would deliver.

Marcy had been an easy prey the first time he had hit her on the eve of their wedding day. That had been the first time he had ever hit a woman and he was surprised at the emotion that spread through him when he landed his first blow, at how much he had enjoyed hitting a woman.

The way things looked now, she was going to be an easy prey once more. Marcy was seconds away from her fate and she was oblivious to his chasing her down. His excitement was so great seeing her sauntering forward, swinging her basket without a care in the world. He could hardly breathe with the anticipation running through him.

He needed to see Marcy's face. He wanted to see the life go out of her eyes, just like he had seen the life go out of his mother's eyes when he heard her neck snap. There had been sheer anger and hatred in her eyes when she advanced on him, but when he had raised his head after the last cruel blow that had landed on his ear and his fist met her chin, Henry saw that all the anger and hatred had disappeared.

There were only seconds before his mother had hit the floor, but it had been long enough for Henry to see his mother look at him with no anger or hatred in her eyes and he had liked that. There had been no love either, but at least it was a start, the hatred had gone and with that he hoped love would develop, he was satisfied, at least for the time being.

Henry had forgotten he intended to take Marcy back to the shack. At that moment in time his need was to see the shock on her face on seeing him. He needed to see the life go out of her eyes as he landed that fatal blow. It would remind him of the revenge he had had on his mother. He had liked that.

Marcy felt a hand on her shoulder and she turned to see Lord Mooreway standing behind her. After the first initial shock, instinct took over and she swung her basket in the direction of his head.

Henry, not expecting this gave a roar of rage and his right hand had turned into a fist, aiming in the direction of Marcy's nose.

Marcy jumped back, but not quite quickly enough for she felt his fist graze her lip but not enough to knock her out. Everything that her aunt had taught her took over. Marcy lifted her knee and placed it between Henry's legs.

His rage was so intense that he barely felt it. His fist came up again and this time landed on the side of Marcy's right eye making her stumble back. The heel of her shoe catching on the hem of her dress and she tripped and fell backwards onto the damp grass.

Henry wasted no time in dropping to his knees, straddling her just like he had done to his mother and he brought up his right fist and took aim.

Marcy was unable to move, but she knew what was coming. Fight until the last, do not give in. That is what her aunt had told her. Do not let yourself be a victim, even if you lose the fight, if you do not give in, you will not be a victim.

So, grabbing the first thing she could with her free hand, Marcy found herself clutching the little finger of Henry's left hand. Before he brought his fist down into her face, she yanked his little finger backwards with a sharp jerk as far as she could bend it and there was a satisfactory crack of bone.

Henry, again taken by surprise and agony, gave a roar of pain and the fist that had been heading for Marcy's face came down to cradle his left hand. All thought of Marcy was gone from his mind, his finger hurt.

Marcy, sensing his pain and lack of concentration on her, pushed him off her with all the strength she could muster.

Henry being off balance fell over onto the grass leaving Marcy free to jump up and she tried to run but her long dress made her stumble when the hem got caught, once again, under her shoe. Instinctively, she grabbed at her skirt and yanked the hem free and she was running away as fast as she could.

She had not gone very far when she heard Henry chasing her down again, this time though he was not silent, his roars of rage brought terror to her face as she sped away.

Henry caught her by her waist, this time pressing her to him and she kicked his shins and punched his left hand, aiming for the little finger until he released her, but not before giving her back a solid punch with his right hand, sending her flying again.

Henry knew he could not go on fighting Marcy. He was in agony; he could no longer use his left hand. He knew he could not hope to overcome her now he only had one hand to fight her with.

She was fighting like a wild cat and it was something he had not expected to happen. None of the other women had fought back, and it muddled his brain. He was no longer in control of the situation. This was not right. His mother had not fought back.

He needed to have a word with his mother, she would tell him what to do, his mother would mend his broken finger, after all, that is what mothers do for their children, nurse them when they are hurt, and love them better.

He needed to get back to his lair, heal himself and wait for the next time. He would be ready for her next time, and there would be no escape.

So, Henry kicked Marcy in the ribs whilst she was trying to get to her feet and she went down again. Satisfied he had taught her a lesson for the time being he set off at a trot, back to the wood, back to the shack and back to try to find his mother. She would know what to do.

Marcy had difficulty in breathing, but she stumbled to her feet and set off for Marchum, shopping basket discarded. She had heard there was a doctor there that would help people in need, one that demanded no money, well she had no money to pay for a doctor and she needed one now. She set off to find him.

Marcy could feel herself getting weaker and weaker, it was sheer determination that kept her feet heading forward. She knew she did not have far to go. Marchum was only a mile away from The Retreat and she must have travelled at least half the distance before Henry had attacked her, so she kept on moving forward.

Her eye was beginning to close, the one he had hit with his fist, she could also feel her lip swelling and her ribs and back hurt when she breathed.

It had been Henry Mooreway. Marcy had recognised Henry Mooreway. Her aunt and the girls back at The Retreat might be in danger, she had to get to see this doctor, she had to get back and warn her aunt and the girls. They did not know what he was like, they had to be warned.

The edge of Marchum was in sight now. Marcy knew West Street was the beginning of it and she also knew that the doctor lived on Haywood Street which was located at the bottom of West Street.

By the time Marcy reached the edge of town, she was exhausted. She saw what looked like a porch covering the entrance to a door and she made for it. She found a wooden bench and she gratefully sat slowly down, her ribs hurting if she moved too suddenly. Marcy sat in the corner and rested her head on the side.

She tried to take a few deep breaths but only succeeded in managing a few short gasps. Marcy closed her eyes; she would rest for a few moments then be on her way. There was no time for self-pity, she had to get back to The Retreat and warn them. No time to waste searching out a doctor, she was needed at The Retreat.

Lord Mooreway sat down on the rickety chair that was placed at the table. He shouted for his mother. She did not come. He waited a while and called again, she was never there when he needed her. She had never been there when he needed her.

His mother had called him names, not very nice names, she had hit him, she had ignored him but one day she would tell him she loved him. One day he would do something right and she would tell him he was a clever boy, a good boy. One day she would take him in her arms and tell him she loved him. The last time she had looked at him there was no hatred in her eyes; at least he had succeeded in that, if nothing else.

These thoughts continually kept coming into his head. When would he get some peace? His mother would not leave him alone, he knows she never will. He had killed her, but he had not rid himself of her.

His rage began to get the better of him again. His mother was never there when he wanted her, when he needed her.

Henry took hold of his little finger that stood up awkwardly on his left hand and gave it a sudden yank. A wailing noise came from his mouth and his senses began to reel, he took deep long breaths until the nausea stilled itself.

He had prepared two splints. He placed one of the splints gingerly under his little finger and the other one gently on top. Then he proceeded to bandage his hand with strips of linen he had torn off one of the old sheets that had been left on the single put-me-up bed that had belonged to the last occupant.

After ten minutes sitting and brooding Henry decided he did not care anymore. He was going back to that Retreat. He was going to see if Marcy had returned. He had unfinished business with her, his hatred for her magnified by his failure once again, to master her.

153

His mother had seen this. That is why she had left him. That is why she would not mend his finger. His mother was disgusted with him and it was all that Marcy's fault. Everything was Marcy's fault, he hated her. She had to be stopped, there was nothing else for it, and he knew that.

Maybe if he put an end to Marcy it would put an end to his torment. Maybe his mother would leave him alone if there was no more Marcy to torment him with.

Henry went outside to the woodpile and picked up a piece of wood then he headed for The Retreat.

Ella had spent the day with Blanche but now she was on her way home. Mr Grundy had told her he would make tea for them both. Give her a break from doing all the cooking. She had raised no objections.

She walked along happily thinking about her wedding day. It would not be long before she would be Mrs Charlie Blurr, and she could not wait.

Ella stepped into the porch and was about to open the front door when she heard a low cough, looking around she saw a young woman sitting with her eyes closed in the exact spot Mr Grundy had found her in on the very first day she had arrived in Marchum.

The young woman was also sitting in the very same spot that Ella had found PC Keyser's daughter, Ruth, sitting, all those months ago.

By the state she was in, this young woman needed help too.

Ella made her way slowly to the sleeping woman and saw blood on her lip and the swelling on her eye.

She turned and ran into the house shouting, "Mr Grundy, Mr Grundy, where are you?"

The portly old gentleman appeared in the hall and enquired, "What's all the noise about Ella?"

"Quick Mr Grundy, I have found another young girl in need of our help."

"The devil you have Ella! Leave her where she is, let someone else find her and help her. You know what happens when you go finding bodies all over the place; we end up with no end of trouble. Come and have some tea, I have made us a nice dinner, sausage and mash with a great deal of beef gravy."

She stood and looked at Mr Grundy, she did not speak.

"Just leave her where she is Ella, someone else will come across her, let them take care of her, you know bodies in distress are nothing but trouble, our dinner is getting cold."

Ella stood and looked at Mr Grundy, she did not move, she did not speak.

"Damn it Ella, you are a very hard young woman keeping a man from his sausage and mash," but he started walking forward and Ella gave him one of her beautiful smiles.

"I knew you would come and help," and as he approached her she slid her hand through his arm and marched outside with him.

Mr Grundy looked at the sleeping young woman and saw the state of her face.

"Better go get Jackson. Give me a hand to get her inside first. It would be best if you went for Jackson, your legs are younger than mine, bring him straight back. Tell him he can have some sausage and mash but don't tell him it might be cold by the time he gets to eat it."

Ella looked at Mr Grundy with shinning eyes. She had come to adore him, and she stood on tiptoes and kissed his cheek.

"You are a very special person Mr Grundy, and I love you."

Mr Grundy said, "You do not have to bribe me with kisses young lady. I am going to help this young woman out of the goodness of my heart. Sometimes I wish I did not have a heart, and this is one of them."

When they did manage to wake the young woman up, it was obvious she was in much pain, they both took an arm each and led her gently into the house and laid her on the couch.

"I shall go and get Jackson," Ella said leaving Mr Grundy to fetch a blanket to cover the young woman with.

Ella ran all the way down West Street and along Haywood Street and into the end terrace house that had once been Mr Grundy's home. A place where she had travelled to and found the best set of friends anyone could possibly have. She had also found love there, and now it was Blanche and Jackson's house, she hoped they would find as much happiness there as she had.

"Is Jackson in?"

"He is cleaning up next door. Something must be amiss for you to return here so quickly. Whatever's the matter Ella?"

"I have found another young woman practically unconscious in our porch. It looks like she has been beaten up. Mr Grundy has sent me to get Jackson."

Blanche burst out laughing, "Rather you than me, good luck telling Jackson he's needed to attend another one of your porch finds." As the two friends' eyes met, both pair of eyes was brimming over with devilment.

"Thanks, I will need all the luck I can get."

Ella found Jackson sweeping the floor of his workshop.

"Hello Jackson, I have another patient for you."

"Don't want one, thanks."

"She needs you, Jackson."

"Well, that is because I am a devilishly attractive man, all women want me, but I do not want them. I love my Blanche, so push off."

"She has been beaten up by the looks of it."

"Not my problem, go and find her a doctor. I am not a doctor, I am a vet."

"She is very pretty. She will be very grateful."

"Don't let Blanche hear you talking like that. Blanche is having my baby you know."

"Yes, I know. What if you have a baby girl and someone beat her up. What would you do then?"

"You cannot blackmail me into coming with you. You are as bad as yon Charlie. He does not believe I am a vet either."

"Mr Grundy told me to tell you there is sausage and mash with lots of tasty beef gravy for you after you have seen to the young woman."

Jackson rubbed his chin, thought for a moment, decided sausage and mash sounded like a good option, picked up his bag and marched out of the door with Ella running after him.

When they entered Mr Grundy's house, Jackson could smell the sausage and mash and his mouth began to water.

He took one look at the young woman lying on the couch and said, "Yes, she has been beaten up alright."

"I will clean her face up but there is not much more I can do for her. We will have to wait until she regains consciousness to find out more," Jackson told them.

Ella went into the kitchen and piled three plates with sausage, mash and loads of tasty gravy. She put two of the plates on trays and taking them, one at a time, into the sitting room, Ella gave the two men a tray each and they both sat in a chair and ate their sausage and mash.

Ella ate her meal in the kitchen while she cut three slices of cake and put them in dishes. She then set about making some egg custard and pouring the custard over the cake she headed back into the sitting room and replaced the two gentleman's empty plates with the cake and custard.

"Well," said Jackson, "I must say it was worth this young woman getting a beating so I could come and have this little put-me-on until it is time for tea. I really enjoyed that Ella."

"Thank Mr Grundy, it was he who did the cooking of the sausage and mash not me."

They heard a moan and saw the young woman stirring. She opened her eyes and looked around her.

"Where am I?" she asked.

"You are quite safe my dear, do not distress yourself, you are amongst friends." Mr Grundy stood up and went and patted her hand.

"You must go to The Retreat. Please, it is most urgent for there is a monster on the loose. My aunt and the girls, they are all at risk, please you must go and warn them, tell them to lock all the doors and windows. There is a man called Lord Henry Mooreway, and he is not right in his head, he attacks women and I think he has followed me from Bossett.

"I think Henry is taking revenge on me for taking his entire guest list from his mother's ball, but they had stolen them from me in the first place. Please, you must go and warn them, you do not know what he is like." The young woman clung onto Mr Grundy's hand.

"Don't you worry your pretty little head over that now; Jackson will call at The Retreat and let them know." Mr Grundy assured her, not understanding a word she had said.

"The devil Jackson will. You go if you want to be a hero. I have had enough of that sort of thing," Jackson told Mr Grundy.

"Take no notice of him, it is his nature to fight against everything, but he is a good chap. He will go and warn them at your Retreat. You rest for a while and you will feel much more the thing in a few hours," Mr Grundy was still patting her hand.

"Why the hell should *I* go to this Retreat? If there is a monster knocking about, I do not want to meet it. I am having a baby and I would rather have a baby than meet a monster. Let someone else go." Jackson dug in his heels.

"If you won't go, then I will," Ella told him.

"And if you go and get beaten up, I will have two patients on my hands. I did not want this patient in the first place and I certainly don't want two. Some friend you are Clarence, volunteering me to go and seek out a monster. That is yon Charlie's job not mine," Jackson complained.

"Well Charlie is not here, is he? It is either you or Ella that has to go to The Retreat and warn them and if Charlie finds out you let Ella go when you knew there is a man out there beating women up, I would not like to be in your shoes. Anyway, you have got a full belly, if you find him and he does you in, at least you will have had a satisfying last meal," Mr Grundy reasoned.

Jackson thought this through and asked, "This Retreat of yours, is it that big stone building about a mile to the south of here?"

"Yes, that's the one. Thank you, I really appreciate it. Hurry, please hurry, they have to be warned," the young woman said.

After Jackson had left, the young woman said to Mr Grundy, "Would Jackson really have allowed this young woman to go on her own knowing there was a women beater hanging around?"

Ella laughed and replied, "No, of course he wouldn't. He is one of my best friends and he is to be my fiancé's best man when we get married in a couple of weeks' time. It is just the way he is, once you get to know him you will find him to be one of the most reliable and dependable people you could ever wish to meet. Jackson will sort things out at The Retreat, you can depend on it."

Lord Mooreway had stood in the grounds of The Retreat waiting and watching hoping to see if Marcy made an appearance. He had no way of knowing whether she had gone back to The Retreat or had run off somewhere else to hide from him.

Henry was beginning to get hungry, he had only had a crust for breakfast and now it was well after lunch. Assuming Marcy had gone back to The Retreat, he decided to go inside and see what he could find out. There must be a kitchen there he could raid.

He would fix Marcy first though, and then he would go and raid the kitchen, take some food back to his shack where he could eat it in peace. Instead of using his own food, he would use theirs.

Henry skirted round to the back of the house and looked in through a window. He had found the kitchen, and there was nobody in sight, the kitchen was empty.

The kitchen door was not locked, and Henry had no qualms in opening the door and walking in, he silently closed the door behind him. Now he knew where the kitchen was situated, it would be easy enough to raid it on his way out.

Walking on tiptoe across the kitchen floor he opened the door opposite the back door which revealed a long narrow corridor, this too was devoid of people, he continued along the corridor.

The house seemed to be deserted. Henry encountered nobody on the ground floor, so he made his way up the uncarpeted stairs. At the top he turned right along the carpeted landing and opened the first door he came to. He came face to face with a young woman wearing a tightly fitted dress, cut so low at the front that it barely covered her breasts. Her face was covered with makeup, red rosy cheeks and thick scarlet lips.

"Now, what have we here? Come in dearie, make yourself at home. These beds are very comfortable, just made for what you have in mind." A smile creased her makeup and there was a gap where one of her teeth should have been.

Lord Mooreway knew at a glance what she was. He had seen enough of them to recognise them from twenty yards away.

Doing as he was told, Henry stepped into the bedroom and closed the door. He tossed the piece of wood on top of the ottoman that was placed at the foot of the bed and his fist automatically became clenched, hard and solid, and the young woman fell backwards onto the soft mattress from the unexpected force that hit her nose and mouth. She lay motionless on top of the clean silk patchwork cover.

Lord Mooreway straddled her inert body and his fist was raised for a second time but the sound of footsteps running up the uncarpeted staircase made him hold off from delivering another blow. He turned his head towards the door but once the staircase had been mounted and the footsteps reached the carpeted landing, Henry had no way of knowing which way the intruder had taken.

Henry jumped silently off the bed, grabbed his piece of wood from the ottoman and shot behind the door just as the door was opened and a short scruffy looking little man appeared.

Jackson, seeing the woman lying at an odd angle on top of the bed with blood running down her nose advanced forward and asked the young woman, "Are you alright?"

That was the last thought that entered Jackson's head because he fell forward from a blow to the back of his head and landed on top of the body on the bed. Where the piece of wood had made contact with his skull, a bloody gash was visible. A stream of blood began to make its way down to the back of his collar.

Lord Mooreway looked at the stranger. He had never hit a man before, well he had bouts of boxing in the ring at The Foxes Club, but that was different. He did not get the same satisfaction from it. What was he going to do with him? What would his mother want him to do with him?

He would take him back to his shack and ask his mother. She might be there waiting for him. It wasn't far back to his shack, he could drag him there. Nobody was in the vicinity as far as he had been able to ascertain. The house was as quiet as a grave.

But then again, he had come across this whore and he had thought the house was empty. Then the scruffy looking little man had appeared.

He shrugged, not as deserted as he had thought. He decided he would do it any way. He would take him back to his shack and decide what was to be done once he had got the little man back there. If he encountered anybody on the way, he would just get rid of them. He was getting good at this.

Henry opened a couple of drawers and found one full of bed linen. He dragged out one of the bed sheets and proceeded to tear it into strips.

He was about to take hold of the shabby man's hands and bind them together when he heard a second set of footsteps running up the wooden staircase, then silence as the feet reached the carpeted landing.

Again, Henry had no way of knowing which way the feet would head so he grabbed his piece of wood and shot behind the door once more, and as before, the door opened and in walked another gentleman. This one was younger, taller and immaculately dressed and instantly recognised by Henry.

Freddie Atton, Henry knew Freddie had come up to Scotland for he had followed him and Marcy here, but he had forgotten all about him. Freddie Atton was no friend of his. He did not have any friends.

Freddie seeing the bodies lying on the bed and covered in blood, went over to them and said, "Who the hell has done this?"

The piece of wood came down on Freddie's head. "I did," a voice said.

Freddie's body fell on top of Jackson's. It was a good job the young woman at the bottom of the pile was unconscious and knew nothing about what was happening on top of her.

Henry calmly continued tearing strips off the bedsheet. Now there were two bodies he had to drag to the shack.

As Freddie was on top of the pile, Henry rolled Freddie off, so he was laid face up on the bed. Taking Freddie's hands Henry brought them above his head and tied them together at his wrists. Dragging Freddie off the bed he proceeded to drag him down the stairs by the strips of blanket that bound his wrists together, for he could not use his left hand, his finger hurt. He dragged him through the house and along the back lawn.

At the boundary wall he hauled Freddie up and laid him across the top of the wall. Pleased that the height of the wall was only shoulder high and he had achieved this with only the minimum of effort and the occasional stab of pain from his left hand if he tried to use it.

Henry pulled himself up and over the wall and jumped nimbly down to the other side and then he reached up and dragged Freddie over. He landed with a thud onto the ground, but Freddie was unaware of this, he was still out cold. Henry had no trouble dragging him through the wood and into the shack.

Taking some rope, he had found in the shack, Henry tied Freddie's feet together, then unfastening his hands Henry pulled them behind his back before making them secure again. He was taking no risks. If Freddie should come around before he got back to the shack with the scruffy little man, Henry had to be confident that Freddie would not be able to escape.

With Freddie's feet bound and his hands tied behind his back, he would not escape.

Henry knew he had to be quick in case the other man he had knocked out came around, so he set off at a trot. The afternoon was beginning to lose its light, evening was drawing in fast and he did not know what to expect when he reached The Retreat.

Finding no obstacles to hinder his progress, Henry ran up the staircase and into the bedroom. He found the scruffy little man still lying inert on top of the young woman who was also still unconscious. Henry glanced at the woman, the blood now drying across her top lip and her bottom lip had a gaping slit in it. This gave Henry a feeling of self-satisfaction.

Henry looked at the gash on the scruffy man's head. To his disappointment he felt no emotion at all, so he proceeded to tie the scruff's hands together with a strip of sheeting, then dragging Jackson down the staircase he made his escape from The Retreat across the back lawn, over the boundary wall and into the wood and finally the shack.

Henry sat on the rickety chair and got his breath back, it had been hard work dragging two bodies along the long damp grass and through the trees with one hand, but he had managed it with no interruption.

His left hand was throbbing. Dragging the two bodies from the house to his shack had not done it much good for on the odd occasion, it had been necessary to use his left hand. But at least the splints had protected his little finger to some extent.

Nobody had seen him. Nobody would know where to look for these two unfortunate men. He was quite safe, here in his shack.

After a while, Henry decided to place his two captives back to back before they became conscious and tie their hands and feet together, then neither could move. He had them safe, they could not escape. He was tired now and hungry, he had not managed to raid the kitchen like he had planned. He drank a mug of cold water and took one of the apples he had bought at the farmer's market over to the table and sat and munched on that.

Henry was tired, so he decided he would go to sleep and decide what to do with the two men in the morning. He would deal with the whore another day.

A moan came from Freddie disturbing Henry's peace, and Henry guessing that Freddie was beginning to come around marched across the shack floor and punched him in the face. No more moans came from Freddie.

Henry was just about to drift off into a peaceful dreamless sleep when more moans disturbed his slumber. This had to stop. So, Henry marched across the floor and this time he punched Jackson in the face, but the moans did not stop. Freddie again, so for good measure Henry silenced Freddie once more.

Henry went and lay down on his put-me-up and was soon fast asleep.

Sylvia Jenson, Marcy's aunt, was taking her time to hitch up the horse to the wagon in the stable at The Retreat. Marcy had been expected back at The Retreat around dinnertime, but she had failed to return.

Sylvia took two of the girls with her in the open wagon and they set off to Marchum in search of Marcy.

They had met nobody on their way into Marchum, but they did come across Marcy's discarded shopping basket lying on the grass and this set alarms bells ringing in Aunt Sylvia's head. After making enquires around the town they discovered that there had been no sighting of Marcy anywhere in the town. Marcy had vanished.

The light was fading when they set off back home and as Henry was dragging Jackson into the wood; their wagon was heading up the drive to their front door.

A search of the house revealed no Marcy and no Freddie, but they did find Lillian's body lying on the bed where Henry had left her.

Aunt Sylvia ran over to the bed and was relieved to find Lillian was still breathing.

Aunt Sylvia went out of the bedroom and down into the kitchen where she found a clean towel and filled a big bowl with water and then she headed back upstairs.

Very gently, Aunt Sylvia wiped the blood off Lillian's face and Lillian groaned back to consciousness. Seeing Aunt Sylvia, Lillian promptly burst into tears.

Aunt Sylvia stood no nonsense, "Lillian, what has happened to you? Have you seen anything of Marcy or Freddie? Has Marcy been back here?"

Lillian shook her head, "I came up here for a little nap and I was on my way back downstairs when my door opened, and this gorgeous man stood there. Well, you cannot let an opportunity like that go by, can you? So, of course, I asked him in and he hit me right on the nose and that is the last I remember."

"It looks like you got what you deserved then. I will not have you using my house as a brothel. You two go and lock the doors, make sure you put all the bolts on while Lillian and I make sure all the windows are shut and secured, then we will all meet back in my bed chamber.

"We will stay together for the rest of the night. There is nothing we can do until the morning it is too dark outside to see anything so therefore too dangerous to be abroad. We will just have to hope and pray that Marcy is safe. Come along now let us make this house as secure as we can."

It was just about to break dawn when Ella was roused from her sleep by a hammering on the door. She jumped out of bed and grabbing her dressing gown she donned it while making for the front door.

She was astonished to find Blanche standing on the doorstep, "Blanche, what on earth is amiss?"

"It's Jackson, he has not come home. I have not seen him since he went off with you. Is he here? No don't answer that, I know he is not here, he would never have left me on my own all night. I dare not come last night in the dark on my own.

"If I had not been so heavily pregnant, I would not have hesitated, but I did not want to put my baby in harm's way. Jackson has never stayed away and left me on my own before. Something bad must have happened to him, I know it has," she could say no more and started to sob.

"Why didn't you go next door to PC Keyser, ask him to see if he could find Jackson?" Ella asked.

"I did," Blanche sobbed, "But he was not in."

"Blanche, you must stay here with this young woman and Mr Grundy, on no account must you venture out, promise me Blanche," Ella held her friend by the shoulders.

Blanche nodded then sobbed, "Where are you going?"

"I am going to get dressed then I am going over to the livery stables and hire a horse. Then I am going to fetch Charlie. Something is going on here Blanche and I don't like it, we need Charlie."

Ella dressed in her father's old riding breeches, headed across the quiet town, keeping a watchful eye out for anything or anyone suspicious. It was just getting light and people were beginning to venture out of their houses and strangely enough, it made Ella feel safer with other people moving about.

At the livery stables Ella paid for the horse and set off at a steady trot until she reached the outskirts of the town, then she set the horse into a gallop and made good time reaching Charlie's estate, nearly two hours later.

She jumped down from the horse, tethered it to the rail at the side of the house and ran into the house heading for the breakfast room, knowing that at this time of day Charlie would still be at breakfast.

Ella found Charlie and his grandmother seated at the breakfast table and exclaimed, "Charlie, Jackson is missing!"

Charlie on seeing the love of his life appear in the doorway stood up and went across the room and taking her in his arms he proceeded to kiss her.

"Charlie, didn't you hear what I said? Jackson is missing," Ella looked up at him, returning his embrace.

"Jackson can take care of himself, on the other hand, have you put glue on your back?" he asked.

"Glue, what would I want to put glue on my back for?"

"Well there is something holding my arms there, they seem to be stuck. For some reason I cannot remove them from your back."

Ella looked up at Charlie's gentle amused face and she put her hand on his cheek and said, "I love you, Charlie Blurr."

"Those are the magic words I wanted to hear, look my hands are free. What is this about Jackson?"

"I found another body Charlie, a young woman sitting in our porch, she had been beaten up and Jackson went to warn the people that live in The Retreat to be careful, there was a mad man on the loose.

"Blanche came and knocked us up early this morning, just as it was getting light and she said Jackson had not been home all night. Jackson has not been seen since he left our house to go to The Retreat, so I have come to get you."

"You have found another body, have you? I bet that went down well with Jackson and Clarence," his eyes were dancing.

Ella matched his enjoyment and she said, "Mr Grundy told me to leave her where she was, to let someone else take care of her, his sausage and mash was getting cold. I had to bribe Jackson with some of the sausage and mash before he would come and have a look at the poor young woman."

Charlie's grandmother had been sitting watching and listening to the conversation between two young people joined together in an affectionate embrace and she was content to sit and watch.

This had been a long time coming. She thought Charlie would never find a young woman to take his fancy, but it had finally happened, and she had to admit she liked Ella, even if her dress sense was sadly lacking. Charlie loved her and that was all that mattered.

Charlie looked across at his grandmother.

"What are you waiting for? Go, find Jackson and make sure he is alive when you do, or don't bother coming back," his grandmother told him.

"I don't know what it is about Jackson, but he has all the women dallying after him, including my grandmother," Charlie told Ella.

"Jackson told me it was because he was a devilishly handsome man, that's why all the women want him," Ella's eyes danced up at Charlie.

"I should have known," he remarked.

Going over to the mantelpiece he pulled the bell and when the butler appeared Charlie instructed him to make sure Ella's horse was given some water, but not too much, and to have a horse saddled for him and brought around to the front of the house.

Looking at Ella from across the room he said, "Nice outfit."

Ella looked down at her legs, clad in in her father's old riding breeches and laughing she said, "My father's. You cannot ride fast if you are frightened your skirt will blow up, so I decided to wear these. I must say they are very comfortable to wear."

"I am going to get changed, meet me outside. We had better set off immediately and go and see what trouble Jackson has landed himself in now."

Charlie's eyes sparkled with devilment, he bent his head and kissed Ella firmly on the lips then off he went to get changed.

Ella watched him go out of the breakfast room door, across the hall and take the stairs two at a time. She had a tender smile on her lips as she watched him. She still could not believe how her world and changed since receiving the letter from Mr Grundy seven months ago, and Charlie was the centre of it.

Ella gave a big sigh of contentment and looked across the room to find Grandma Blurr watching her and Ella felt her cheeks go crimson.

Ella found it hard to look away and after a few seconds Grandma Blurr said softly, "You'll do. Come and grab yourself a slice of toast and eat it while you are waiting for Charlie to come down. Help yourself to a glass of milk before you go charging back to rescue Jackson. I bet you had nothing to eat before you came, did you?

Ella shook her head as she walked across the room to partake of a bite of breakfast.

"When you have eaten your toast, go and join that grandson of mine and find Jackson, but make sure you bring them both safely back."

Ella shot her a grateful smile and said, "I will, I promise."

She buttered herself a slice of toast and greedily guzzled down a glass of white creamy milk.

Chapter Fourteen

Freddie was the first to recover his senses. He could not see a thing at first, he thought he had gone blind, but gradually he became aware of darker shapes and he realised he was in a darkened room.

His head hurt, and he could not seem to move his arms or legs. After a while he could feel the rope restraints at his wrists, he was tied up. Not only was he tied up, but he was tied to someone else, back to back, he could not move, one way or the other.

He tried to nudge the person behind him. That did not work. The person he was tied to did not move. So, Freddie fearing the worst found a finger of his fellow captive and tried to twist it but Freddie could not get enough movement to achieve any significant pressure because the rope that bound them together was too tight.

Still holding the finger, Freddie gave it a quick hard nip. That had the required effect and he let the finger go.

A yelp came from behind him.

"Hello old chap, are you alright; we seem to be in a bit of a pickle. Do you know what is going on?"

Jackson tried to open his eyes without much success or, so he thought.

"I can't see," he mumbled.

"I thought the same, but I think we are in a dark room, I can just about make out dark shapes. Can you move?" Freddie asked.

"Leave me alone, let me go back to sleep."

"Go back to sleep, what are you talking about, we have to get out of this mess. Going back to sleep is not going to solve anything."

"No, but I could not feel my head when I was asleep. My body hurts, back and front, I would rather be asleep. Besides, I have just been bitten on my finger by a rat. I hate rats. If I am going to be eaten alive by rats, I would rather be asleep."

Although Freddie's face hurt too, he could not help finding the situation funny and he started to laugh. He tried his best to stem the flow of laughter for it used the muscles in his face and this did not help.

"You have not been bitten by a rat, it was me nipping you to try and find out if you were alright. I see you are."

"Well, you see wrong, I am not alright, I want to go home."

"So do I, going home is an excellent idea right at this very moment. But first we will have to get these ropes off somehow."

"Who are you? Is it your fault we are trussed up like dead chickens?"

"Certainly not, I have no idea why I am here or how I got here. My name is Frederick Atton."

"I have never heard of you."

"No, I don't suppose you have. I doubt if I have heard of you either, but we seem to be in the same mess for our sins."

"I don't have any sins, so it must be because of your sins. What have you done to deserve this?"

"As far as I know, I have not done anything. The last thing I remember was I was at The Retreat and could not find Lillian, so I went upstairs to see if she was in her room. Lillian was the only one left at The Retreat because the others had gone into Marchum to try and find Marcy."

"At the Retreat, were you? That is interesting."

"When I got to her bedroom, the door was slightly open and there was this man laid on top of Lillian. At first, I was shocked at what I saw because I thought he was up to no good. Then I saw his hair was matted with blood, so I rushed over to see what it was all about, and I felt a blow at the back of my head."

"Even more interesting," Jackson said.

"The next thing I knew, I was being pulled down the stairs and my body was rattling down each step and because my hands were tied above my head I could do nothing about it. I must have passed out again for I woke up here and found myself tied to you. What the devil is going on?"

"I have no idea. But it is interesting to hear you say you felt a blow to the back of your head. I had been sent to The Retreat to warn them there was a dangerous man on the loose. He had beaten up a young woman, and she wanted someone to go and warn them at The Retreat.

"When I got to The Retreat I found no one in either, so I too went upstairs to see if I could find anybody and saw a young woman lying on the bed with blood coming out of her nose. I went over to see if I could help and that is the last I remember, somebody hit me on the back of the head too."

"This young woman that was beaten up, I bet it is Marcy. She had vanished and her aunt and two other women that are staying at The Retreat now went to look for her. Lillian stayed behind to look after The Retreat in case any other unfortunate young woman came knocking on the door. They don't turn anybody away at The Retreat."

"My face feels as though it has been rattled down a set of stairs too. This woman you have lost has found her way into my life. Ella picked her up. She is like that Ella, finds all sorts of dodgy characters and involves Charlie and me. Look where it has landed me this time."

"What woman?" Freddie asked.

"How the devil do I know who she is? She said she had to get back to The Retreat and let them know there was a monster knocking about, and that they were in danger. If you have lost a woman and Ella found one, it must be the same woman. Mr Grundy said I had to come and tell them to make sure all the windows and doors were locked.

"I didn't want to come, fought against it, but he threatened me with Charlie, so I didn't have much choice. If I had known I was going to be rattled down a set of stairs, then I should have opted for Charlie's wrath."

Freddie started laughing again and he gasped, "Stop making me laugh, it hurts."

"Then do the same as me and go back to sleep. It doesn't hurt when you are asleep."

They heard a rasping noise as a flint was run across a stone and a candle was lit allowing a faint glow to provide light.

Freddie saw a pair of knee length boots approaching him across the floor; they came to a halt by his side. He saw the pair of knees bending and a face appeared just above his. The face that came into view seemed familiar.

"Hello Freddie. Comfortable, are you?" a voice asked.

"Henry! Henry Mooreway, I say old chap you are the last person I expected to see but thank God you are here. This gent and I seem to be in a bit of a situation, could you cut these ropes? We would be most grateful." Freddie's spirit's rose.

"You know what Freddie; I have a surprise for you. I have got to kill you. I cannot let you go now you have seen my face. No witnesses, that is the rule. But I don't think I am going to enjoy it very much. I did not get any pleasure from knocking you out. Not like I get when I hit the ladies, they like being hit do the ladies, some of them beg for more. I ask them to beg for more and when they do, I give them more, oh yes, they like it alright," explained Henry.

There was silence for a while, Henry letting this information sink in.

"I am waiting for my mother to appear you see. She is displeased with me again for letting Marcy get the better of me once more. I thought if I brought my mother two men, she would realise what a good boy I am.

"I am going to let my mother decide what she wants me to do with you both. My mother does not like men, so I thought it might please her if I let her decide what is to be done to you. She might even tell me what a good son I am. I cannot keep you alive though, even if my mother wants me to. You would tell tales on my mother and me. I cannot allow that, can I?"

"You did this to us, what the devil for Henry? Why are you here in Scotland?" Freddie asked.

When there was silence Freddie continued, "How long have you been here?"

"Not long, I followed you and Marcy here, so I have been here as long as you have. I have seen you many times, but you did not see me, for I am invisible.

"I found your conversation with this little man very illuminating. So, Marcy has been telling tales on me, has she? Your scruffy little bedfellow here says she has been telling everyone that I am in Scotland and to keep their doors locked against me.

"You cannot deny it for I heard it all. Marcy will have to go, I thought I had her yesterday, but she foiled me a second time. There is not going to be a third time. Would you like me to bury you both together, you and Marcy, in the same grave? It would save me having to dig two graves; in fact, if I dump all three of you in one grave, it will save me having to dig three graves." Henry felt pleased with himself for thinking of this.

"What is going on Henry, why are you doing this?" Freddie repeated the question.

"I killed my mother and it is all Marcy's fault, I knew she was travelling to Scotland the morning after her party, so I followed her. I had to get away because if I had stayed in Bossett, the constabulary would have come for me. As things stand now they have no idea where I am. They will never think of looking for me in Scotland.

"That is why I have to kill you both. You can see that can't you? I cannot let you live or you will tell the constabulary where I am, and they would put me in jail with all the other criminals. My mother wouldn't like that. I saw Isaac and his new bride travelling with you. I must say it was a stroke of good luck for me, when they turned back," Henry told him.

"You killed your mother?" asked a shocked Freddie.

"I had to; I had to get some peace. You do see that, don't you? My mother went on and on and on about Marcy. She gave me no peace, even when I was out and about, my mother was in my head, she would not leave me alone.

"Now my mother is dead, but she is still here, in my mind, telling me what to do, no peace, no peace. If I kill Marcy then there will be no mother and no Marcy to obsess my mind, to torment me like they do, I need some peace. When am I to get some peace?" Henry wanted to know.

Jackson had seen these symptoms many times before, soldiers living in a world of their own, refusing to come to terms with the horror of the battlefield. By the sound of it, this young man's mother is his battlefield.

"You are very lucky to be on such good terms with your mother," Jackson told him. "Me, I hated my mother, she beat me, left me without food, called me names and showed me up in front of her friends.

"I could never do anything right for her, I came to hate her and now I hate all women, especially the whores. They try to manipulate you, try to tell you how good you are in bed and all the time you know they are lying, you know they are only after your money. They deserve all you hand out to them.

"I wish I had the nerve to do what you are doing, you are very brave, and I admire you," Jackson told Henry.

Freddie was shocked at this turn of events, the last thing he had expected to hear was these remarks from this other man to whom he was tied. His spirits sank even further, he was doomed.

Silence reigned once more in the shack, no one spoke until finally Henry went around to face Jackson and he said, "I think my mother will like you. I think I will give you to my mother, she can take it out on you instead of me."

"I have a better idea. Why don't you and I go into partnership? You could teach me how to knock a whore around without killing her. We could work as a team, lure women back here to the shack and give them what for.

"If we work as a team, it will be easier to get away with it, give your mother something to watch. She will enjoy that won't she?"

171

Jackson's heart was beating against his ribs, making his blood flow faster which was not doing much to help his head. The rush of adrenalin was making his head hurt, he wished it would stop pounding.

Jackson knew Henry was unstable. He had to try and make friends with him, let him know he was not the only person in the world that had been ill-treated by their mother. Not that Jackson had been ill-treated by his mother. He'd had a very happy childhood.

Henry went to sit on his rickety chair at the table, to have a think about this for a while. It sounded exciting. Two of them working together, nobody would ever be able to pin them down, not if there were two of them.

But where was his mother? She had not appeared yet. She must still be angry with him. He had been a bad boy, he had let Marcy escape and his mother was displeased with him.

Why was she not here now, in his hour of need? Why would she not tell him what to do? What if his mother did not like these two men? After all, she did not like his father and she did not like him. There he had said it. His mother did not like him, he knew that, he had always known it, but it did not alter things. He loved his mother.

If his mother did not like him, whose fault was that? Hers! She was the one that had brought him up. She was the one that had made him what he was today.

Henry was going to have to think about this, he felt no resentment against these two men and it was making it hard for him to deal with them. One of them wanted to be his partner. He had never had a partner before. He had never had anyone that he could call his friend. His mother did not like him having friends.

His mother was dead now; he knew that for he had killed her, but she was still here, still in his head, he could not rid himself of her. When was she going to go, let him have some peace? He did not know. What if his mother liked his new partner more than she liked him? He had some thinking to do. He had to think.

Charlie and Ella had ridden hard and fast back to Marchum. They called first at the livery stable and returned Ella's horse. Ella mounted behind Charlie held him around the waist as they cantered on to Haywood Street where Charlie took his horse into the new paddock Jackson had created, and after checking there was some water for the horse, he shut the paddock gate and left his horse to graze.

Taking Ella's hand, they walked rapidly to West Street to see the young woman Mr Grundy was keeping an eye on.

When they arrived at Mr Grundy's, Blanche rushed across to Charlie and threw herself on his chest and cried, "Charlie, Jackson is missing."

"I know Blanche, try not to worry. I am going to set off and find him, I need to have a few words with this young woman first." Charlie looked across at Ella who came and took Blanche by the arm and led her to a chair.

Marcy told Charlie all she could, and Charlie set off for The Retreat.

On arrival at The Retreat, Aunt Sylvia let Charlie in and he informed her who he was and where she could find Marcy. Charlie then went on to ask about Jackson, but Aunt Sylvia could tell him nothing for she was more in the dark than he was. She had never heard of anybody called Jackson.

When questioned neither could Lillian, she told Charlie she had not known who the young man was who had attacked her; she had never seen him before. Nor could she tell Charlie where the young man had gone after the attack because he had knocked her out.

A description of her attacker was all Lillian could provide. She knew nothing of any Jackson, for she had never seen him at all.

What Charlie did find out was that someone else had gone missing. Someone called Freddie Atton had not been seen since yesterday afternoon. Things were not looking too good.

Charlie began to panic, he had no leads, and he had nothing to go on. Something must have happened to Jackson he would never have gone missing without leaving some sort of clue for him to follow had it been possible, but there was nothing.

Looking at Aunt Sylvia he asked, "May I look at Lillian's bedroom?"

"If it is going to help you in your enquiries, you have my permission to look anywhere you like. I shall leave these two young women here with Lillian to keep her company while I go and fetch Marcy home. You do not require me for anything else, do you?"

"No, there is nothing you can help me with, thank you," Charlie said.

Up in Lillian's bedroom Charlie made a thorough search but came up against a blank wall, he found nothing to help him. All he found was the remains of a shredded bed sheet. He walked over to the window and looked out. The bedroom was at the back of the house facing towards a wood, there was no movement of any kind to be seen. No clues for him to follow, he began to panic again.

If anything had happened to Jackson, Charlie did not know how he was going to tell Blanche, Clarence and even Ella. They were all a close little group whom he classed as his family and Jackson was the main pivot, Charlie loved them all dearly. *Please God, don't let anything have happened to Jackson,* Charlie made a silent prayer.

Charlie was about to turn away from the window when a darker shade of green caught his eye. It looked like something had been dragged into the wood. It could easily have been a badger or rabbit run, but then again it could easily have been Jackson. There was only one way that Jackson would have gone quietly, and that is if he was being dragged.

Charlie decided it was worth a try. He had nothing else to go on, and he had to do something, he could not just sit and wait for something to turn up.

On closer inspection of the run Charlie's spirits rose. It looked like something had been dragged into the wood; he could just make out the odd footprint indented into the damp grass. The sun was drying the dew and the grass was starting to spring back up, but he could see the impressions of footprints.

Charlie was lost again in his detective reasoning. Things for Jackson were beginning to look up, *Hold on old boy, I am on my way,* Charlie thought, and he vanished into the wood.

Aunt Sylvia knocked on the door in West Street and Ella ran to open it.

"Hello," Aunt Sylvia said, "I believe you have my niece here, I have come to take her home."

"Please come in, she is in the sitting room. I am afraid she has had an accident and her face is a bit of a mess, but it looks far worse than it is. She has been talking about going back to The Retreat, but Mr Grundy said it would be better if she stayed here until we find out what is going on," Ella told her.

"Aunt Sylvia, thank God you are safe." Marcy held out her hands in the elderly lady's direction.

Aunt Sylvia taking one look at her niece's face advanced forward and took Marcy's hands in hers, "What did his face look like?"

Marcy smiled, "Don't make me smile Aunt Sylvia, it hurts. Your training came in handy for I fought him off and broke his little finger. He let me go and I staggered here."

"Who is he, why is he doing this?" her aunt wanted to know.

"The man that did this is the same man who I was going to marry. The one that attacked me on the eve before our wedding day. He is the reason why I am here, but I will explain everything later. I want to go home. Is everything alright at The Retreat, are you alright, and are all the girls alright?" Marcy wanted to know.

"Slow down child, yes, everything is alright. Lillian had an encounter with your monster, but she is alright. These poor girls are used to being smacked around, just another day on the job for her. I hate to tell you my dear, but Freddie is missing as well. There is also someone called Jackson missing. Someone called Charlie is trying to find them. I am sure he will. He seemed to be a competent sort of person."

"Freddie is missing. How has it come about that Freddie is missing too?"

"We have no idea. There seems to be no way of finding out either. No one has seen or heard anything. I left this Charlie person searching Lillian's bedroom, let us all hope he finds something.

"I think we should be going back to The Retreat if you are feeling up to it. I left the three young women we have stopping with us there. I don't want to leave them on their own for very long. Although I did tell them to keep together, all stay in one room until we get back, so they should be alright."

"Yes, of course I am feeling up to it. I want to get back to The Retreat myself I have taken up too much of these good people's time as it is. If I come across Henry a second time he had better think twice before he attacks me. I am just a bit sore and bruised but apart from that, and the sight I must look, I am perfectly alright," Marcy confirmed.

"May I come with you?" asked Blanche.

"Do you think that is wise in your condition my dear?" Aunt Sylvia wanted to know.

"Jackson is my husband, I want to know where he is and what has happened to him," Blanche told her, tears brimming in her eyes.

"In that case, of course you must come with us," Aunt Sylvia relented.

"If Blanche is coming with you then so am I, Jackson is my friend and I got him into this. If anything has happened to him, I shall never forgive myself. I want to go too, and to be with Blanche," Ella insisted.

"While you are all getting into the wagon, I will just run upstairs and change into something more appropriate." Ella went to change out of her father's riding breeches.

"Then let all who are coming back to The Retreat pile into the wagon, so we can be on our way." Aunt Sylvia helped Marcy stand.

Ella, running back down stairs tucked her hand through Blanches arm and they followed the little group out to the waiting wagon.

Mr Grundy insisted on accompanying the ladies and he too took his seat in the wagon with Aunt Sylvia at the reins.

After asking directions in Marchum, Lord and Lady Singleton's coach made its way up West Street passing a horse and wagon that was tethered to a rail of the end house. Not giving the wagon a second glance their coach carried on, out of town along the dirt road heading into the countryside.

Lord Singleton sat on top with the coach driver at the reins and he held a shotgun across his knees, keeping a lookout for any highwaymen that might jump out at them along the way. None had, and their journey had been uneventful but nevertheless, Lord Singleton was happy the end was in sight.

Charlotte and Miss Tubby both had their heads out of a window, one on either side of the coach.

"I bet I will be the first to see it," Miss Tubby was full of excitement. Although she was nearer sixty years old than she was fifty, Miss Tubby had lived all her life in Bossett and this had been an experience of a life time for her and secretly she would not have missed it for the world.

Charlotte glanced across the coach at her and smiled. Charlotte knew how hard the death of The Dowager Lady Singleton had hit Miss Tubby and she was pleased to see the old lady enjoying herself.

"I bet you don't," Charlotte replied getting into the swing of things.

It wasn't long before Charlotte spotted the old rambling house, but her eyesight was better than Miss Tubby's, and Charlotte could not bring herself to spoil the old ladies pleasure, so she kept it to herself.

A few seconds later as the coach rumbled its way towards The Retreat, Miss Tubby shouted, "There I see it, there up front. Can't you see it Miss Charlotte?"

Lord Singleton had admonished Miss Tubby about calling his wife Miss Charlotte, but it had fallen on deaf ears.

Charlotte stretched her neck out of the coach window to get a glance at the building and pretending it was the first time she had seen it she exclaimed, "Yes, I believe you are right Miss Tubby. That must be The Retreat for there is no other building to be seen."

Miss Tubby clapped her hands with glee. "I win, I saw The Retreat first."

Charlotte smiled kindly. "Yes, you did Miss Tubby, well done."

The huge wooden gates stood open and the coach proceeded up the long straight drive, coming to a halt in front of the pillared entrance.

Lord Singleton stepped down from the coach and held the door open for his wife to alight and then Miss Tubby.

Going over to the front door Lord Singleton pulled on the bell. They heard it jingle faintly somewhere inside the house, but nobody came to answer it. He tried again, but still nobody came to let them in.

Having come all this way Lord Singleton was not about to be put off, he tried the door and to his surprise it opened. He went in and Charlotte and Miss Tubby followed but, once inside they were greeted by silence.

"Hello," shouted Isaac. "Is there anyone about?"

Again, there was silence.

"You two wait here, I will go and have a look around. Someone might be in the back and had not heard us arrive." He strode across the hall to the back of the house. He found no one.

Charlotte and Miss Tubby, still standing close together in the hall, watched Isaac return to the hall and head up the stairs.

What happened next made Charlotte and Miss Tubby freeze on the spot.

Hysterical screams came from somewhere above stairs. Isaac did not reappear.

Henry let the silence linger while he thought about having this strange little man as a partner. What if his mother liked his new partner more than she did him, her son? Dare he risk it? No, he decided he could not, he wanted his mother all to himself. They would both have to go.

The silence in the shack was broken by the screech of on owl, not once but twice, and the noise of the screech made Jackson close his eyes.

Charlie, he thought, *why the hell do you have to be so loud, it hurts my head?*

"What was that?" Henry stood up and looked nervously around.

"It sounded like an owl hooting to me. You can tell you are a city boy if you can't tell that was the hoot of an owl. You can't mistake the hoot of an owl, any self-respecting country born man would be able to tell you that," Jackson told him.

"I know about owls, they only come out at night and that was no owl," Henry said.

"They make mating noises once they have gone to roost. Didn't they teach you that in your posh city school?" Jackson was trying to bluff his way along.

"No, they did not. I don't believe you." Henry was still looking nervously around.

"Please yourself," replied Jackson, "if you prefer to believe it is your mother or one of the women that you have knocked around after your blood, carry on. My head hurts. Did you have to rattle it down those steps?"

"It was easier for me to drag you with your hands bound together above your head, it could not be helped, my hand hurt." Henry defended himself. "You don't really think it is my mother, do you?"

"No, I think it is an owl. Listen this is what an owl sounds like," and Jackson hooted twice, cringing in pain when he puckered up his lips.

Charlie's spirits rose, Jackson was alive. "Thank you, God," he whispered and began to make his way towards the shack. He had been all around the outside and there was only one door, so he had no option but to creep towards it.

Charlie listened at the door until he heard Jackson say, "Where exactly is your mother? You are sitting in the middle of the shack with your back to the door. Is she behind you?"

Charlie took the hint, whoever was in that room at that moment in time had his back to the door and Jackson had the man's attention.

Charlie took hold of the latch and slowly lifted it up. Inching the door slightly open he could see the shape of a man's back sitting at a table so he thrust the door wide open and flung himself on the unsuspecting back and the two men fell to the floor.

Henry was winded, and Charlie banged his shoulder hard on the floor as they landed but Henry was not about to give in. His rage instantly rose not only against his attacker but against the man who had pretended to be his friend.

All Henry could think of was to get free from the strong pair of arms that held him down. He tried to push his arms out to slacken the hold that held him fast, but that did not work, the hold did not slacken.

Charlie tried to think of his next move, if he slackened his hold, his captive could make a run for it, so he said, "I would appreciate a hand here Jackson."

"You and me both, I am trussed up like a dead chicken, one of my arms and a leg has gone numb and my head hurts and you need a hand, typical, self-first every time," Jackson said.

Freddie, who had been left speechless, finally came to his senses.

"Hit his left hand, I saw he had a dirty bandage on it and he was tending not to use it."

Charlie did not recognise the voice, but he took his advice. He made a grab for his captive's left hand and all fight went out of his opponent.

The culprit gave a roar of agony and started to cry.

Charlie took out the handcuffs he had brought with him and cuffed Henry's, hands behind his back.

"Tie his legs as well, Charlie," Jackson said, "he is not fully stable, mentally that is, and as such he is dangerous, and he could run off. But be careful with him, he is a sick young man, he is going to need a lot of help."

Charlie did as his friend bid. Once Henry was tied to the table he went over and opened the shutters on both windows on either side of the shack to provide more light for them to see by.

This action failed in providing more light for it was dark in the wood, but at least they could see a little better than before.

Taking long strides, Charlie knelt beside Jackson and began undoing the ropes. Once Jackson was free he bent over the second young man and proceeded to release him too.

Jackson rubbing his sore wrists and trying to stand up said, "You took your time in getting here."

"You forget, I am not a policeman anymore," Charlie countered.

"Yes, you are not a policeman any more, just like I am not a doctor but who the hell listens."

"You have a policeman living next door to you, why didn't you go to him for help?" Charlie wanted to know.

"Yon PC Keyser is no policeman. All he does is walk around making notes in that damned occurrence book."

Looking over at his friend he said, "I hate to admit it Jackson, but I have missed working with you."

179

Jackson looked back at him, "Sod off."

This afforded Charlie much pleasure and undoing the last knot of the shocked young man that had been tied to his friend he grinned at him, "It's alright, he is from Mars."

Charlie held out his hand to the speechless young man, "Charlie Blurr."

The young man held out his hand and they shook hands, "Freddie Atton."

"Well Freddie Atton, shall we go back to The Retreat and let them all know you are safe? They have been worried about you." Charlie told the young man.

"Good idea, but can I have a moment to let the circulation get flowing again, like your friend over there, we have been laid on our side all night and there isn't much feeling in my arm and leg."

"Do either of you have any ideas about what this is all about?" Charlie asked no one in particular.

"I haven't a clue," Jackson replied, "But I know I have a bad headache."

"Your captive's name is Lord Henry Mooreway, he comes from a town called Bossett which is roughly three days' drive south of here. Henry told us he has killed his mother and he followed Marcy here. He blames her for all his downfalls and he is out to make her pay.

"I don't know how true all this is so don't take my word for it. I am only telling you what he told us, but I do know he intended to kill your friend and me and put us in the same grave as Marcy. He must have gone off his head because he was never like this when I knew him back in Bossett," Freddie informed them.

"So, you knew him from Bossett, did you?" asked Charlie.

"Although he is not what you would call a friend, he is a member of The Foxes Club in Bossett that Isaac and I frequent. I have travelled up here with Marcy who runs The Retreat with her aunt. It looks like Henry followed us all up here and he is out to get her."

"Oh yes, I have met her, and her aunt," Charlie told him.

"Are they all alright at The Retreat? Are Marcy and her aunt safe?" asked Freddie.

"Yes, they are all fine, but Marcy's face looks a bit like yours and Jackson's, she has suffered cuts and bruises, but she is alright."

"Thank goodness for that at least. I had been fixing the door of the stable block for Aunt Sylvia and when I had finished I went into the house to see if Marcy had returned from Marchum. But the house was empty, so I ran up the stairs to see if I could find anyone in.

"I went past Lillian's bedroom and the door was slightly open. I found your friend here, lying on top of her, so I went to drag him off because I thought he was up to no good. Then someone hit me over the head and I went out like a light."

"You thought I was up to no good, did you? Let me tell you I am pregnant, and I do not go around getting up to no good with other women, even if I am a devilishly handsome fellow," said an irate Jackson.

"How was I to know? How can you be pregnant?"

"My Blanche is having my baby," he told Freddie.

"Never mind that, carry on with your story," Charlie told him.

"When I became aware of my surroundings, I was being dragged down the stairs, I was being bounced against every step on the way down, and I passed out again. I didn't regain consciousness until I found myself tied to your friend, Jackson.

"The feeling has returned to my leg and arm now so if you don't mind me saying so, I think we should set off back to The Retreat, there could be carnage there."

"Could be carnage, have you seen your face? If my face looks like yours then I don't want to see it. I cannot stand the sight of blood," Jackson moaned.

Freddie looked at the comical, middle-aged man with unruly hair matted in blood and remembered his conversation with Henry. It had disturbed him at the time and it disturbed him now.

"What do you know about this man?" Freddie asked Charlie.

"Which man?" Charlie wanted to know.

"This man you call your friend, the one I was tied to," Freddie replied.

"He was kicked off Mars and landed on his head on a rubbish dump in Marchum," Charlie replied.

Freddie digested this and asked, "Where is Mars?"

Charlie pointed skywards.

"You mean the planet Mars?" asked a shocked Freddie.

"The very same," confirmed Charlie.

Freddie could think of nothing to reply to this, he thought he had come to live in a lunatic asylum, so he continued, "I think you should take him in for questioning as well. He has got some very funny ideas. He wanted to go into partnership with Henry, join up as a team and prey on unsuspecting women. It is not normal."

Charlie looked over at Jackson, and their eyes met, well one of Jackson's eyes met Charlie's, his other eye was swollen and closed but Charlie didn't miss the mischievous glint in the one good eye that met his.

"No one, even Jackson, has ever said he was normal."

"My Blanche does," objected Jackson.

"With the exception of Blanche, oh, and his father-in-law, he has a fondness for him too."

"Sod off Charlie," Jackson told him.

Charlie laughed. "Everything will be alright at The Retreat. All was well when I left them this morning so if Henry has been here, then nothing untoward will have gone off at The Retreat. But let's get this poor Lord Henry what's-his-name untied and make our way back there and let them all know you are both alright."

On arrival at The Retreat they found not only the wagon belonging to The Retreat, but a large, well sprung coach tethered up alongside it.

"This is Isaac's coach. They must have arrived sometime this morning. They are friends of mine from Bossett."

Charlie indicated to Henry to get into the wagon and he complied with the order. For the moment there was no more fight left in Henry and Charlie jumped up beside him, taking up the reins he said to Jackson, "Tell Aunt Sylvia I am borrowing the wagon and I will be back to pick you all up once Henry has been delivered to the police station. I will not be long; I do not want to distress Marcy and Lillian any more than is necessary, best not to let them see their attacker again." Charlie headed back down the drive.

Isaac tapped on the first bedroom door he came to and when he got no reply, he gingerly opened the door.

Once the door was opened, three women standing at the bottom of the bed all huddled together began to scream like banshees. Then one of them dashed forward and punched him in the stomach sending him staggering back onto the landing.

As if some sign had been sent to the other two women, they both threw themselves screaming at Isaac too.

Finding himself in a restricted place on the landing and three screaming women punching him, Isaac found it difficult to disengage himself from them. He had never hit a woman in his life and he did not intend to do so now. He began by trying to grab hold of one of them, but the others had other ideas, Isaac was losing the battle.

Charlotte and Miss Tubby had frozen on the spot at the sound of the screams from above. They were then scared witless by the door behind them opening. They turned to see, to their relief, Marcy standing next to an elderly lady with white hair, a lovely young girl standing next to a heavily pregnant woman and a portly, jolly faced man of indefinable years.

"Marcy, whatever has happened to your face?" asked a shocked Charlotte.

"What is going on up there?" Marcy wanted to know ignoring Charlotte's question.

"We don't know, Isaac went upstairs to see if anybody was around and all hell broke loose as you can hear," they were informed.

"Oh dear," the lady with white hair said.

To Charlotte's surprise, the old lady moved at great speed up the wooden staircase and disappeared round the same corner that Isaac had disappeared round.

Almost instantly the screaming stopped, and Isaac appeared at the top of the stairs being supported by two very well endowed young women, one on either side of him. He did not look in the best of health.

Footsteps were heard behind the little group of people standing in the hallway and they turned to see two very dishevelled and battered gentlemen walking towards them.

"Jackson, oh my Jackson, what have you been up to now?" Blanche strode across to him and pulled him into a firm embrace and he gratefully rested his aching head on her bosom. It was the nicest, softest pillow he could have wished for. Her bulging belly was pushed into his and Jackson feeling the bulge of his baby pressing into him, the comforting arms of his wife around him and the best pillow in the world for his head to rest on, was in heaven.

Freddie saw Marcy and the state of her face. He rushed over to her and took her hands in his, "Did Henry do this to you?"

"He did, but this time I fought back, and I broke his little finger and he could not keep hold of me, so I managed to get away, again," Marcy told him.

"He also had a gash at the side of his face. Did you do that as well?" Freddie wanted to know.

"Yes, I walloped him with my basket. I was frightened Freddie. He was the last person I expected to see up here in Scotland," Marcy clung onto his hands.

"You have no need to be frightened of him any more Marcy. Henry has murdered his mother, and someone called Charlie has carted him off to jail. I don't think you will ever see Henry again," Freddie informed her.

"Did Henry do that to your face as well?" Marcy asked looking up at Freddie's cut lip and bright red eye.

"He did, so now I know how you feel. When the people back in Bossett learn of this I think you will find all the gossiping will stop about you leaving Henry waiting at the church, their loyalties will have changed sides," he told her.

Isaac, at the top of the stairs was feeling like a punch bag but when he saw the state of his friends face he said, "It would seem your party was hell of a lot better than mine, Freddie."

Freddie tried to smile but found it too painful, "Welcome to Bedlam Isaac old boy, nice to see you."

Jackson, still with his eyes closed and wrapped in this wife's arms said, "Clarence, the first thing you have to do when you get back home is knock that blasted porch down."

The old gentleman demanded, "What? Why should I knock my porch down?"

"Then no more stray dogs can make their way in there for Ella to find. I am getting too old for all this," was the reply.

"I think it would be best if we all went into the sitting room and sat down. I shall go and make some tea for us all then we can get this chaos sorted out," Aunt Sylvia said then added, "and I think these two gentlemen, sorry three gentlemen could do with their wounds attending to."

"I'm alright, thanks," Jackson told her.

Aunt Sylvia could not help laughing and the tension disappeared.

Charlotte waited at the bottom of the stairs for Isaac to descend and took charge of him. He was pleased to be out of the care of two of the women that had rendered him helpless and to feel the arms of his bride around him.

The same two women offered to make the tea and went off to the kitchen and the rest followed Aunt Sylvia across the hall and into the sitting room.

Miss Tubby was happily tending to the wounded and fussing about from one to the other and Charlotte was informing them all of Henry's crime back in Bossett.

Isaac had apologies from the three women who explained to him that Aunt Sylvia had told them all to stay together in one of the bedrooms in case Lillian's attacker returned and if he did, to strike first and ask questions later. So, when they saw this strange man standing in their bedroom doorway that is what they did.

Ella came forward and said, "Well, this has been an interesting experience."

Jackson opened his one eye and looked across at her. "Yes, a very interesting experience. We never had these experiences before you landed on our doorstep, just look what the experience has done to my face."

Clarence piped up, "It could have been worse Jackson, and you could have ended up like Henry's mother, dead. Anyway, I think it has improved your face, it has given it more character."

"Go to the devil Clarence. It is your damned porch that sets Ella off, and it is not your face that has been rattled down a staircase." Jackson's head was still resting on his best pillow in the world while he sat beside his wife on the old tatty sofa. His eyes were closed. All the same he was happy to know his friends were around him keeping him safe.

"Why don't we introduce ourselves? We do not know any of you and we are greatly in your debt. Marcy, you seem to know everyone. Why don't you do the honours?" her aunt said.

After the introductions were over Isaac informed them, "Charlotte and I were going to carry on and see some of the beautiful sights that Scotland has to offer after we had dropped Miss Tubby off, and then join Freddie for the journey home. But considering the circumstances, I think we will head home and come back when I feel more the thing."

Marcy glanced over at Freddie, and her heart sank. She had tried her best to think of him as just a friend, but she had failed miserably. She had got used to having him around, he had grown on her. She did not want him to leave.

Freddie looked over at Marcy and found her looking at him and his decision was made, "I am going to sell my house in Bossett and come and live here if that is alright with you, Aunt Sylvia. There is still a lot that needs to be done here, both inside and outside of the house, besides, after this, life would seem very dull back in Bossett. Nothing like this has ever happened to me before."

"You may stay here with pleasure young man, I have got used to you being around," Aunt Sylvia replied.

"Well, I for one can do without this sort of thing, I don't mind dull. It does not make your ribs and face hurt," Isaac responded.

"You don't know the half of it Isaac. You came off lightly, you only had three women on top of you, me, I was tied up to a deranged Martian," Freddie told him.

"Did your deranged Martian scream?" Isaac wanted to know.

"Not that I was aware of."

"Then give me a deranged Martian anytime. Have you ever innocently opened a door and had three screaming women chasing you? It was terrifying. There ought to be a law against it."

Freddie tried to stop himself from laughing but he did not quite succeed, "And you a newly married man as well," he joked.

"It has its compensations," Jackson said still content in the arms of his loved one.

"If I get my hands on whoever did this to my Jackson, he will be walking around minus his unmentionables," said Blanche with feeling.

"That's my girl," said a proud Jackson.

Charlie pulled up outside the police station and took Henry inside. "Hello sergeant, look what I have brought you."

"Well met Charlie, we have missed you. Who have we here?"

"He goes by the name of Lord Henry Mooreway, so I am told. He is from Bossett, we don't know for sure why he is in Marchum but Marchum is bearing the signs that he has been our way," Charlie told him.

"Still solving crimes, are you?" the sergeant asked.

"Jackson says your guest is mentally unstable and he needs a doctor. You had better get him one but keep an eye on him because if he is mentally unstable it can make him very dangerous. He has not uttered a word since I arrested him, not that I have arrested him, for I am no longer a police officer, nor has he made a move to escape.

"As soon as I overpowered him he retreated into himself. He is a very violent man sergeant, so let your men know to be very wary of him, you never know when he might go into one of his rages and lash out."

"What crime has he committed on our patch?"

"Assault, abuse, kidnapping, breaking and entering, threatening murder, take your pick." Knowing how much paperwork this was going to generate Charlie was glad he was no longer a policeman.

"How long has he been in Marchum? I have never seen him before."

"I would say around two or three weeks, if that."

"Three weeks and he has done all that? Thank God he wasn't here a month."

"There has been carnage up at The Retreat. You need to send one of your officers up there to take statements."

"I shall send PC Keyser, he likes making notes in his occurrence book."

"So I have heard."

"He is not as good as you Charlie. You are well and truly missed. Is there any chance of you coming back?"

"Not a chance in hell sergeant. I have surprised myself, I enjoy running the estate and in a couple of weeks I am to be married, which I am also looking forward to. I can milk the cows, feed the pigs, plough the land and at the end of the day, no paperwork, no there is not a chance in hell of me coming back."

Charlie waited until they had Henry safely under lock and key before he made his way back to The Retreat. He entered the sitting room and looked around to find Ella.

He saw her sitting on a hardback chair near the window next to Clarence.

"Is everything alright Ella?" he asked.

"Yes, everything is under control now."

"Good," then he added, "I see Jackson has managed to get himself the best seat in the house. You spoil him too much Blanche, just look at his face, he is in seventh heaven."

"Me too," Blanche told him.

"I can't argue with that Blanche," and Charlie gave her an affectionate smile and felt for Ella's hand.

"If it wasn't for your Ella, I would not be here, sitting in the state you found me in. It is about time you got married and gave Ella half a dozen nippers to look after. That will keep her out of Clarence's porch."

"I had come to take you all home, but PC Keyser is on his way to take some statements, so I think we should all stay here and get it over with," Charlie told them.

"If yon PC Keyser is heading our way with his occurrence book, you might as well get the spare blankets out, Aunt Sylvia. We are in for a long stay," Jackson informed them all.

Charlie laughed. There was no one on this planet like Jackson and he would be eternally grateful he was his best friend.

When PC Keyser arrived, Isaac informed him that the Bossett police were looking for Henry for the murder of his mother and PC Keyser made a note in his occurrence book.

Two days later saw the departure of Isaac, Freddie and Charlotte. Freddie was going back to Bossett to put his house on the market, but he would be back.

Charlotte had asked Miss Tubby what she wanted to do, whether she wanted to stay at The Retreat or to go back to Bossett with them. Miss Tubby opted to stay; she had decided that life was going to become most exciting from now on.

Chapter Fifteen

Mrs Moyer had invited Blanche, Jackson, Mr Grundy, Charlie and Ella to dine with them and they were all happy to do so.

Since Charlie had left the police and gone to work his grandmother's estate, these little get-togethers were becoming less and less frequent.

Jackson's face, although the swelling had gone down, was still showing just a trace of a yellowy green colour, it would soon be back to normal. The bump on the back of his head only hurt him when he laid his head on the pillow, or he ran the comb through his hair, so he did not bother using the comb on the back of his head. That would have to wait until it was fully healed, but nobody noticed any difference.

Charlie and Ella had been married three whole days and the honeymoon was still new.

Ella and Mr Grundy had moved into Charlie's grandmother's house after the wedding so at present Mr Grundy's house on West Street was empty. Mr Grundy said he did not want to sell it in case he didn't like living in the country and he could always go back to West Street to live.

Mr Moyer looked over at his son-in-law, "Caught a murderer, did you? Not many can boast that."

"More like the murderer caught me. Look at the state of my face? He didn't get his face rattled down a flight of wooden steps, nor was he trussed up like a dead chicken," Jackson complained.

"Yes, but if you hadn't called at The Retreat when you did that poor girl would most likely be dead by now, so that is another life you have saved," Mr Moyer told him logically.

Jackson cast around in his head for something to say and failed.

Charlie's eyes lit up and Jackson did not miss the smile that Charlie tried his hardest to hide.

"It is about time Clarence knocked down that damned porch. I have already told him to get rid of it, it is like a magnet to any waif and stray in Marchum and Ella is bound to find them, and who ends up with um, Charlie and me. And I would just like to point out to you Clarence; you will not bribe me with sausage and mash a second time. I am having a baby you know, and it isn't good for the baby to see his father looking like this the minute he is born. It will frighten the little thing to death."

Jackson waited for someone to reply to his remarks but what he got was an "OUCH" from Blanche.

Jackson shot out of his chair as though he had been struck by lightning, panic showing on his bruised face.

All eyes turned to Blanche. She was rubbing her tummy and breathing deeply.

"I think it is time," she said.

"I will go for the doctor," Jackson panicked.

"You are the doctor," Charlie told him.

"I am not a doctor, I keep telling you. I am a vet. I am not having my baby delivered by a vet," Jackson informed them all.

All eyes were now on Jackson until Blanche said "OUCH," again.

"I will go for the doctor," Jackson insisted.

"I want you Jackson," Blanche told him.

"What if I do something wrong, what if something happens to either of you, I would not be able to live with myself," Jackson told her.

"My daughter is in the safest hands in Marchum when she is in your hands Jackson. Blanche wants you and she will damn well have you," Mr Moyer said.

"You could always head back to Mars," Charlie told him.

"Sod off," Jackson said.

"Language boy, baby on the way," Clarence said.

Mrs Moyer stood up and helped Blanche to her feet, "While you lot are deciding what to do, Blanche and I are going to the bedroom and we are going to have a baby, with or without you."

Ella jumped up and opened the door, "May I come too?" she asked.

"Of course, my dear, let the men fight amongst themselves." Mrs Moyer guiding her daughter through the doorway, turned and said, "Mr Grundy, you seem to have a slight sense of understanding about you. Would you be so kind as to pull the bell and ask the butler to see there is hot water and clean towels sent up to Mrs Jackson's bedroom?"

Mr Grundy's chest puffed out with satisfaction, he had not expected to be involved in having this baby, so he willingly went over to the fireplace and pulled on the bell, and he waited for the butler to appear so that he could to do his bit.

After two hours of pacing the carpet Jackson could stand it no longer so he went to see what was happening above stairs. He found his wife well into her labour and his medical instincts took over.

Mrs Moyer with a pleased smiled on her face, stepped back and let Jackson do his job.

Mr Moyer watched his son-in-law leave the room and then he looked across the room at Charlie and Clarence, "He is a fine lad, that son-in-law of mine."

"He is indeed Mr Moyer, we love him, don't we Clarence?"

"We sure do, and my Fran loved him too," Clarence confirmed.

"As does my Ella," agreed Charlie.

"And Blanche of course, we all love Blanche, isn't that right Charlie?" Clarence asked.

"Of course, we all love Blanche, that should go without saying, she is one of our gang, has been from the very first day we met," confirmed Charlie.

"Mind you, she does tend to encourage Ella in her escapades you know," Clarence confided in Mr Moyer.

Mr Moyer nearly burst the buttons on his waistcoat when his chest swelled out and he stood two inches taller, *Blanche has bagged herself a good catch after all,* he thought, and carrying on with his thoughts, he decided to buy Jackson a present.

Mr Moyer cast around in his head for a suitable present he could buy for his son-in-law until he finally hit on the very thing, '*a comb*', he would buy Jackson a comb.

Blanche had a little boy. He had a healthy pair of lungs that he exercised while Jackson bathed him gently in warm water then wrapped him up in a clean white towel before he took him over to Blanche and laid him on her chest.

Blanche cradled the little bundle to her and the baby stopped crying, but Blanche started.

After a few minutes, Jackson took the baby from Blanche and handed him to his grandma then he went back to his wife and wiped the tears from her face before kissing it soundly.

"That's my girl," and they hugged for a while.

"Right, while you ladies clean up here I will take my son downstairs to show the men. Charlie will be green with envy."

Jackson walked into the dining room where Charlie, Mr Grundy and Mr Moyer were still gathered. All three men looked over at Jackson.

Jackson announced, "It's a boy."

"I knew it, I damn well knew it." Mr Moyer slapped his leg to show his approval.

"Congratulations Jackson, are mother and baby doing alright?" Charlie asked.

Jackson took his son over to his grandpa and handed him over.

"Mother and baby are doing just fine," Jackson told them with satisfaction.

Mr Moyer looked down at the tiny bundle in his arms and asked, "What are you going to call him?"

Jackson looked at all the Charlies gathered in the room and said, "Charles, because he is a proper little Charlie."

Mr Moyer lifted the tiny bundle up to his lips and he kissed the baby's soft forehead and as he did so the towel fell away to reveal an unusual amount of hair for a newly born baby and the thought that went through Mr Moyer's head was, *TWO COMBS.*